Eternal Youth . . .
Eternal Damnation

Cynthia's brother found her on the floor next to the toy chest, with her hands over her mouth.

"What? What's wrong?" Richie cried.

Cynthia pulled back and ran out of the room. Richie watched her in confusion and then turned his attention to the chest. He walked to it and slowly lifted the lid. The stench hit him immediately. It wasn't an unfamiliar putrid odor; he had smelled it whenever he passed a dead animal on the highway or came across one while working on telephone lines.

He held his breath and looked down into the trunk to see what it was . . .

There on the floor of the chest were the remains of what looked like a doll. The hair was still intact, but the face looked like a tiny, rotted human skeleton . . .

Look for Andrew Neiderman's
The Devil's Advocate
Available from Pocket Books

Books by Andrew Neiderman

Brain Child
The Devil's Advocate
The Immortals
Imp
Night Howl
Pin
Someone's Watching
Tender Loving Care

Published by POCKET BOOKS

The IMMORTALS

ANDREW NEIDERMAN

POCKET STAR BOOKS

New York   London   Toronto   Sydney   Tokyo   Singapore

An *Original* Publication of POCKET BOOKS

 A Pocket Star Book published by
POCKET BOOKS, a division of Simon & Schuster Inc.
1230 Avenue of the Americas, New York, NY 10020

ISBN: 0-671-70454-0

First Pocket Books printing July 1991

10 9 8 7 6 5 4 3 2 1

POCKET STAR BOOKS and colophon are trademarks of
Simon & Schuster Inc.

Cover art by Lisa Falkenstern

Printed in the U.S.A.

For Abe Wasserman
my teacher, my friend

— 1 —

Paul Stoddard drove up to the gate and rolled his window down as the security guard approached the car.

"My God," his wife Brenda said, gazing at the ten-foot-high fence. "He likes his privacy, doesn't he? Fences, security guards. Is that a television camera aimed at us, too?" she asked, pointing.

"Uh-huh."

"Good evening," the security guard said. He had fair skin with freckles, green eyes, and strawberry-blond hair. Brenda didn't think he was more than eighteen or nineteen, yet when he scrutinized her and Paul he had the look of a much older man, a man of experience. It was as if there were someone else living within that pretty college-boy body. It gave her the chills.

"Paul Stoddard," Paul said. "I'm afraid we're a bit late. We had to fly in, and you know how the airlines are these days. Besides, the traffic on I-95 was murder."

Brenda wondered why Paul felt he had to apologize to a security guard, especially since the man didn't seem the least bit interested. He checked his clipboard and nodded.

"Go right on in, sir, and turn to the right. There are places to park all along the driveway there."

"Thank you."

The gate groaned and swung open as if it had heard the security guard's approval, and Paul continued up the circular driveway. Brenda noticed more television surveillance along the way and even heard a chorus of barking guard dogs off to the right. The sprawling hacienda was as magnificent as Paul had described, she thought, with its palm trees, hedges, fountains, and flower beds.

There was another security guard waiting at the top of the driveway. He directed them to an available space, and when they stepped out of their car he approached with a metal detector. He ran it over both of them. Brenda didn't know whether to laugh or to express her annoyance, but Paul's serious expression kept her from doing either.

"What's going on, Paul?" she asked as they headed toward the Leon mansion. The front patio was all lit up, and there were spotlights puncturing the darkness everywhere.

"Mr. Leon is a careful man," he said simply.

"Careful or paranoid?"

"Just forget it," Paul snapped as they stepped up to the front door.

The party had already begun. Paul and Brenda could hear the music and laughter coming from Mr. Leon's living room.

"Sounds like everyone's two drinks ahead of us, Paul," Brenda said. He smiled and nodded. Then he pushed the doorbell and took a deep breath before looking up at the dazzling night sky.

"Beautiful night," he remarked.

"Yes, it is," Brenda agreed. She gazed back at the security guard, who continued to study them closely. She noted that this guard looked just as young as the man at the gate. Then she turned to the door, surprised it hadn't yet been opened.

"They're having such a good time in there, they never heard the bell ring," Brenda said. Paul shook his head and smiled.

"There's always a good time to be had at Mr. Leon's," he replied. When was the first time he had heard someone say that? When was the first time he had said it to someone? He couldn't remember.

The door was finally flung open. A tall, handsome man with light brown hair and cerulean eyes stood before them.

"Good evening, Gerald. This is my wife," Paul said. "Brenda, this is Gerald Dorian, Mr. Leon's secretary."

"Hi," Brenda said.

"Welcome." Gerald brought his head back and shouted, *"The Stoddards are here!"*

Behind him the chatter ended, and someone turned down the music.

"Well, don't just let them stand outside, Gerald," a deep, resonant voice declared. Brenda looked at Paul. The voice boomed as if it had come over a microphone and through speakers planted in the ceilings and walls. "Show them in. Mr. Stoddard is the guest of honor."

That was followed by a wave of laughter.

"Welcome to Florida," Gerald said, and he stepped back.

"Thank you, Gerald. Sorry we're late. The delays at the airport . . . the traffic . . ."

"I told him to book us on an earlier flight," Brenda said, entering and gaping at the luxurious residence. Her eyes flitted from the chandeliers to the paintings to the rugs and tiled floors. "You just have to anticipate delays," she muttered.

Gerald nodded. "Right this way," he said, and Paul and Brenda followed him, stepping down into the living room. Instantly there was a burst of applause, and the others began to greet them. Some of the guests Brenda recognized from company gatherings, but she didn't know most and had to be introduced.

"Mr. Leon is eager to see you," Gerald coaxed gently. Paul nodded. Brenda raised her eyebrows. Where was Mr. Leon? she wondered. "Please follow me," Gerald said, and Paul took Brenda's arm.

3

She continued to glance about curiously, impressed with the works of art, the sculptures, the glass pieces on pedestals. What a wonderful place and a great party, she thought, but when she looked back at the guests she saw one of the women she had recognized looking as though she would burst into tears.

Gerald led them through the large living room to a corridor, stopping finally at a pair of large oak doors. He knocked, and they heard Mr. Leon cry, "Enter." Gerald opened the doors and stepped back.

It was an enormous room, almost as big as most houses, Brenda thought. She looked about quickly, taking in the room's simple decor with its beige Berber rug and whitewashed stucco walls. Directly before them was a large desk behind which sat the man she assumed was Mr. Leon. To his right was a glass wall that looked out on the well-lit patio tiled with Mexican pavers. It surrounded a kidney-shaped pool and a circular tile hot tub.

Brenda's gaze returned to Mr. Leon. He looked like a man in his early forties. She had assumed he would be much older. He wasn't particularly handsome. His face was a bit too lean, his jawline too sharp, and his nose too thin, but he had deep-set dark blue eyes that fixed so intently on her, she couldn't help but be drawn to him. He smiled and gestured with his long hand, moving his fingers gracefully, reminding her of a bishop or cardinal, even a prince beckoning someone to approach.

"Welcome, Paul and Brenda," Mr. Leon said as they stepped forward.

Suddenly a muscular Doberman appeared at the corner of the big desk. It produced a low, guttural growl.

"Sit, Thor," Mr. Leon commanded, and the dog sat back, its eyes still blazing suspiciously. Even though it was obedient it remained primed to pounce, Brenda thought, seeing how the dog's legs trembled and the muscles in its jaw twitched.

As soon as Mr. Leon stood up and extended his hand

4

over his desk Paul rushed to take it, and they shook hands.

"I'm sorry we were late, but—"

"That's all right, Paul. There was never any doubt in anyone's mind that you would appear," he said with a knowing, sharp turn upward on the word "appear." His eyes brightened. "You look good."

"Thank you."

"Doesn't he look good, Gerald?"

"Yes sir, he does."

"And I see you have a very lovely wife, Paul. You were very modest when I asked about her." He extended his hand to Brenda.

"Thank you," she said. "You have a beautiful house!" She started to look around and saw the bank of video monitors on the wall behind her. From his desk Mr. Leon could see every part of his house and grounds. Two monitors were devoted to the guests in his large living room.

"Thank you. We'll show you more of it in a few moments," Mr. Leon said. He turned back to Paul. "Everything going well back in New York?" Mr. Leon asked.

"To the letter," he replied.

Mr. Leon smiled warmly and turned to Brenda.

"I knew Paul would be successful for us in that territory. You should be very proud of your husband, Brenda."

"Oh, I am," she said, beaming.

Mr. Leon nodded. "Well, let's not lose our momentum. This is a party. My guests are here to eat and swim and enjoy themselves," Mr. Leon said. Smiling, he put his arm around Paul and threaded his other arm through Brenda's. Then he led them out and to the living room. All the guests stepped back as they approached.

"It's time for a toast," Mr. Leon announced.

Gerald moved forward quickly to hand Brenda her glass of champagne. Then he brought glasses to Mr. Leon and Paul.

"To Paul," Mr. Leon said, raising his glass. He winked at Brenda.

"To Paul," they all chorused. Everyone drank. Paul hesitated a moment and then drank his. He and the others gulped theirs down quickly. Brenda took a long sip of hers, saw everyone had emptied his glass in a gulp, and then emptied hers. She returned the empty glass to Gerald, who waited at her side. Gerald set the glass down on a coaster on a side table. Everyone's eyes followed his movement and stayed with the glass for a moment. Then they all turned to Brenda expectantly.

It began immediately.

"Oh dear," she said. "It must be the rushing around or something. I suddenly feel so dizzy."

"Just sit down," Mr. Leon said. He helped her to a chair and then turned to Paul, who stood staring with a look of deep worry on his face.

Paul nodded and turned to smile at the others, who were all watching him intently now, watching his reaction.

"Paul!" Brenda called. "I . . . feel so faint." She lifted her hand toward him. Paul stepped forward and took it. He patted it once.

Brenda sat back and closed her eyes. When she opened them again she saw they were all staring at her, but they had fallen out of focus. Soon she couldn't tell one from the other. She couldn't even tell which one was Paul. But she had no trouble recognizing Mr. Leon's voice.

Mr. Leon began to sing.

"For Paul's a jolly good fellow, for he's a jolly good fellow . . ."

Soon they were all singing.

She heard the words, "which nobody can deny." She tried to cry out, but she was unable to move her lips. She was paralyzed. Even her eyes wouldn't open. It was as if she had been buried alive in her own body.

Gerald lifted her from the chair gently, as gently as one would lift a baby. Paul followed as Gerald made his way to the rear of the house. The others were right behind him, walking out into the warm Florida night. They went a dozen yards or so to the right of the pool. Mr. Leon owned a little over twenty acres, and all the land was fenced in, with lights and alarms everywhere.

Paul stood beside Mr. Leon and watched Gerald lower Brenda into the open grave.

Mr. Leon put his hand on Paul's shoulder.

"You start it off, Paul."

Paul stepped forward obediently to take the shovel Gerald handed him. He dipped it into the pile of dirt and threw the shovelful into the grave, not looking to see where it fell on Brenda's body.

Then he turned hopefully to Mr. Leon, who smiled.

"I have something special for you, Paul. I bet you know what it is," he said. Everyone laughed. Paul laughed, too. He followed Mr. Leon and the others back into the house, looking back only once to see Gerald finishing the burial.

The light blue Mercedes sedan jerked to a stop in the driveway, and Harris Levy practically leapt out of the vehicle. He rushed down the walkway, cursing the distance between the driveway and garage and the front door of his Weston, Connecticut, home—an eight-room, restored turn-of-the-century farmhouse with a wrap-around porch. He hated his home; it was really his second wife Selina's dream house, not his. He preferred city life. He fed off the noise and the movement and even enjoyed crowds. He was a great walker and thought nothing of trekking thirty or forty blocks to shop or go to a restaurant.

Harris shoved the door key at the lock and missed the keyhole. The wasted movement frightened him. He shook his head and tried again, and again he missed.

He blinked at the porch lights. He knew those bulbs weren't dimmer.

"Oh, Jesus," he cried. This time, as would a much older man with fading sight, he knelt down and slowly brought the tip of the key to the lock. His hand shook but he succeeded in fitting the key correctly and then straightened up to turn it and open the front door.

After he stepped in he closed the door behind him and took a deep breath. He put his small, rich Italian leather case on the marble-top oak table under the hat and coat rack, one of the many antiques Selina had found during her frequent safaris through the small towns around them. The embossed gold letters on the case, LEON ENTERPRISES, glittered in the illumination of the entryway light.

He opened the briefcase and rifled through his papers until he located a small pillbox. He opened it and turned it upside down, shaking it madly. He threw the pillbox back into the briefcase and brought his palms to his face. He started to sob and then stopped and took another deep breath.

He looked at himself in the oval hanging mirror, framed in dark pine wood. As he did so he brought his fingers slowly to his face and ran the tips of them along the deep wrinkles across his brow, down to the crow's feet at his eyes. Then he turned sideways to get a better view of his temples. That was gray hair, and it looked as if it were spreading even while he gazed into the mirror.

"No," he told his reflection, shaking his head. His face looked dark, foreboding. "Jesus, no," he said, and he turned to look up the stairs. He looked back at the empty pillbox in his briefcase and quickly started up the stairway, pulling himself along the mahogany balustrade until he reached the second landing and turned sharply right. He paused before the doorway, closed his eyes, opened them, and jarred open the door.

A small lamp on the nightstand beside the bed cast a pale glow over Selina's body. She was folded in the fetal position, her right hand clenched in a small fist and brought to her chin. He stared at her for a moment and then groaned and rubbed his jaw.

It felt like a toothache. Definitely. He walked farther into the bedroom and approached Selina's vanity table mirror. Kneeling down, he stared at himself, bringing his face closer to the mirror as he widened his lips. His teeth had lost their gleaming whiteness, and the upper corners of some looked . . . rotted.

He pulled back from the mirror as if he had gotten a whiff of his own stale breath. The abrupt movement sent a sharp pain down through his lower back, making him groan aloud.

Without further hesitation he approached the bed and stared down at Selina. He looked at the nightstand. Her bottle of tranquilizers was open. He took it, emptied most of it into his hand, and put the tablets into his pocket. Then he slipped his hands under his wife's body.

She moaned softly, but her eyes didn't open. She wasn't a big woman, only five feet four and a little over a hundred pounds, but the effort to lift her nearly brought him to his knees. He struggled and strained, clamping his lips down on his own cries. His eyes bulged, but he finally stood up with her in his arms. Her head fell back against his chest.

He carried her out of the bedroom and turned right in the hallway. He went down to the end of the corridor and opened another door, nearly dropping her when he reached for the knob to turn it. He struggled to balance her, again subduing his agony, and walked through the door to another, shorter stairway. Each step was harder than the previous one, but he made it to the attic.

He sandwiched her between the wall and himself and flipped a light switch. A single light bulb dangling on a thick black wire illuminated the attic and revealed a chair directly under a ceiling beam. Dangling from the beam was a clothesline, the bottom looped and knotted into a hangman's noose.

Harris took a deep breath and brought Selina to the chair. He set her down and held her against the back of the chair while he caught his breath. Then he looked up at the rope. He moved around to the front and scooped Selina up so that her head was above his. As carefully as he could, he slipped her head into the loop. The bottom caught under her chin. Moving awkwardly around her body and still holding her, he stood up on the chair. Then he released his hold on her, and she was supported only by the rope. It held. He pushed her head forward so that the rope slipped off her chin and around her neck. Finally he tightened the knot.

As soon as he did so he stepped off the chair and looked up at her. Her eyes fluttered. He had been hoping she wouldn't regain consciousness, but apparently the cutting off of oxygen had done something to stimulate her, and her eyes opened. She gaped at him madly for a moment, her eyes bulging, the attic light making them glow with a sickly yellowish tint.

He stepped back.

"I'm sorry!" he cried. Her eyes snapped closed just like a toy doll's eyes. He didn't wait to see anything else. He turned and started down the attic steps, but he missed one and tumbled the rest of the way. At the bottom he pulled himself up to a sitting position and moaned aloud. Pain coming from everywhere over his body sucked the breath out of him. He gasped, placed his hand over his chest to keep himself from wheezing, and struggled to a standing position. Then he made his way back to the bedroom and collapsed on the bed.

He lay there for a moment. Every joint in his body ached, and he had a horrible ribbon of pain just above his eyes. It was as if he were wearing a crown of thorns.

He brought his hands to his head and ran his fingers through his hair. When he looked at his hands he saw they were filled with strands, only the strands were completely gray.

"No," he said to his bony-looking fingers and thin palm. "Please." He reached for the phone and tapped out the numbers, incorrectly pecking at the pushbuttons twice before he put all his concentration on the series of digits and got it right.

"Leon residence," Gerald Dorian shouted. Harris heard music and laughter in the background.

"Gerald, thank heavens." His voice was cracking. It was hard to speak. "Gerald, please . . . it's Harris Levy."

"Mr. Levy, how are you?" Gerald asked cheerfully.

"Not well. Terrible."

"What?"

"Not well," he repeated. "Gerald, tell him I did it. Please . . ."

"Hold on a moment, Mr. Levy. I have to close this door." A moment later the background noises were subdued. "Sorry about that. Now, what were you saying, Mr. Levy?"

"Gerald, I've got to talk with Mr. Leon. I did what he wanted."

"I'm afraid that's out of the question. He's quite occupied at the moment, Mr. Levy."

"But Gerald, I'm getting old . . . sick."

"You waited too long, Mr. Levy. I pleaded with you."

"Please, Gerald," he cried. "Speak to him. Tell him I did it. He told me I still had time if I acted promptly. Well, I did."

"All right, Mr. Levy. I'll talk to him. We'll call you back."

"But I need immediate attention, Gerald. Please."

"Stand by."

Before Harris could interject another word Gerald hung up his receiver, and the line went dead. Harris pressed the phone harder to his ear, as if he had just heard his own death sentence.

His face began to stretch, the skin thinning out until he felt it tearing at his cheek and jawbone. The receiver dropped out of his hand and bounced on the pecan-brown carpet. His arms fell to his sides as if they had weights attached to the ends. He couldn't lift them.

Soon his eyes were watering. Just before his vision became blurred he turned to see himself in the pearl-framed vanity mirror. That couldn't be his face, he thought. The man who looked back at him was as gaunt as a hundred-year-old man. His skull was pressing out, rising up through his scant layer of skin, skin that looked more like thin parchment. Veins were rupturing in his cheeks. There was a ripping just at the crest of his right cheekbone. He screamed with pain, and then his vision blurred and the images before him merged into one liquid mess, colors blending into others, shapes taking on adjacent angles and dimensions.

He moaned and lay back on the bed, taking the same fetal position Selina had been in. He felt as if he were literally shrinking in his clothing. His body seemed to be retreating toward some center deep within.

The last sense to go was the sense of smell. It was awful . . . decaying flesh, putrid liquids oozing from his eyes and his mouth. His beautiful sports jacket folded in as he continued to diminish on the bed. The blur was replaced with darkness. For a moment all was quiet.

Then the peace and quiet he had assumed was death was shattered with the sound of his own bones crumbling. Yet when it was over, he was still there, imprisoned in the dust. Where was he? What was he? He had no form; he saw nothing, felt nothing, yet he was still there. He wanted to scream, but he had no voice.

Outside, stars glittered and the moon slipped out from behind a thick charcoal-gray cloud. The silvery rays shot through the office window like a spotlight and fell over the sports jacket and pants collapsed and folded over the small pile of dust within.

Mr. Leon was gazing through the glass doors, sitting in his high-back leather desk chair and turned in the direction of the pool so he could watch his guests. He always wondered what sort of things they said to each other when he was not nearby.

No sense in wondering, he thought, reaching under his desk to turn a knob. Instantly the voices of the men and women around the pool were brought into his office. He could direct the microphones and center in on anyone he wanted.

The fools were talking about their investments, laughing about how much wealth they would be able to accumulate with so much time at their disposal. Some of the women were comparing hairdos and talking about clothes. One of the men was thinking about getting a nose job, maybe even having most of his face changed. The people around him thought that wasn't a bad idea. They were showing signs of boredom, Mr. Leon noted. It was difficult to hold on to employees these days or to find just the right ones, ones who had his vision, ones who had imagination and an insatiable hunger for life.

Paul Stoddard looked a bit pale around the gills. He wasn't very talkative, either, and he continued to look to the right, where they had put Brenda. Mr. Leon hoped he hadn't misjudged the man. Perhaps with more responsibility he would grow and forget. Nothing like a little power to make a disciple more devoted, he thought.

All of the women were very beautiful. He had chosen well. Everywhere there were floodlights illuminating them, showing their bodies smooth and brown with softly curving necks and perky white bosoms. Some had long legs, their thighs inviting and as pure and rich in promise as birth itself.

One of the women laughed, her voice musical, innocent, wholesome, yet as sweet and tormenting as rich cream. She made his heart throb the way it had when he first set eyes on a beautiful young girl he knew would be his.

How long had it been? He laughed, thinking of all the clever ruses he had created to eradicate time, including staging his own death and attending the funeral like a dutiful, loving son. How many times had he died? He laughed at his momentary lapse of memory. What difference did it make if he had died seven or eight times? It kept people from wondering, didn't it?

Still, there had been three attempts on his life over the years; admittedly not that many, when you consider the prize and the number of years, but still, any one could have succeeded. Was there a potential assassin in this new group of disciples around his pool? No one had shown any signs of wanting more than he had been given, and yet . . . it was human nature to be greedy, wasn't it?

Thank goodness for modern technology and all this protection, he thought. Most of the time he lived in a cocoon. True, but he lived, and how he lived!

Movement on one of his television monitors caught his eye, and he turned to watch Gerald Dorian cross the living room and head toward his office. The cameras followed Mr. Leon's personal assistant to his office door, where he stood waiting to get Mr. Leon's attention. Gerald knew better than to interrupt one of Mr. Leon's moments.

Mr. Leon spun around slowly to greet him. He leaned back in his chair and pressed the tips of his fingers against each other.

"Yes, Gerald?"

"Mr. Levy just phoned, sir."

He sat back farther and pressed his palms against his chest. Gerald knew Mr. Leon was in one of his meditative moods, his face complacent, thoughtful; his eyes philosophical, the blue in them deep, dark. Even when he was in deep thought his forehead remained smooth, his eyebrows straight. He wasn't a very tall man, barely six feet, but to Gerald he sometimes looked gigantic.

"Oh yes, Mr. Levy. And?"

"He wanted you to know he had done it. He said you told him if he took action, there was still time, but it sounded too late," Gerald said. Mr. Leon nodded.

"Poor man," he said. "But he who hesitates . . ."

Mr. Leon reached into the top drawer of his desk and brought out a soft-looking leather-bound book; the brown had faded into a rust. Without looking up, Mr. Leon spoke as he wrote something in it. "Well, then, you had better send Mr. Stoddard in to see me." He looked up to admire himself in the wall mirror on the left. He looked so much bigger than he had yesterday. He turned back to Gerald. "As I recall, Mr. Levy had made a recommendation to us. Now we'll act on it." He smiled. "We need a replacement," he said.

"Yes, sir."

Mr. Leon went back to his leather-bound book and wrote something else in it. After a proper pause, Gerald asked, "Will there be anything else, sir?"

Mr. Leon sharply punctuated whatever he had written in his book and closed it. Then he returned it to the drawer and looked up. For a moment he seemed distracted, his eyes gazing through Gerald, beyond the room, beyond the house, beyond the time. He was like a seaman on the port side of the deck gazing at the horizon, dreaming of home.

"What? Oh, yes, yes," he said, gazing through the glass doors again. "Please see how our lobster bake is coming along. Suddenly I'm very hungry. Ravenously hungry."

"Yes, sir," Gerald said softly. Mr. Leon thought he heard a discordant note in Gerald's voice.

"Gerald?" Gerald turned back.

"Sir?"

"They come and go, Gerald. You of all people must never forget that," he added, not disguising the threat.

"I know, sir."

"You're not getting tired, are you, Gerald?" Mr. Leon asked, smiling.

"Oh, no, sir. No," Gerald said emphatically.

"Good. Anyway, it's a myth, you know."

"Sir?"

"To suggest that if we lived forever, we would grow tired of life. A myth," Mr. Leon repeated, turning back to look at his guests.

"Yes, sir," Gerald muttered.

He stared at Mr. Leon a moment, fascinated by how still he sat and how intensely he studied the young women. Then he shook his head slightly and left to do all that he had been told to do while Mr. Leon turned up the volume on his speakers and continued to eavesdrop on their conversations.

— 2 —

Drake Edwards groaned at the sound of the buzzer. He was in the midst of a great dream. He was going up for a jump shot; there were seconds left, and Sandburg was one point behind. Beyond the backboard and all around him the crowd was standing. Cynthia was in his dream, even though she hadn't attended Sandburg Central. She was holding her fingers to her lips, and her girlfriends were clutching her arms and squeezing themselves together in a clump of hope.

The ball left his hands as if it had a mind of its own and cut smoothly through the air. It dropped through the hoop so sharply it made no sound and hardly disturbed the netting just as the buzzer sounded.

But it wasn't the buzzer of the court's time clock; it was his alarm clock, waking him and telling him it was time to get up and get ready for work. Cynthia heard him groan and ran her fingers through his hair. Then she leaned over and kissed him on the back of his neck.

"Sorry, honey," she said. "It's seven."

He groaned again and turned over, keeping his eyes closed.

"It's getting harder and harder to get up in the morning," he complained. When he moved his legs his old

16

knee injury reintroduced itself, as it had been doing for the last year or so. The doctor suspected he was becoming arthritic.

"I'm only forty years old," he had protested, but then he remembered his forty-four-year-old brother Michael and his receding hairline. With his paunch and baggy eyes he looked sixty. It was in the genes. The Edwards boys took after their grandfather. He and Michael would be completely bald by fifty and look years older than they were.

He moaned and rubbed his knee.

"Oh, poor Drake. Is your knee bothering you again this morning?" Cynthia asked sympathetically.

"Not again, still," he said.

He knew why he always dreamed of heroic scenes on the basketball court. He had almost been a star for his high school, but just at the start of his senior year, when he was primed and ready to go, he took a terrible fall during the first quarter of the first game of the season. He had been hit just as he had gone up for a jump shot, and when he came down he fell on his right knee. There was no chance to break his fall, no time to hold his hands out, nothing to fall on but the knee.

The injury not only took him out of the season, it put him on crutches for half the school term, and when he finally got free of the crutches he was still limping so badly that his friends called him Hopalong Edwards.

Very funny.

He groaned again and pulled himself into a sitting position. It was Monday morning, and he wanted to go to work at the insurance company as much as he wanted to dig a twenty-foot ditch.

"I'll get the kids started," Cynthia said. She put her hand on his shoulder. "You all right?"

He nodded and then felt bad for not acknowledging her concern. He turned and kissed her. At thirty-five Cynthia was aging far more gracefully than he was, he thought. But again, that was in the genes. Her mother certainly didn't look sixty-two, and her father was a hardy, vigorous man at seventy-one. Drake's parents were dead; his father from a heart attack at sixty-four and his mother from a stroke and heart attack at sixty-six. Some prognosis for the siblings, he thought mournfully.

Drake hoped his son Stuart and his daughter Debbie had inherited Cynthia's genes and not his.

"Do you remember what today is?" she asked as she caressed his rough, unshaven cheek with her soft one and drew his lips back to hers. They kissed again, and he shook his head. Then he nodded and smiled.

"Sure." He leaned toward her to kiss the bottom of her chin. "Our real anniversary," he whispered.

They both laughed. It was silly, but after fifteen years of marriage, no one knew but them. They had decided to get married impulsively one night while she was still a senior at SUNY-Albany. Of course, she was old enough, but they both knew Cynthia's parents would be heartbroken if she told them what they had done. Instead she and Drake continued to date, became engaged shortly after graduation, and got married again the following September.

"Your father's still not sure I can support my family," Drake complained.

"Every father's like that, honey. You'll be the same when it comes to Debbie. You'll hope for a doctor or a lawyer, too."

"Certainly not a salesman, eh?" he said, pulling the blanket off. His back felt so stiff this morning, he thought. Maybe he could try acupuncture treatments.

"Unless, of course, he's one as good as you."

"Sure, sure." Drake paused before getting out of bed and smiled to himself as he reminisced. "When I was younger I could sell anything to anybody. Just like my father, maybe better," he added, nodding.

"You needed my help once," she reminded him.

"What? Oh." He shook his head. "I staged that whole thing." He stood up and pretended he was back in Albany, New York, selling used cars. "Oh, miss, can we borrow you for just a moment? Only a moment, please."

"I thought you were crazy."

"Then why did you stop?"

"Crazy, but handsome," she admitted.

"That poor schnook." He postured again. "I've got a young man here, miss, who doesn't think his girlfriend would go for this car, and I've been telling him it's such a good deal, he would be foolish to pass it up. But he's afraid it's a"—Drake turned to the imaginary customer—"what did you call it, sir? A family car?"

"I remember. You practically twisted my arm to say the right things."

"Well, you said, 'It's nice.' What kind of a thing was that to say?"

"The truth. It was nice, but not much more. It was a station wagon," she added, arms out for emphasis. Her nightgown slipped off her smooth left shoulder.

"At least I got you to say the gearshift was cool. Cool!" He turned back to his imaginary customer. "Did you hear that, sir? Cool, and that's from a"—he turned back to Cynthia, still reenacting the scene that had taken place more than fifteen years before—"you go to college here, right?"

"So that's what you were doing? Finding out who I was and where I lived. Sneaky, Drake Edwards, very sneaky."

"You didn't turn me down when I came by to ask you to dinner," he pointed out.

No, she thought, she didn't. What beautiful dark eyes he had, she thought, and he had that firm "I know who I am" look that most college boys lacked. Drake was the first really mature man she had known. The others were still on the way to becoming someone or something.

He swept me off my feet, she thought. But it was fun, and how could she ever forget the looks on her roommates' faces? It was worth going out with him for that alone.

One date led to another. Drake had energy; he seemed unstoppable. This man will become rich and famous, she thought. He was driven, ambitious, but not so mono-

ANDREW NEIDERMAN

maniacal that he was oblivious to her needs. Most other
men she had dated spent most of their time talking about
themselves. Sometimes she felt as if they saw her as
just another ornament to wear on their arms, a mark of
conquest—not that she was ever an easy prize.

But Drake was different. He always considered her
feelings first. From the start they were simpatico. His
mood was dependent upon hers. If she was depressed,
he would spend all of his energy working at cheering
her up.

"I can't be happy if you're not happy, Cyn," he told
her. And he would cheer her any way he could, including gifts of flowers or deliveries of stuffed animals.

She laughed, remembering.

"What's so funny?" he said, unbuttoning his pajama
top. He was heading for the bathroom. He was hoping
a hot shower would awaken his sleeping muscles and
restore at least a semblance of youth and vitality to his
worn and battered body.

"I was just recalling Mom's face when she came to
visit and saw all those stuffed animals you bought me.
'You could open up your own store! Why don't you get
rid of a few?' " she said.

"Why didn't you?" he asked. "I did go a bit
overboard."

"Not to me. Each one was special, each one repre-
sented a memory. Mom didn't understand."

Cynthia had to wonder. Was her mother as much in
love with her father as she was with Drake? Maybe it
wasn't possible for two other people to love each other
as much and as completely as she and Drake did.

"I was a bit crazy in those days," Drake confessed.
He smiled to himself, recalling. "It was fun, though,
being impulsive, uncaring. No mortgage payments, car
payments, not worrying about the water heater leaking," he added, smirking.

"Everyone has to grow up sometime, honey," Cynthia said, rising.

"You mean everyone has to grow old," he corrected. He went in to stand dumbly under the shower.

Mornings had a debilitating sameness to them these days, Drake thought. Schedules wore you down. You became imprisoned by the clock, subdued by minutes and buried in hours. He had to finish breakfast by seven-forty, be out the door by eight o'clock the latest to drive to Goshen and board the commuter bus into New York. Falling off schedule meant he would be two hours late for work, and that meant staying at the office later and not getting home until eight-thirty at night.

But this was the sacrifice he and thousands of others were making so that their families could live in a nice environment while they worked in the city. What we do for our children, he thought, and he sped up the morning rituals.

There was never a question about Drake and Cynthia having children. They hadn't dated a dozen times before they started to talk about a family. They agreed that two children would be enough.

"If only we could be lucky and have a boy and a girl," he had said, and they were.

Stuart was born fourteen months after they had their official wedding. He took after Cynthia's side of the family: cerulean eyes, hair as bright as sun-kissed hay, a fair complexion with a patch of freckles under each eye. But he had Drake's congenial personality. He was outgoing and eager to socialize. When he was four he enjoyed sitting and listening to Cynthia and Drake and their friends, and by the time he was eight he was contributing to the conversation. One of his elementary school teachers had the nerve to write, "Stuart suffers from diarrhea of the mouth" on his end-of-year report. Cynthia stormed into the elementary school and demanded a meeting with the principal and the teacher, who later apologized, but she insisted that Stuart had a problem keeping quiet.

When Cynthia returned home and told Drake about it all later, he only shook his head.

Debbie was born three years after Stuart and was slightly underweight. She would be forever known as "the peanut" as far as Drake was concerned. She had Drake's rich dark hair and hazel eyes, but she had Cynthia's diminutive features. Debbie was soft-spoken, but as precious and as huggable as a teddy bear. She doted on Drake. From the day she could walk she had listened for his entrance and run into his arms to be swept up and kissed.

"Peanut!" he would cry.

Cynthia gently pleaded with him to stop calling Debbie that.

"When she's a teenager she's going to hate it, honey. Boys won't take her seriously," she warned.

"Are you kidding? Look at those eyes. She's going to break hearts, leave them shattered throughout the halls because she won't love anyone but Daddy. Right, Peanut?"

Debbie was quiet, Cynthia thought, but she was shrewd. She saw it in the way Debbie shot her a knowing look before she turned back to Drake and nodded. Maybe Drake was right. Maybe Debbie would be a femme fatale.

Cynthia usually had no difficulty getting her children up and ready for school. She had them both seated at the dinette table by the time Drake came down for breakfast.

The Edwards family had a modest three-bedroom, two-story, colonial-style home with a downstairs office-den, living room, dining room, kitchen, and breakfast nook. Their home was in Sandburg, a small upstate New York community that was suddenly booming because of the rash of commuters who spread over the landscape. Drake said it was the greatest thing that could have happened to real estate values. Their house was worth at least ten to twenty thousand more because of it.

"Morning, everybody," Drake said. Cynthia grimaced at the way he was limping when he came down the stairs. He saw the look on her face. "Still a bit stiff," he explained.

"Hi, Daddy," Debbie cried. Drake kissed her and mussed Stuart's hair.

"Hi, Dad. Dad," he said quickly, "today's my class meeting to organize the party for Saturday. You're still going to be a chaperon with Mom, right?"

"Check," Drake said. "Make sure they play something from our generation, though, okay?"

"Like what?"

"I don't know." He looked at Cynthia. " 'Camptown Races'?"

"Oh, Drake." She poured his coffee, but before he could bring the cup to his lips the phone rang. Everyone turned toward the wall where it hung. "No one calls this early unless there's something wrong," Cynthia declared.

"No way to find out without answering," Drake said, and he got up. "Hello." He listened and then shook his head to indicate it wasn't anything bad. Cynthia breathed relief and coaxed Debbie to finish her cereal. "Yes, you've got the right Drake Edwards. Well, I do have a pretty tight schedule here, so I can't talk . . ." He listened. Cynthia raised her eyebrows and looked at him as he turned his body away.

"Well, I do remember a Harris Levy. What's it called? I don't know, I . . . one moment," Drake said, and he put the receiver down to get his date book from his briefcase.

"What is it, Drake?"

"Someone named Paul Stoddard wants to take me to lunch." He snapped open his briefcase and checked his date book quickly. Then he returned to the phone. "Yes, I can make it. Twelve-thirty at the Grand Hyatt. Fine. See you then." He hung up the receiver.

"Who's Paul Stoddard? What did he want?" Cynthia asked quickly.

"I don't know him, but he says Harris Levy recommended me, and whoever Harris Levy recommends they take seriously."

"Take seriously for what?"

"A position at their firm."

"What firm? Who's Harris Levy? Why would you be interested in another job?" Cynthia fired her questions in staccato fashion.

"Whoa." Drake shook his head. "All I said was I would meet the man for lunch. I don't know any more than you do, but since he's buying . . ." He shrugged and sat down. He gulped his orange juice and swallowed the vitamin Cynthia had left beside it.

"Do you know Harris Levy?" she asked, sitting down herself.

Drake paused and thought as he started to pour some cold cereal into his bowl.

"The only Harris Levy I can recall—and you know how good I am with names—was a friend of Dad's who worked with him when he was selling those World Book Encyclopedias. But it can't be the same Harris Levy," he added, and he poured his cereal.

"Why not?"

"That guy was at least twenty years older than Dad. Dad died, what . . . twelve years ago? That would make Harris Levy close to a hundred. Can't be the same one," he repeated.

"Why can't he?" Stuart asked.

"Because this Harris Levy is regional director of this firm's Connecticut office, and even George Burns doesn't have that much energy."

"Then who is he, and how come he recommended you, Drake?" Cynthia asked.

"I don't know, honey, but you know that saying about looking a gift horse in the mouth."

"What happens, Daddy?" Debbie asked, wide-eyed.

"You smell the horse's bad breath," Drake said, and he grimaced. Debbie squealed with laughter, but Cynthia stared, not sure why it all made her feel so anxious.

The commute was a dull nightmare, especially on rainy days. The weather was supposed to improve by mid-afternoon, but there was nothing as dreary as sitting on a bus with other commuters, most reading the papers or catching up on work they were supposed to complete before arriving at their offices.

No one else at Burke-Thompson, Drake's insurance firm, lived where he lived. Most lived in Connecticut, a few in Jersey, and a very lucky few in Manhattan. Old man Burke lived in Queens, and his son-in-law partner, Larry Thompson, lived in Yonkers and had a mere half-hour commute from home to office.

Drake had been with the firm for nearly twelve years and had been honored with the title Agent of the Month six times, each time bringing a plaque and a small raise in pay. Last week Larry Thompson had suggested Drake was up for a vice-presidency soon. That would give them a few thousand more a year, and Cynthia could go ahead and renovate the kitchen. Of course, a vice-presidency meant more responsibilities, more hours, more paper pushing, which meant more stress. Stress, Drake was well aware, aged you faster, and if there was one thing he didn't need to do, it was to further accelerate his biological clock.

But what was he to do—turn down a promotion when it finally came? Funny how life puts you in a corner, he thought as he sat back and closed his eyes. The light chatter and the hum of the bus's engine nearly put him to sleep. He did fall into a deep daydream, imagining himself winning the lottery and retiring before it was too late to enjoy retirement. He wished he could spend more time with his children.

Drake was worried about Stuart, worried that he wasn't manly enough, wasn't enjoying his boyhood enough. He was growing up too fast. Drake was determined that his son would go out for the eighth-grade basketball team next year. Schoolwork and student government were fine, but he needed exercise; he needed the physical side of life as well.

His daydreaming and his worrying made the commute seem much shorter than usual. After they pulled into the station Drake walked quickly to the subway and made his stop in record time. He was at the office just before nine-thirty. Tina Patterson, the receptionist, was just getting herself situated. All the men in the office drooled over the shapely twenty-year-old redhead who paraded about in tight skirts and sweaters. Drake certainly wouldn't disagree about how attractive she was, but he didn't find himself panting and longing for her as intensely as the other men in the office did. Maybe that was another sign of aging, he thought sadly.

"Morning," Drake called as he walked by. She gave him a big, warm smile, bigger than she gave the others because he didn't pay her as much attention. He tried to explain that to Marty Collins.

"Don't let her see how interested you are, and she'll be easier to get," he advised.

"Easy for you to say," Marty replied. "You're married, getting it regularly."

"So get happily married," Drake responded.

"That's a contradiction in terms," Marty quickly replied.

Drake began his day, diving into his work completely as always, making the calls, going over the policies, advising clients about the changes they should have—selling, selling, selling. Or schmoozing, as his father used to call it. You chatter about everything under the sun and slip in your sales pitch subtly, so subtly the client doesn't even realize he's being sold. That takes personality, instinctive psychology, talent. And Drake was good at it. No question about that.

Maybe that was why this Harris Levy, whoever he was, had recommended him, Drake thought when he resurfaced and noticed the time. Why shouldn't other people be considering him from time to time anyway? He had made his mark in the insurance industry.

Billy Decker and Marty asked him to join them for lunch. He was going to lie and say he had to meet with a client. Why should they know he was talking to a prospective employer? he thought. It will probably lead to nothing, and rumors will fly for no reason. On the other hand, if Larry Thompson knew he was in demand, he might up the raise in salary and speed up the promotion. Drake opted for the second possibility and told them he was having lunch with an executive from a competing firm. Their eyes widened with envy.

He laughed to himself as he left the office and headed up Madison Avenue to Forty-second Street. It was only five blocks up and two over to get to the Hyatt—not enough to justify a cab—but the walk on a cool gray May day was taking its toll on his leg. When he caught sight of himself in a storefront window he saw he was actually limping the way he had limped in high school.

I guess I have to see the doctor again, he thought, and he plodded on.

During lunch hour Madison Avenue and Forty-second Street became terrifically congested with traffic and people. Many were like him, white-collar workers, men in suits and sports jackets, women in suits and designer clothing. New York was full of attractive women, he thought when one particularly elegant-looking girl, not much more than twenty or so, passed him. Her laugh had a pure, innocent ring to it, and the sound took him back to his earlier days with Cynthia. How do you recapture that feeling? he wondered—that sense of excitement and wonder when something as simple as a walk in the park made your heart pound with anticipation.

He shook his head, regretting the depressing turn his thoughts were taking. He waited at the light with the clump of pedestrians around him and moved on the green just as automatically, if not as quickly, as the others. He turned down Forty-second Street and continued to the Hyatt. Once inside, he took a deep breath and relaxed. The cool air, the sound of the piano, the refinement of the polished lobby and the slower pace of the people moving up and down the steps made him feel as though he had just stepped out of one world—a maddening, hot and cluttered one—and into another where people could be . . . people.

"I'm meeting a Mr. Stoddard," he told the maître d'. The young man snapped to attention.

"Oh, yes. Right this way, sir," he said without checking his chart.

Drake followed him down the aisle and toward a table in the far corner by the windows that looked out over the street. A man who looked no more than thirty at the most stood up to greet him. He was wearing a light blue Cardin sports jacket and matching slacks with a hand-painted tie. There was a diamond tie pin glittering at the center.

Paul Stoddard had light brown hair swept up and back in soft waves. Cynthia would love this guy's deep blues, Drake thought, and he reached for his extended hand.

"Drake. Glad you could make it."

"Thank you."

"Sit down, please," he said, indicating the chair across from him. "I always like it here—like the open, bright feeling—don't you?"

"It's nice," Drake said, looking around. Actually, he hadn't been there before.

"Great salads. Got to watch that waistline," Paul said, patting what looked to be a rather flat stomach. Drake smiled weakly, regretting his own developing paunch. Just like Michael, he was destined to come apart at the seams if he didn't keep at it. But he often felt like the Dutch boy at the dike, holding it all back with a single finger. It took more and more time at the gym to hold his own as it was, much less improve.

"So," Drake said, "what is Leon Enterprises?"

"Would anyone care for a drink?" the waiter inquired.

"I'll have a martini, extra dry. Drake?"

"Oh, just a mineral water."

"Come on, you can have a cocktail. Believe me, this is a special occasion."

"If I drink at lunch, I'm asleep by three. Mineral water," he repeated. The waiter grimaced and turned his shoulder as he jotted down the order. Why were there so many fags nowadays? Drake mused. Paul seemed to be able to read his thoughts. He raised his eyebrows as the waiter left them.

"I thought I knew all the insurance firms in the Northeast," Drake said.

"Well, we don't sell insurance, exactly, Drake. I took some liberties when I used that term on the phone."

"Pardon?"

"I guess you could say we sell youth insurance, something that keeps people looking younger. And if they look younger, they feel younger."

"I don't understand. What do you sell?"

Paul Stoddard smiled and dug into his jacket pocket to produce a small silver tin with the words "Youth Hold" written on top. He placed it between them on the table. Drake stared down at it.

"What is that?"

"It's a skin cream that removes wrinkles."

"Oh." Drake started to sit back.

"Guaranteed," Paul added.

"Uh-huh." Drake took the tin in hand and turned it over. On the back was a simple line of directions: "Apply lightly once a day to the affected areas." Under that was written "Leon Enterprises, Coral Springs, Florida."

Drake unscrewed the top and looked at the clear contents. It looked like a tin of Vaseline. He brought it to his nose and smelled.

"No odor."

Paul shook his head.

"What's in it?"

"Mr. Leon's secret," Paul said. "When people ask, you simply tell them it's secret. They like the mystery and think it means the stuff is more valuable. Not that it isn't expensive. That tin sells for fifty dollars."

"Fifty dollars?"

"Keep it," Paul said. "Use it," he added. Drake looked up sharply.

"Do you?"

"What do you think?" Paul smiled, and when he did, his eyes twinkled mischievously. But his skin did look baby-smooth, especially around and under the eyes, where Drake's skin was most wrinkled and baggy. His brother Michael's face was becoming a road map, he thought, and he looked at the cream.

"I never heard of this. Never seen it advertised."

"That's because Mr. Leon doesn't advertise. The best advertisement is word of mouth. You know that; you're a good salesman."

"Never saw it in any stores, either."

"It's not in stores. Mr. Leon doesn't want it placed side by side with crap and phony products."

"So then . . ." The waiter served their drinks.

"Are you ready to order?" he asked.

"I'll have the shrimp salad special," Paul said. "Drake?"

"The same."

"Very good," the waiter said, plucking the menus off the table as if they were unpleasant to touch.

"So how is it sold?" Drake asked.

"Door to door. The old-fashioned way. Mr. Leon is an old-fashioned sort of guy."

"Door to door?" Drake stared incredulously. "You want me to go selling this stuff door to door? That's why you called me and asked me to lunch?"

"Mr. Leon is very particular about who his salespeople are. We've been looking into you, and it was decided you would be a prime candidate."

"Well, I'm very flattered, but—"

"You'll begin working at three times your present salary, and you will earn commissions on sales. Once you start, you will see that Youth Hold sells itself anyway. Believe me, people will come to you. We're going to give you the entire Mid-Hudson Valley of upstate New York."

"Three times my present salary? Do you know how much I make?"

Paul bit into a bread stick.

"Of course. You've been with Burke-Thompson for twelve years. Last year you earned approximately thirty-eight thousand dollars, not counting a few perks here and there. Look at me," he continued. "I drive a Porsche, have a magnificent home in Westchester, an apartment on Riverside Drive, and I just invested in some real estate in Beverly Hills. Purely for the speculation," he added, and he sipped his martini. Drake noticed the large diamond pinky ring with the thick gold band on his right hand.

"But money's only the beginning, Drake. What you're going to get from Mr. Leon you couldn't get anywhere else on this earth, and believe me, it's beyond any price tag."

Drake looked down at the skin cream.

"Try some. A little dab'll do ya," Paul said. "Go on," he coaxed.

Drake dipped his right forefinger into the cream and rubbed some of it around his temples. Paul indicated he should put some under his eyes as well. Drake did so and then looked around to be sure no one was watching.

"I feel stupid doing this."

"You won't once you see the results," Paul assured him.

"If it works, why would anyone buy another jar? You might make one sale, but—"

"Because it doesn't last forever. They've got to keep using the stuff. It's as if you sell a legal addictive product. Once they're hooked, they're hooked for life," Paul declared, and he widened his smile.

Drake nodded. That made sense. If it really worked. He looked at Paul with a great deal more interest.

"How did you get to be the director of the entire Northeast for this company?"

"I made a few sacrifices," Paul replied, his eyes sharp, almost cold for a moment. "But it was worth it, believe me. You're going to feel the same way when you're working for Mr. Leon."

"I don't know," Drake said. "There's a good chance they'll make me a vice-president next week, and—"

"You won't be there next week, Drake. You'll be with us."

Drake looked at him sharply. How did someone so young get to be so confident and cocky? he wondered.

"Drive a Porsche and have a home in Westchester County, huh?" Drake knew how expensive real estate was there.

"Don't forget my New York apartment."

Drake shook his head.

"I've got to hand it to you. You don't look much over thirty, and you're way ahead of me," Drake said enviously. Paul laughed.

"I'm older than you are, Drake."

"Huh? This stuff might work on wrinkles," Drake said, "but there are other ways to tell someone's age."

"Don't I know it?" Paul looked around as though he were about to reveal something highly secret. Then he dug into his inside coat pocket and came out with his wallet. He snapped it open and presented Drake with his driver's license. Drake read it and looked up.

"Fifty-two?" Paul nodded. "You're fifty-two?" Drake said again. Paul closed his wallet and put it back in his jacket. "I don't get it."

"You will," Paul said with a coy smile.

The waiter served their food, but Drake didn't pick up his fork. He sat staring at the youthful-looking man across from him.

"It's good," Paul said, chewing. "Relax, enjoy. That's all you're going to do from now on. Believe me."

Drake lifted his fork slowly and began to eat.

"I'll tell you more about it all when I drive you to your commuters' parking lot today," Paul said. "You're never going to have to commute to work again," he added. "No more time to waste, and even if you do waste some, you won't mind.

"Not as long as you work for Mr. Leon," he added, and he sipped his martini.

3

Cynthia turned into her driveway just as the school bus arrived and opened its doors to permit Stuart and Debbie's exit. Stuart squinted at the bright May sunshine as he came bouncing down the steps with Debbie following demurely behind. They turned to wave to their bus driver and then ran to greet Cynthia.

"Hi. How was school?"

"I had my class meeting," Stuart reported officiously, "and the party's definitely this Saturday night. I told them you and Daddy would be our parent chaperons."

"Uh-huh." She opened the back of the station wagon and reached in for the bags of groceries. She looked at Debbie and saw the excitement in her eyes.

"How was your day, honey?"

"I got a hundred on a spelling quiz," Debbie said, pulling the paper out of her notebook quickly. Cynthia paused to gaze at it.

"That's wonderful. Here, each of you can take in one bag of groceries, okay?" She chose the lightest one for Debbie and then gave Stuart the nearest. He was a good-sized twelve-year-old boy, firm and athletic like Cynthia's younger brother Richie, whom Stuart loved almost as much as he loved Drake.

The children charged ahead, entering the house on the garage side. Cynthia hugged two bags to her bosom and followed. Although the house was only ten years old, the kitchen desperately needed remodeling. The cabinets were chipped and faded, but more than that, they were awkwardly constructed. She had to stand on a small ladder to put away her dry goods, and the doors of one cabinet couldn't be opened if the refrigerator was open at the same time.

She had been shopping for a new kitchen, subscribing to magazines that featured furniture and house designs. Drake kidded her about it.

"These magazines you leave nonchalantly about in every room, even on my work desk in the garage . . . that's not a hint, is it?"

She knew he wanted to invest in a new kitchen as much as she did. It was only a matter of saving the money. Despite his good job, they were not unlike most middle-class families. They had their car payments, their mortgage, their regular monthly expenses. And the children needed more and more. Stuart was growing out of his clothing practically from week to week these days, and Debbie needed new things, too, not to mention her and Drake's clothing needs. It was time for him to get some new suits, and there was a pants and blouse outfit at Kandy's Boutique Cynthia couldn't stop drooling over, despite its five-hundred-dollar price tag. Besides all this, Drake insisted they put away money for a winter vacation every year.

"We've got to have something to look forward to," he insisted.

Stuart ran out to bring in the rest of their groceries while she started to put things away. She smiled in his wake. From visiting their friends and neighbors, she knew how difficult it was for most of them to get their children to do anything other than things purely for themselves. She was proud of how considerate and compassionate her two were. Surely it was a result of the cheerful home atmosphere. When there's love in the house . . .

"Dad's home!" Stuart announced, returning from the garage.

"Dad? But it's only"—she looked at the clock on the stove—"only three-thirty," she remarked. Her mind went instinctively to bad thoughts: He was sick. Maybe it was his leg. It had been bothering him so much that morning, it must have become unbearable.

She put down the jar of mayonnaise and went to the garage just as Drake drove in. He waved, smiled. He didn't look sick.

"Hi, Dad," Stuart cried from behind her. "We're having the party Saturday."

"Great. Now I have to find a date," he kidded.

"What's wrong, Drake?" Cynthia asked quickly. "Why are you home so early?"

"Nothing's wrong; everything's fine," he replied. She saw he was carrying a new black leather briefcase. He kissed her on the cheek. "Where's Peanut?"

"She doesn't know you're home, Dad," Stuart said. "She went right to her telephone to call Dottie Mednick and talk about Johnny Wilson."

"What's this? She's talking about a boy?" He winked at Cynthia. "And she's only in the fourth grade. You better have a mother-daughter talk with her, Cyn. Explain the facts of life. You know, how holding hands leads to chapped skin."

"Oh, Drake." She shook her head at him but continued to scrutinize his deep brown eyes for signs of trouble. She saw nothing but a brighter sparkle. "Where did you get that new briefcase, and what are you doing home so early?" she repeated, her voice a little more insistent.

"Hey, you sound like you're complaining," he teased, smiling impishly. He had gained about fifteen pounds since they'd first met, and his dark brown hair had become sprinkled with gray. Some days he looked tired and years older, but she always hesitated to mention it because she knew how sensitive he was about aging. He was terrified he would soon look like his brother Michael. This afternoon, though, she thought he looked free of stress. What was going on?

"Drake!" she whined. He laughed and embraced her. "Come on in and we'll talk. I have some great news."

"What?" she asked as they entered the kitchen.

"You'd better sit down," he advised, pointing to the dinette. "Oh, we've got groceries to put away," he said.

"They can wait. What is it?" she pursued.

"Can I stay, too, Dad?" Stuart asked.

"Sure, Mr. President, but just listen, okay?"

He nodded, elated that he would be included in a serious grown-up conversation.

"Well?" Cynthia demanded. She folded her arms under her bosom and sat back. "I'm sitting."

Drake pulled back his shoulders and took a deep breath.

"Remember that phone call this morning?"

"Of course. You went to lunch with that person?"

"Uh-huh." He paused, holding his smile.

"So? You're driving me crazy, Drake," she said when he still hesitated.

"I'm going to take the job."

She felt her heart skip a beat and a warm flush come into her face. Instinctively her hands went to the base of her throat. It was a family thing—her mother had the same gesture when anything made her nervous.

"What kind of job? Where?"

"The company's called Leon Enterprises," he said. "I'm going to be a salesman for them, and I've been given prime new territory. Our territory," he said, holding out his arms. "No more commuting!"

"What kind of salesman? What would you sell for them? Is it still insurance?" He stared at her, a cat-ate-the-mouse grin on his face. "Tell me," she insisted.

Drake placed the new briefcase in front of her on the table and snapped the brass fasteners open. Then he lifted the top of the briefcase and turned it to her, exposing the row of shiny silver tins.

"What is that?"

Drake plucked out a tin and unscrewed the top. He handed it to her and she looked at the clear, creamy contents. Then she read the cover.

"Youth Hold? What is it for?"

"It removes wrinkles anywhere they appear on the body."

"Wrinkles?" She sniffed the contents.

"No odor," he said. "No one can tell you have put it on."

She read the directions for its use and the words "Leon Enterprises."

"You've heard of dozens of lotions and creams that are supposed to keep your skin young and wrinkle-free. Well, this is the real thing. This works!" Drake announced.

She smirked and sniffed it again. Then she shook her head.

"Drake . . ."

"No, listen," he said. "I've had the most extraordinary day today." He seized a chair and pulled it back quickly to sit down. "I met Paul Stoddard for lunch at the Grand Hyatt. You should see this guy. He drives a Porsche, has a house in Westchester, a New York apartment, and property in Beverly Hills."

"From selling this?" Cynthia asked, indicating the Youth Hold.

"Uh-huh. He's regional director now for Leon Enterprises."

"How old a man is he?" she asked. Drake smiled and nodded softly.

"He's older than I am, but he looks years younger than I do. Happy in his work, that's the secret. This job is stress-free. Nothing to exacerbate my already accelerated time clock," he emphasized.

Cynthia glanced at the tin and then reached for it to look at it more closely.

"Can I smell it, too, Dad?" Stuart asked.

"Sure, son." Drake handed him another tin after opening it. Stuart sniffed and shrugged.

"You've got a long way to go before you need this, Stuart."

"I've never heard of this stuff, Drake," Cynthia said, turning the tin around in her hand.

"That's because it isn't in stores and it's not advertised."

"Why not?"

"Paul Stoddard says they don't have to advertise, and Mr. Leon doesn't want to put his product on shelves beside phony merchandise."

"Really? But why not advertise?"

"Because," Drake said sitting back and smiling widely, "they don't have to. I told you . . . this works."

"This works?" Cynthia started to laugh. "I know you're a crackerjack salesman, Drake, but you're talking to someone who is familiar with just about every cream and lotion on the market."

"I know, and that's the beauty of this product. I really don't have to be a crackerjack salesman. Gone are the days when I had to use psychology, manipulate, be shrewd and even a bit dishonest in order to make a sale," he added, winking at Stuart.

"But—"

"If a product is really good, truthful, and honest and does what it's supposed to do, people will buy it just because of that. It sells itself," Drake explained, aware that he was using Paul's exact words.

"But if it's not in stores, how do people get it, Dad?" Stuart asked.

"That's the beauty of this company, son," Drake said, and he leaned toward Cynthia again. "It is sold only by our own people, people who have been screened and chosen carefully, and it's only sold door-to-door, the old-fashioned way.

"Paul Stoddard explained that Mr. Leon is an old-fashioned gentleman. He is the sole owner of the company and the sole creator of the product, a real American success story."

Cynthia's skepticism began to dissolve. She dipped the tip of her forefinger into the cream and studied the contents.

"What's in it?"

Drake shrugged.

"Secret formula. That's what we're supposed to tell people if they ask. Paul says keeping it mysterious helps sell it. People have the feeling they have something no one else has."

She shook her head.

"You're going to give up a good job at Burke-Thompson to go door-to-door and sell a youth cream that dissolves wrinkles?"

"Uh-huh. I already quit."

It was as if a clap of thunder had shaken the house. Her heart paused and then began to pound. She felt her face redden.

"Stuart," she said, "please go do your homework."

"Huh? But Dad said—"

"Stuart, go do your homework," she commanded. He rose obediently but sadly.

"Go on, son. We'll talk in a few minutes, and you can tell me all about the seventh-grade meeting."

"Okay," he said, somewhat placated. The moment he was out the door Cynthia turned on Drake.

"I can't believe what you're telling me. You quit your job without discussing it with me."

"It all happened so fast, Cyn," he explained. "I knew once you heard the details you would be just as happy and excited about it as I was."

"But Drake . . . you were building something substantial at Burke-Thompson. You told me Larry indicated you would be made vice-president next week, and we were planning on that added income—"

"Forget Burke-Thompson," he declared, pulling his chair closer to the table. "Opportunity has come knocking—no, pounding—at my door."

"But you're getting a raise."

Drake sat back, widening his smile.

"Cynthia, I'm already going to make three times more than I'm making now. I could never make this kind of money at Burke-Thompson even if they made me president."

She gazed at him incredulously and then looked at the tin of cream.

"But to give up a job with a respected insurance firm to sell something nobody's heard of . . . not one person I know talks about this, Drake." She couldn't help sounding as if she was whining. He didn't change his expression.

"When you grimace like that, Cynthia, you deepen the crow's feet, and they shatter your temples."

"Crow's feet?" She had just the faint beginnings of facial wrinkles and never imagined Drake saw them as unattractive. Most of her friends, even beautiful Steffi Klein, were envious of her complexion.

Drake dipped his finger into the cream and reached out to pat her temple, but she backed away.

"It won't hurt you."

"I told you, Drake, I have a half dozen of one thing or another upstairs on my vanity table. I don't think I have a serious problem yet anyway."

"You don't, but this will ensure you never do."

"Oh, Drake, nothing really works."

"This does," he insisted. He closed the tin and pushed it toward her. "Try it or not, this is going to support us and give us things we've only dreamed of having. I have the entire Hudson Valley territory, and people here are just as vain as they are everywhere else."

Cynthia shook her head, still disbelieving he had gone ahead and made a major life decision without discussing it thoroughly with her. It was so unlike him; he seemed so different, as if his new job had already changed him in some mysterious way.

"Why did they come to you, an insurance salesman, to sell a cosmetic cream? I don't understand."

"It all began with a recommendation from Harris Levy. I mentioned that this morning. He's their Connecticut regional director, and—"

"But you didn't know him, did you? Is he a former client?"

"No." He shrugged. "As I told you, the only Harris Levy I can recall is a Harris Levy who worked with my father in the old days. That's not important anyway. What's important is that they want me very badly."

She nodded. Drake was a good salesman. He was talented when it came to persuading people to buy things. He had natural talent and knew who was a potential customer and who wasn't, and he was so personable that everyone who met him liked him. It was understandable that another company would want him, but this was such a dramatic step, and one he had taken so abruptly.

"What if you don't make as much as you think you will, Drake?"

"I told you, my salary will be almost triple what I'm making now, and I get a commission on sales, too. I can't do badly," he replied, arms out.

"You really told them at Burke-Thompson that you're taking another position?"

"That's why I'm home early," he said, smiling. "Paul Stoddard drove me to the commuters' parking lot to pick up the car and—"

"How much notice did you give them?"

"No notice. I'm finished with Burke-Thompson."

"You just packed up and left?" He nodded, holding his smile, which she thought was annoying now. "After twelve years?"

"Uh-huh."

"But that's not right. You shouldn't burn bridges, Drake. You always say that yourself."

"I'm not going back, Cynthia. This is one bridge I don't mind burning." He pushed the tin of cream at her and stood up.

"Daddy!" Debbie cried from the doorway. "I didn't know you were home."

"Hey, Peanut. Come give your old man a kiss. I did well today and came home to share the news." He beamed and glanced at Cynthia to indicate that he thought she should be more supportive. Debbie ran into his waiting arms. Cynthia watched them a moment and then looked at the tin of cream.

To risk their futures, their lives on some new foolish cosmetic . . . what had come over him? Could he apologize to Mr. Burke and get his job back? she wondered.

"Well, I guess I better go up and talk with Stuart. We've got class business. Come on, Peanut."

He started out with Debbie and then stopped and turned back to Cynthia.

"Oh. There's a get-together of employees and their spouses at Paul Stoddard's home a week from this Saturday. You can meet all the other salespeople. From the way Paul describes them, it's like one big family."

She nodded, still in a daze, and began to put away the groceries and prepare dinner. Drake was so excited about his job that she had to remind him why their dinner was special. He laughed and apologized. He was so happy, she didn't have the heart to be upset.

Just before going to bed Cynthia sat at her vanity table and studied her face in the mirror. Everyone her age had crow's feet. Why make a big thing about it? Of course, in time, age would catch up with her, just as it did with everyone else. Even Mom was starting to look her years. You couldn't hold it back forever, even if you had great genes and used pounds and pounds of skin creams.

Why do we have to grow old? she thought. Why can't we remain young and beautiful and just die that way? Age, she had read somewhere, was a disease, just like any other disease, and if that was so, perhaps it could be cured.

She looked down at the tin of wonder cream—Drake's promising future. She hesitated and then opened the tin and dipped her forefinger into the soft clear cream. Then she spread it evenly over her temples.

Nothing happened, except that the cream disappeared.

She smirked. He was going to go door-to-door. No matter how good a salesman he was, he would eventually have to give this up and return to a regular job, she thought. She covered the tin and prepared for bed.

After Drake tucked Debbie in for the night he joined her, slipping under the blanket gracefully.

"I'm getting up early to meet Paul Stoddard in Manhattan tomorrow," he said. She didn't reply. "You're angry, huh?"

"Frightened is more like it."

"Don't be. I know this is going to be great for us. I just know it."

"But what if it isn't, Drake? What will you do?"

"Hey, I'm not exactly a nobody in the insurance business. I'll get another position."

"But you would have to start at the bottom," she insisted, "and at your age—"

"What am I, ninety?"

"You know what I mean. You're always complaining about how this country puts such an emphasis on youth. Didn't you tell me about your friend Sam Cohen? You said he's a great salesman, but just because he's in his early fifties he can't find a good job. They would rather hire someone green at a low salary and build on him. Didn't you tell me that?"

"Yeah. So what? That's not going to happen to me, Cynthia," he said bitterly.

She was sorry they were arguing. It was their real anniversary night; they should be affectionate toward each other. She should be in his arms.

"I'm sorry," she said. "I'm just scared."

"Hey, did I ever let you down? Huh?" He put his arm around her, and she pressed her face against his shoulder.

"I love you, Drake," she whispered.

"And I love you. Hey, we've got some celebrating to

do, don't we?'' She didn't reply. He kissed her cheek and then slid down the bed so he could place his lips between her breasts. She moaned softly. ''Happy anniversary, honey,'' he whispered, running his hands gently under her nightgown. He caressed her naked thighs softly. She sat up and pulled her nightgown up and off her body.

They kissed again, and he took off his pajamas.

''The way we fit,'' he commented as they brought their bodies together, ''it's as if we were designed for each other.''

''Fated to be?''

''Like Romeo and Juliet.''

She reached up and put her hand behind his head to bring his lips down on hers again, and then they made love as passionately and as lovingly as they ever had before.

In the morning Drake was up before she was. She opened her eyes and saw him coming out of the bathroom, his towel wrapped around his waist.

''Good morning, sleepyhead,'' he said.

Her eyelids fluttered, but she couldn't keep them open. Sleep was tenacious.

''Morning,'' she said, sitting up slowly and yawning. He sat on the bed and pulled on his jockey shorts and socks. Then he turned to kiss her. After he did and she opened her eyes, she smiled incredulously. His face had a glow and a smoothness to it.

''You look bright and chipper this morning.''

''I feel it.''

''No, I mean you look . . . different.'' What was it? There was something.

He smiled.

''My wrinkles,'' he said. ''And those characteristic Edwards bags under my eyes . . . they're gone.''

''Gone?'' Yes, she thought, they were.

He took her hand and kissed her fingertips.

''I used Youth Hold yesterday,'' he said, ''when I met Paul Stoddard for lunch.'' He admired himself in

44

the mirror over her vanity table. "And as you can see, it works! And you know what that means, don't you?" he asked as he stood up to finish dressing.

"What?"

"We're going to be rich," he replied. "Very rich."

Thor's sharp, guttural bark wrenched Mr. Leon out of a delightful post-lovemaking doze. He sat up abruptly in his bed. A red light on his security monitor was blinking madly, and a buzzer went off, crying out an alarm. His dog strutted angrily from one side of the room to the other, frustrated by the sounds and his inability to attack.

Instantly Mr. Leon hit the intercom switch and screamed into the microphone. His voice would be heard virtually everywhere on the compound like God screaming down from the heavens.

"Sector four!" he cried. "I have an indication of a penetration at sector four!"

Another alarm sounded, and then another. Outside his bedroom suite and all along the corridors of his great house the scurry of footsteps and the shouts of security personnel could be heard as they converged on sector four. Thor began to scratch at the double doors to join the pursuit.

"Stay," Mr. Leon commanded. He wanted his dog to remain close to him. Thor retreated from the door obediently but whined and barked at it.

Mr. Leon reached down at the side of his bed and came up with his .357 Magnum. He cocked it and spun off his bed, crawling in commando fashion over the rug toward his patio door. The gold silk curtains had been drawn closed, so he moved a corner of the material away with the barrel of his pistol to peer out at the grounds. He saw one of his men carrying an Uzi machine gun and rushing across the lawn. Two Dobermans ran alongside him, barking madly.

"What is it? What's wrong?"

The girl in the bed was awoken by the noise and

45

tumult. She turned her head slightly to come up out of sleep the way a diver might emerge for a quick intake of air before returning to the depths of wonder. She closed her eyes again but grimaced when Thor's barking became even more shrill. "What's going on?" she cried.

"Shut up," Mr. Leon growled. He couldn't recall which one he had taken to bed, just that she was one of the brunettes.

The young woman closed her eyes and pulled the downy quilt over her head.

Mr. Leon waited impatiently. Finally he went back to his intercom.

"What is it?" he demanded. "Gerald!"

Gerald Dorian responded instantly.

"It looks like some kids in the nearby field lost control of one of those remote-control airplanes, Mr. Leon. It flew into the fence and caught on fire because of the electric current. We're taking care of it, sir."

Mr. Leon released the air in his lungs and relaxed. He lowered the hammer on his pistol and placed it securely in its holster. Then he turned to Thor.

"Quiet," he commanded. "Quiet!"

The dog gazed up at him as if it were being betrayed and then lowered its head and retreated to its bed.

"It's all right," Mr. Leon muttered as if the dog could understand. "False alarm," he added.

He straightened up, feeling somewhat silly and embarrassed by his own overreaction now, but the woman he had taken to bed still had the blanket pulled over her head. Later she would probably tell the others about this silly dream she had had. It brought a smile to his face.

Now he recalled. Her name was Sandra; she was that Jewish girl Gerald had found at the Fontainebleau a year or so ago, the one from New York who had been working as a receptionist in the hotel, hoping to find a rich doctor or lawyer on vacation. Frustrated with her failure and terrified she would turn twenty-nine and still be unmarried, she was susceptible and vulnerable to all that he could offer. Like the others, she was more than satisfied with the accommodations, the charge accounts, the chauffeur-driven limousines. Of course, she didn't know anything. None of them did. It wasn't necessary that they know. He kept them until they bored him, and then he let them go.

Whenever he thought about them and about ridding himself of one or the other, he imagined his fingers on the end of a balloon, holding in the air. Tired of it, he released his grip, and the air escaped. The balloon shriveled up, lost its form and its beauty. Now it was something to discard.

Just like them when he released his hold. They wouldn't understand what had happened. They would think they had remained young and beautiful, healthy and strong because they had lived in a wonderful place, where everything had been provided for them and where they had no worries, no obligations, nothing to concern themselves with but looking beautiful and sexy for him. No harm done, as long as he didn't keep them beyond their natural life spans. Once they had gone beyond that, like his disciples, like poor Harris Levy, they would have the terrible dream, live and die the nightmare.

He knew it awaited him if he should ever be put in the same predicament. Next to being assassinated, there was nothing he feared more. But since he was the one in control, the one with the power, he felt confident. After all, he had kept the nightmare simply a nightmare for centuries, hadn't he?

He laughed quietly and opened the drapes. The bright light washed out the shadows and poured warmth over the large room with its marshmallow-soft cream carpet, its clean white stucco walls, and its handmade Spanish antique furniture.

Sandra groaned under the blanket.

"I'm getting up," he said, and he went to the oversized walk-in closet to get his black silk robe. He wrapped it around his firm, sleek body, taking pleasure in his own muscularity, and slipped his feet into soft black leather moccasins.

Whenever he had a scare of any kind he instinctively wanted to visit the spring. Its trickle reassured him the way a mother might reassure her child after he had suffered a nightmare. It brought him the same warm comfort, the same sense of security, the same feeling that all would be right, forever and forever.

He laughed at that: "Forever and forever." It was his ritual toast. When he lifted his glass the disciples repeated the words: "Forever and forever."

Forever, he thought, is only as long as I want it to be.

— 4 —

Cynthia's two closest friends smiled at her across the table in the booth in Steine's Diner in Sandburg, where they had stopped for coffee and a nosh after a matinee movie. When they had met they barely had enough time to buy their tickets and get inside before the show began. Afterward Ellen and Steffi got into an argument about the way the wife in the movie handled her husband's infidelity. Ellen thought she should have cut his balls off, but Steffi thought she should simply run up his credit card bills. Cynthia hadn't been able to reveal anything about Drake's new job until the three of them were seated and served. Unable to contain herself any longer, she burst out with the news.

The late afternoon sky had turned gray. There was the chance of thunderstorms. As the clouds slipped over the sun the shadows in the parking lot expanded and spread over the cars. It tempered her elation.

"Of course, I'm excited," she continued after they offered congratulations, "but Drake's never done anything this radical without first talking it over with me and thinking it out carefully," she added pensively.

Ellen and Steffi stared at her, surprised at how quickly she had interjected a dark note.

"Maybe it was a take-it-or-leave-it proposition, and he had to act quickly," Steffi said. "Anyway, I leave all the important stuff to Sheldon. He's so much more intelligent than I am. You should do the same," Cynthia's petite, dark brunette friend counseled.

"It's not just a matter of who's more intelligent. These decisions have a major effect on both your lives. Sheldon shouldn't make any of them without consulting you first," Cynthia lectured gently. Out of the corner of her eye she saw Ellen shaking her head as if to say, "Why waste your breath?"

"Oh, he consults me," Steffi said, "but I usually say, 'Whatever you think, Sheldon.' That way, if we make a mistake, it's his fault," she emphasized with a sly smile.

"But what if it's a good decision?" Ellen asked quickly. "You won't be able to take any of the credit."

"Sure I will. I agreed to let him decide, didn't I?"

All three laughed loudly.

Ellen eyed the slice of blueberry pie à la mode they were all supposed to share as the waitress placed it at the center of the table. Cynthia understood.

"At war with your scale again?"

"Does Gucci sell perfume? Maybe Drake has something that will keep you from getting fat as well as getting wrinkles," Ellen quipped. "I'd kill for it."

"There is something," Steffi said, cutting off almost a third of the piece for herself.

"What's that?"

"A role of adhesive tape," she said. "Put a piece over your mouth." She giggled as Ellen scowled. "Just kidding."

"I don't understand why some people," Ellen said, nodding toward Steffi and widening her eyes as she bit into her chunk of pie, "can eat anything they want and not gain an ounce. And I know she doesn't do much exercise. She never wants to go to aerobics with me," she complained.

"It's all metabolism," Cynthia replied. "Probably the

same reason why some people age sooner than others—
the clock they inherited ticks faster. Anyway," she said,
reaching into her pocketbook and producing the tin of
Youth Hold, "science is starting to come up with
solutions."

"That's it?" Ellen asked, eyeing the tin covetously.
"That's what made your face glow like a teenager's
today?"

"Uh-huh."

"May I?"

"That's why I brought it along. Just wipe some over
your temples from the corner of your eyes back. Rub it
in gently," Cynthia instructed. Ellen dipped her finger
into the cream and brought the dab to her nose. "It
has no odor," Cynthia said. "That's another plus," she
added.

"You sound like *you're* the salesman," Steffi quipped.
Cynthia smiled.

"I do, don't I? Maybe it comes from living with one
so long," she explained, although she couldn't remember ever having pushed anything Drake had sold before.
She didn't want her friends thinking she wanted to make
money off their friendship.

"I wonder why I've never heard of this stuff," Steffi
said, studying the cover.

"The company is owned by an eccentric man who
doesn't want to advertise," Cynthia said.

"Sounds crazy," Steffi said.

"I'll try anything to change my life," Ellen said. She
rubbed the cream in and turned to Steffi. "Well?"

"It takes a while. Overnight," Cynthia said.

"If it works, send Drake over for his first sale. Of
course, young Venus here doesn't need any," she
said, indicating Steffi. She was unable to disguise her
resentment.

"I'll do what Cynthia did and use it as a preventa-
tive," Steffi said, dipping her finger in and spreading the
cream over her temples, too. She had a peach complex-

ion with skin so soft and blemish-free it was as if she had stepped off the pages of a glamour magazine.

Cynthia closed the tin and dropped it back in her pocketbook. Then she cut into the pie.

"I'm curious," Ellen said, and then she drew the right corner of her mouth up. "And I know George is going to grill me when I tell him anyway. How did Drake get this wonderful opportunity? Why did a cosmetics company come to an insurance salesman?"

"Someone recommended him."

"Oh."

"But that was very strange," Cynthia said, more to herself than to her friends. She held her piece of pie before her and thought. In the midst of all the excitement, the drama of Drake's starting an entirely new career and their suddenly becoming a lot better off financially, as well as the wonder of Youth Hold, she had completely forgotten Drake's earlier comments about that.

"What was strange?" Ellen pursued.

"Drake doesn't know the man who recommended him, a Harris Levy. Or at least, he doesn't think he does."

"Huh?" Steffi said. "Either he knows him or he doesn't, right?" She looked at Ellen, who nodded, but fixed her eyes on Cynthia.

"What does that mean, Cynthia?"

"The man with that name Drake knew couldn't be alive today. Or if he was alive, he certainly would be too old to be working."

"Well . . ." Ellen shook her head. "Shouldn't Drake be more curious about that? I know George would be. If I should switch our brand of margarine, he wouldn't dip his butter knife into it without first putting me through an interrogation as to why I changed."

"I don't know. I guess with all the excitement—"

"But before you changed jobs, wouldn't you want more assurances, references? It's not like my changing margarine," Ellen pursued.

Cynthia nodded thoughtfully.

"I should have asked more questions, too," she said, the concern wiping away the brightness in her face.

"What are you bugging her for?" Steffi interceded. "Look at her. She was happy a moment ago, and now you've got her worrying. See," Steffi said, holding up her blueberry-stained fork as if it held the point she was making, "that's why when your husband asks for your advice, it's best to say, 'Whatever you think, honey.' Then it's his fault, and you don't have to sit there worrying that you didn't ask enough questions."

Cynthia lifted her eyes toward her beautiful, happily self-centered friend, and for the first time she wondered if she wasn't the smartest of the three after all.

Although Drake had not given her any indication when he left to meet with Paul Stoddard in the morning, Cynthia had assumed he would be home about the same time as before. By the time she returned home, the children had already arrived from school. Stuart appeared at the door as soon as she stepped out of her car.

"Dad called. He won't be home for dinner," he announced sadly.

"Really?"

Stuart's face darkened with disappointment as he nodded. "I wanted to tell him the details about the party."

"So? You'll tell him when he arrives. Did he say what time that would be?"

"No. He just said it would be late."

"Late?" She shook her head. "Did he say why?"

"Nope. And Debbie's not feeling well," he added nonchalantly.

"What? What's wrong?"

"She's upstairs with a headache and stomachache."

"Oh, no. Stuart, why didn't you say so right away?"

"She said she was going to be all right after a nap," he called as she charged past him.

She found Debbie in bed, hugging the stuffed Mickey Mouse Drake had bought her two months earlier. It was nearly as big as she was. Her cheeks were streaked with tears.

"What's wrong, honey?" Cynthia sat beside her on the bed and felt her forehead. It was too warm.

"I threw up," Debbie moaned.

"Oh, you poor thing. Let me get you out of your clothes and get you some sweet tea to settle your stomach. I want to take your temperature, too, sweetheart." When she took the temperature she found Debbie had a little over a hundred and one.

"Looks like flu," she predicted. She had been through it a half dozen times before, but that didn't make her any less anxious.

"My stomach hurts, Mommy," Debbie complained.

"I know, sweetheart. I'll call the doctor."

"You better call Daddy and tell him to come home," Debbie cried through her tears.

"He's not working where he used to work, Debbie, and he's coming home late. But don't worry," she added quickly. "Mommy will help you."

Stuart came to the bedroom door. Too often when one of her children came down with something, the other followed suit.

"Better stay away from Debbie for a while, Stuart. I'm sure she has the flu."

"Ugh," Stuart said. "I can't get sick now," he added in a panic. "We're having the party tomorrow night!"

"Well, then that's all there is to it," she said, smiling back at him. "You can't get sick. Can he, Debbie?"

Debbie shook her head but grimaced with another jolt of stomach spasms.

"I'll call the doctor," Cynthia repeated, and she returned to the kitchen. When she described the symptoms to their pediatrician, he agreed it sounded like the flu and prescribed the usual: some sweet tea, aspirin for headache, and some warm Coke for nausea.

Cynthia became so busy with Debbie, she forgot all about dinner for herself and Stuart, but her twelve-year-old son surprised her by coming to Debbie's doorway to announce he had prepared a salad and spaghetti for both of them. Although Cynthia had little appetite, she was too proud of him and saw he was too proud of himself for her to turn down the dinner. Debbie finally drifted into a slumber, so Cynthia went to the dining room. Stuart had already set the table.

"This is wonderful, Stuart. Wait until I tell your father!"

Stuart pulled out her chair. She smiled at his firm, serious face. He looked like Drake when he concentrated on something, she thought. She took her seat and let Stuart serve. He had prepared an attractive salad and even warmed the garlic bread. When she saw how well he had cooked the spaghetti she was sincerely impressed.

"It's delicious, honey. I'm going to have you make dinner more often."

He took her seriously and shook his head.

"I can't Mom. I'm going to have to stay after school a lot more these days. Class presidents sit on the student judiciary committee and the student government executive council," he reminded her. Cynthia nodded. How quickly responsibility was maturing him, she thought. And then she thought about how burdens and obligations tend to make one older so much faster.

"Don't take on more than you can handle, honey. You have your schoolwork, too. And you were talking about going out for the basketball team, right? You and Daddy practiced all summer." She recalled the two of them out in the driveway, Drake patiently explaining the right techniques. She knew he had been an excellent athlete in high school and was often frustrated by his knee injury. Just tossing a basketball with his twelve-year-old son made him grimace in agony, but he tried not to show it for Stuart's sake.

"I know. I won't," he said with Drake's same self-assurance.

She smiled and finished her dinner. Stuart wanted to clean up, but Debbie was still sleeping, so she decided to do it all to keep her mind off things. It didn't work.

The clock ticked on, and still Drake did not return or call again.

Debbie woke up, still having stomach cramps. When Cynthia took her temperature again it had risen to one hundred and three, and this with her taking aspirin. She debated calling the doctor one more time, but she didn't. She didn't want to be a panicking mother, and she knew it was best to save the doctor for when things really looked serious.

Temperatures always go up at night anyway, she told herself. She gave her another aspirin and a half. She sat beside her and comforted her until she fell asleep once more.

The polished black limousine pulled up in front of Antonio's restaurant on Macdougal Street in the Village, and the driver got out quickly to open the door for Drake and Paul Stoddard. Drake smiled and nodded at the driver, who seemed impervious to any gratitude or courtesy.

"You're going to love this place," Paul said. "It opened months ago and is still relatively unknown, but it's a real find."

"I'd better call home," Drake said after gazing at his watch. "We've been so busy, I didn't have a chance since I spoke with my son."

"Sure. Do it inside. Give us three hours, Charles," Paul told the driver.

"Three hours!" Drake exclaimed.

"Hey, when you dine at Antonio's, you dine. This isn't one of your mom-and-pop diners in Sandburg," he added in a derisive whisper, and then he followed it with a loud laugh. He slapped Drake on the back. Sometimes, Drake thought, Paul seemed so unrefined for a man with so much responsibility and wealth. It was as if he had gained it all overnight.

"Come on," Paul coaxed. "The others are eager to meet you. Whenever someone is added to the Leon family it is very exciting for the rest of us." He opened the door and indicated that Drake should enter first.

It was a small restaurant with no more than a dozen or so tables, many just big enough for two. The decor consisted of gray stucco walls, three gaudy brass chandeliers, two false windows dressed with light blue drapes, and a cream tile floor. All the tables had candles in bell-shaped lamps and were covered with white cotton tablecloths. The waiters were dressed in black and white with black ties.

There was a small bar to the left of the entrance, but there was no one at it. In fact, only four of the tables had people at them. Paul had been right about the place's remaining undiscovered, Drake thought. One of the larger tables in the far right corner had three people at it. Drake assumed they were the other Leon sales personnel. Paul gestured in their direction.

Two women and one man stood up as they approached. Neither of the two women looked much older than their mid-twenties, and both were rather attractive. The one introduced as Patricia Stanley was a tall, bright-eyed, auburn-haired woman with a sleek, full-breasted figure well revealed in her thin, light blue cotton dress. Drake thought her waist was so small, he could place his hands on her hips and touch his fingertips.

Estelle Brown looked to be the older of the two, but not by much. She was a good four inches shorter than Patricia and had dark brown hair. Her figure was smaller, but no less tantalizing in her frilly turquoise Spanish blouse and pleated peasant skirt. Either of these two could be in show business, Drake thought. They were both outstanding.

Brad Peters, the man in the middle, looked about thirty. He stood a little over six feet tall and had a firm athletic build, svelte in his light blue sports coat and slacks. Even in the dim light Drake could see he had a tan, healthy look and was quite attractive with his bright blue eyes. Later Drake would learn that Brad had just returned from a two-week vacation in Florida, visiting with Mr. Leon.

"The Leon compound is like a major resort anyway," Paul said when it was mentioned, and everyone agreed.

They began with wine, two different kinds. Everyone seemed so knowledgeable about wines—the years, the different tastes. From the conversation Drake gathered they were all well-traveled; they knew restaurants in Paris, Madrid, London, and Rome. They got into an argument about Greek food and the best restaurant in Athens.

Most of the evening Drake was an observer and listener. What could he contribute anyway? His and Cynthia's travels were limited to motor trips up and down the Eastern seaboard and a few Caribbean holidays. Once they had gone to Mexico, but Europe, the Far and Middle East—all loomed somewhere on the dream horizon, to be visited when the children were older. If they could afford it at the time, that was.

Well, now they could, he thought, and in time they would be as well-traveled and as sophisticated as the people around him. He couldn't help being a little bitter about it. The three looked years younger than he and Cynthia and had apparently lived twice the life. Boy, how he had buried himself, he thought, and he became even more grateful that this opportunity had presented itself.

He had spent most of the day learning about the financial benefits associated with working for Leon Enterprises—the employee participation in stock and other perks as well as the other businesses, professionals, and tradespeople who provided services and products free as a courtesy to employees of Leon Enterprises. When Drake questioned why, Paul replied, "Because we give them something they can't get anywhere else." He left it at that for the time being, and when Drake looked at the list of what was available to him and his family he didn't question any further. The biggest freebie at Burke-Thompson had been the key to the men's room.

He and Paul then went over the territory he would be assigned, mapping out where he would go and what he would try to accomplish. At lunch Paul told him a little about himself, how he had been married twice and how his second marriage wasn't going well. In fact, he was in the midst of a rather tragic situation, even though it was impossible to tell from his demeanor. His wife had literally disappeared.

"She's been suffering from a deep depression," Paul told him. "Actually, she had become suicidal. The doctors thought it was something chemical, an imbalance. One day I came home from work and she was gone."

"How long has it been?" Drake asked.

"A little over two weeks."

"My God. I never would have known anything was wrong. I mean . . . you seem so well adjusted, so—"

"It's part of our training," Paul explained. "How to deal with crisis. Mr. Leon wants his people to be stress-free, to keep their temperaments even, not to suffer anxiety and get sick and old from it."

"Training?"

"Workshops. I'll explain it to you this afternoon," he said, smiling.

Drake nodded.

"Still . . . what have the police been doing about your wife?"

"All that they can. I didn't mind telling you about it, but it's not healthy to dwell on it," Paul said somewhat curtly. "I don't want to be rude, but it's something we've been taught, and it works."

"Of course," Drake said, but it was as though a small, dark cloud had crossed the warm, promising sun. That was the only depressing note of the day, however.

Drake was impressed with the beautiful office Leon Enterprises kept in Manhattan. It wasn't large, but it was plush—thick, rich nylon carpets, oak-paneled walls, comfortable real leather sofas and settees. The view from Paul's window was one of the most breathtaking views of Manhattan Drake had ever seen. At Burke-

Thompson he had a view of another cubicle on his right and a dark gray wall on his left.

Paul explained Drake's territory to the others at Antonio's, and the conversation centered on how best to begin in a new area. Each related his own experience, what succeeded, what made things harder.

Another bottle of wine was ordered, and then another. Each of the three had to impress everyone else with his or her choices, Drake concluded. He remained as diplomatic as possible when they turned to him for his opinions.

"I can see you have found a perfect Leon Enterprises employee," Brad Peters declared. "He knows how to avoid offending anyone. That's good sales psychology." The two women laughed but stared at Drake with such interest, he found himself flattered. That, along with a half dozen glasses of wine, made him lose track of time and place. By the time they had ordered and been served their meals a little over two hours had passed. Paul's estimate of three hours to dine was beginning to look accurate, if not underestimated.

Once, just before they ordered their coffee and dessert, Drake thought about calling home, but somehow he lost track of that thought, too. Perhaps it was because of the way Estelle kept patting him on the knee, or because of the glow in Patricia's crystalline green eyes when she spoke to him. She fixed her eyes on him so firmly he couldn't look away, and he even became self-conscious about how often he gazed down at her deep-cut, promising cleavage and the rosy tops of her breasts, bubbling out of her revealing neckline.

Finally the dinner ended. The women hugged and kissed him, and Brad welcomed him warmly with a vigorous handshake.

"You're one of us now," he said. "And that makes you very special."

Feeling a buzz from the wine, the wonderful meal, the exciting conversation, and the beautiful women, he never noticed the lateness of the hour when he and Paul finally emerged from the restaurant and got into the limousine.

"How are you doing?" Paul asked.

"Great. I feel great."

"You're going to feel better. Don't worry about your car. I'll have someone bring it home for you. I'd rather take you home in the limousine tonight. Don't want anything to happen to our newest prospect," he explained.

"Well, that's very kind of you."

"No problem." He leaned forward and opened the small bar. "How about something cold?"

"Sure."

He poured two mineral waters over ice and handed him one.

"How'd you like the Northeast group?"

"Great. Can't get over how young and good-looking everyone is. Especially Patricia and Estelle," Drake said. Patricia's eyes still loomed in his.

"They're both about my age," Paul remarked.

"What? Those women are over thirty?"

"Early fifties, to be exact."

"No way," Drake said.

"Yes, there is a way. Mr. Leon wants his salespeople to look young and be healthy, for obvious reasons. You don't mind, do you?"

"Mind? Mind what?" Drake held his confused smile.

"Looking young and being healthy?"

"What?" He laughed. "I'll put up with it, only there's just so much this cream can do for me."

"Of course, and that's why I'm going to ask you to do one more thing. I'm asking for Mr. Leon, actually."

"What's that?"

"Start taking one of these every day," Paul said, drawing a small plastic case out of his pocket. He opened it carefully and revealed a dozen clear capsules. They looked empty.

"What is that?"

"Our special brand of vitamins, you might say. It

won't hurt you; it will give you more energy than you've had in a long time."

Drake nodded, a bit apprehensive.

"There is one setback," Paul confessed. "Once you start with this, you won't want to stop."

"It's addictive? An addictive vitamin?"

Paul shrugged.

"It's only natural that we would become addicted to good health and youthful vigor, isn't it?"

"I suppose so, but—"

"You saw those three tonight."

Drake stared at him. What was he trying to say?

"How old is Brad Peters?"

"Truthfully?"

"Yes, of course."

"Brad's seventy-one."

"Seventy-one! I don't believe that."

Paul shrugged.

"It's all right. You will believe it eventually." He held out the plastic container. "It's up to you, Drake. The choice is simple—money, health, youthful vigor, or . . . what you had before."

"You mean I've got to take these things, this addictive vitamin?"

"You won't regret it," Paul said. "I don't," he added.

Drake thought for a moment.

"Well, if it's that good, what's the problem?" He plucked a capsule out of the case. "I'll get my wife to take them, too, and—"

"No," Paul said, shaking his head. "You can't. She's not working for Mr. Leon."

"Really?"

"I'm afraid so. You're going to have only enough for yourself, Drake, and if you should share what you have and fall short, you won't be happy, and neither will she. Do you understand?" The threat was clear.

"For that reason," Paul continued, "it's best you

don't ever tell her about this. Don't even let her see them."

Drake held the capsule inches from his mouth.

"Well," Paul said sitting back, "that's all of it. If you can live with it, everything we've described is yours, just as you see it's been ours."

Drake looked at the capsule and then looked at Paul, who waited with a tight smile on his face.

"Doesn't seem to me like I'm sacrificing anything," Drake concluded. "Like you said, it's not an addiction anyone would complain about."

He placed the capsule in his mouth and chased it down with the cold mineral water.

"Welcome," Paul said, reaching forward and taking Drake's hand firmly in his. "Welcome to Leon Enterprises."

— 5 —

Cynthia glanced at the clock on Debbie's nightstand and saw it was nearly ten o'clock. Drake had still not returned or called. Even though he had given the message to Stuart, he should have called her to let her know when he would be home if he was going to be this late, she thought. Where could he be?

Stuart was just crawling into bed when she went to his room.

"I was hoping Daddy would come home before I went to sleep," he complained. "He couldn't talk long on the phone."

"You and Daddy will talk in the morning, honey," she promised.

"What if Debbie's still sick tomorrow? Will you still be able to chaperon?" Stuart asked.

"We'll see. Besides, Stuart," she chastised gently, "you should be worried more about her than about your party, right?"

He nodded. She saw he regretted sounding self-centered. How easy it is for all of us to become that way, Cynthia thought.

She tucked him in and kissed him on the forehead, partly to reassure herself that he wasn't coming down with something, too. He felt cool. "Daddy didn't say anything more than that he would be late?" she inquired again. Stuart shook his head.

"All right, honey," she said, standing. "You better go to sleep."

Stuart nodded, still despondent.

"Stop moping," she said, and she ran her hand through his hair. "I was very proud of you tonight, honey, and Daddy's going to be, too, when he hears how helpful you were." She kissed him again and left the room.

When she looked in on Debbie she found her still sleeping, but her cheeks were crimson, and she felt even warmer than she had before. She would sponge her down with cool water when she awoke, Cynthia thought, and she went into the den, hoping to distract herself with some reading. She didn't want to turn on the television, afraid that she wouldn't hear Debbie.

Just before eleven she heard a car pull into the driveway, and she heaved a sigh. Drake was finally home. But when she didn't hear the garage door go up she rose with curiosity and hurried to the window just in time to see a limousine back out and start away. Drake was walking toward the front door of the house, swinging his briefcase and whistling.

Confused, she went to greet him at the door. He entered smiling.

"Hi, honey." He reached out to embrace her, but she stepped back.

"Drake, where have you been? What happened to your car?" she exclaimed.

"Someone's bringing it up for me tomorrow. They didn't want me driving. I'm not drunk," he added quickly. "It was just more convenient this way. Besides, we have all sorts of people to handle these gofer jobs." He reached out for her again, but she remained implanted.

"How did you get home?"

"The Leon Enterprises limo," he said proudly.

"Chauffeur and all. Neat, huh? Now where's my wel-come-home kiss?" He stepped forward. She still didn't go to him, even though they were inches apart in the foyer.

"But where have you been? It's after eleven," she said, grimacing. He looked strange, his eyes so bright they were nearly luminous, and his face glowed with a youthful vibrancy, reminding her of the very first time they had met. It was as if the years between had been only a dream and they were yet to live them.

"Honey," he said, shaking his head, "I had the great-est day, met the greatest people. This is the best move I could ever have made."

All these superlatives, she thought. He sounded like a teenager.

"But where have you been all day, Drake?" she repeated, her tone somewhat more demanding. "And what have you been doing until now?"

"I wasn't playing," he replied with unexpected agita-tion. He turned to put his briefcase on the small foyer table.

"I know," she said softly. "It's just so late, and—"

Drake spun around so abruptly that she brought her hands to the base of her throat and stepped back.

"Here's what I did all day," he began with an aggres-sive verbal energy. "Paul and I worked on strategies for the territory. He explained the job in more detail, had me fill out the required business forms, tax forms, and so on. I learned about the perks. We went to lunch. I went back to his office, and we talked about the product, its history, plans for the future, and then we went to dinner to meet with some of the other northeastern sales representatives." He flashed a smile. "Okay?"

"You stayed in the city for dinner?"

"Uh-huh. Paul took me to this fabulous Italian place in the Village. Don't ask me what I ate. I never heard of any of the dishes, but everything was fantastic!" He smacked his lips.

"This company," he said, rattling on, "is like a big

family, Cynthia. I never met so many strangers and in so short a time felt as if I had known them all my life. I mean, everyone is down-to-earth but enthusiastic about the work. You just get the feeling you can do wonders, live forever," he cried, looking around as if first realizing he had arrived in his own home.

"That sounds very nice, Drake, but—"

"Cynthia," he proclaimed, his hands on his hips as he turned slowly toward the kitchen, "I've decided we should forget about redoing this kitchen."

"Forget about redoing it? But why? You said we were going to be able to afford it, and—"

"We're going to be able to afford a lot better than this dump," he said disdainfully. He almost spit out the words.

"Dump?" The house needed some work, but Drake had never called it a dump before, she thought.

"We're going to build a new house, one nearly twice the size," he declared. "And the kitchen will have the most up-to-date appliances. And furniture"—he glanced at the living room and shook his head—"we need new furniture. I want us to have a playroom, too. You know, pool table, Ping-Pong. After we finish building the house we should build a tennis court, don't you think? I know you're going to want a swimming pool. I mean, that will be built when we build the house. We will be doing a lot more entertaining. It's important.

"As soon as I get back I want to start looking for some land, land with a view, in one of the communities closer to New York City," he concluded, nearly overwhelming her with his energetic outburst. Working all day, riding to New York and back, having dinner and drinks . . . she expected all that would have made him tired, but he looked as fresh as he had in the morning.

"Get back? Back from where?" She realized they hadn't moved from the entryway yet, and Drake hadn't asked about the children, but he had tossed surprises at her one after the other so quickly that she had barely had a chance to catch her breath.

"I've got to go to a weekend session of workshops sponsored by the company tomorrow. It's the way they break in all their salespeople."

"Workshops? You didn't mention any workshops before."

"Well, I just learned about them," he said, looking a little annoyed that she would be even slightly critical or upset. "This is a very special product, Cynthia," he said, tapping his briefcase and lowering his voice until it was almost a whisper. "And Mr. Leon is very particular about how we approach people, what we say, and so on. There are sales techniques and there are sales techniques. Leon Enterprises does things in a unique way. We work with psychologists, sociologists, marketing researchers. It's a very sophisticated operation."

"How long has this company been in business, Drake?"

"Why?"

"It sounds so big, so successful. How long?" she pursued.

"A while," he said, smiling. "A long while."

Cynthia shook her head.

"But Drake, why is it no one has publicized this? Why hasn't it at least been in the news, or written up in magazines? You know Steffi Klein subscribes to just about every fashion and cosmetic magazine published, and she's never heard of it either."

"I told you. It's Mr. Leon's way to downplay. He despises publicity and has never granted anyone an interview. So," he said, finally entering the house, "everything all right? The children are asleep?"

"Debbie's sick," she finally revealed. "I think it's the flu."

"Oh, really?" He looked more annoyed than concerned. "Did you call the doctor?"

"Yes. He prescribed aspirin and sweet tea, but she's burning up. I'm thinking of calling him again."

He nodded.

"Whatever you think." He seemed distracted, as if

he couldn't concentrate on anything but his new job, and it certainly wasn't characteristic of him to say "Whatever you think" when she told him one of the children was sick. More often than not, he was more doting and concerned than she was, especially when it came to Debbie. By now he would be in her room and at her bedside, so worried he would bring tears to her eyes.

Drake loosened his tie and started through the living room, Cynthia following behind.

"I didn't really realize until today just how much territory they're giving me. It's a big responsibility, and it's very flattering that they have such confidence in me, Cynthia. You should be very proud," he admonished. He gazed back at her disparagingly.

"I'm proud of you, Drake," she said defensively.

"Well, you don't sound it."

"What do you mean? What did I say?" she whined.

"It's not so much what you say, it's how you say it. And you keep harping on the fact that none of your friends know about Youth Hold. Well, you know, Cynthia," he added, turning on her, "those friends of yours are not the most sophisticated and intelligent people around."

She felt her cheeks redden.

"They're your friends, too, Drake. You like Sheldon Klein, and you've always enjoyed being with Steffi," she added, not intending to sound jealous. But she couldn't help it this time. She had seen the way Drake gawked at Steffi. Oh, there was never any question about his fidelity; it was just a woman's natural resentment and insecurity coming to the fore when her husband looked at another woman as appreciatively as Drake and the others looked at Steffi.

"What's that supposed to mean?" he snapped.

"Nothing. Just that . . . that you like being with these people. You like George and Ellen, and Gary and Lucy. And just the other day you wondered why we hadn't been with the Brands, right?"

"It's company," he shrugged. "What are we supposed to do, hibernate up here because most of our friends are simplistic?"

"Simplistic?" She shook her head. "Who were you with today? What sort of things did they put in your head, Drake?"

"See?" he said accusingly. "You're doing it again. Instead of finding joy in this, you're finding something to criticize. Just listen to yourself. Listen," he commanded, and he shook his head.

She felt the tears fill her eyes but held them back. Why were they arguing? She didn't understand what they were disagreeing about or why he was suddenly so upset. She took a deep breath.

"Okay," she said. "Let's not talk about it. I'm nervous about Debbie."

He nodded and finally headed up the stairs to her room. Cynthia paused in the doorway and watched. Debbie stirred when he put his hand on her forehead, but she didn't open her eyes.

"When did you give her an aspirin last?"

"About an hour ago."

He gazed down at their daughter and ran his hand softly over her hair. This was more like him, Cynthia thought: loving, concerned. Then he pulled his hand away quickly, as if Debbie were on fire and he was afraid to be burned.

"She feel very hot?"

"No. She's got fever, but it's not unusually high." He shook his head. "Sickness is so debilitating, so horrendous," he said with surprising vehemence.

"I think it's just the flu," she said softly, hopefully.

"It doesn't matter." He looked up at her. In the light spilling in from the hallway his eyes blazed. "Anything, even the common cold, is intolerable." He looked back at Debbie, muttered something under his breath, and started out. "Let's give the aspirin a chance to work," he decreed, and he went to their bedroom.

She checked Debbie herself and thought she didn't

feel any hotter than before. Maybe the fever had reached its peak and would break before morning. She fixed her daughter's blanket, surprised that Drake hadn't done so. There were many times when Debbie was sick that Drake would plant himself on a chair in her room and watch her for hours. His fear came from her being so small and fragile.

When she entered their bedroom she found him undressing. He was sitting on the bed, slipping off his socks. He smiled up at her, but so licentiously that it brought a smile of curiosity and surprise to her own face.

"Missed you," he said.

"I was hoping you would call to let me know exactly what was going on. I was worried," she replied softly. He slipped his pants off and set them aside.

"I was going to call you from the restaurant, but I got so involved with these people that by the time I thought about doing it, it was time to leave. Then I was going to call you from the limousine, but Paul said it might frighten you to receive a call this late. I thought he was right, so I figured I'd just come home. Sorry," he added, and he smiled lasciviously again, this time patting the bed to indicate she should come sit beside him. He was sitting in his briefs.

Despite his old football injury, Drake had been able to maintain a firm, athletic-looking body most of his life. Just lately he had developed "love handles" and a small paunch, but the muscles in his shoulders and arms were still quite dense and well-defined from his sessions at the health club. Cynthia had always admired his physique and told him he had cute buns. It was about as kinky as the two of them ever got.

Usually their lovemaking was gentle, straight, spontaneous. They petted and held each other lovingly before and after, and they were always considerate of each other. From listening to her friends reveal details of their own sexual relationships, she was sure they would find hers and Drake's quite uninteresting.

He reached up to take her hand and pull her closer to him when she hesitated.

"Hey, I'm sorry I yelled at you before," he said, sounding more like the Drake she knew.

"I didn't mean to sound like I was criticizing, Drake. It's just that this is a big decision, and—"

"I know," he said, and he ran his hand under her skirt. The move surprised her, for he brought his fingers quickly to her thigh and squeezed it gently.

"Drake, I'm still so nervous . . . Debbie." She turned back toward the open doorway, but his traveling fingers brought her back to him.

"She's got the flu. Kids get the flu," he said, moving his fingers to her crotch. She started to pull back, but he seized her other leg with his other hand and jerked her forward so that she fell awkwardly over him. Instantly he was at her, kissing her neck while he pulled his right hand out from under her skirt and ran it under her blouse, cupping her breast roughly. She groaned and tried to turn away, but he held her so tightly it hurt.

"Drake, you're squeezing too hard. What's wrong with you?"

"Wrong with me? Nothing," he said. "Don't you want to make love?"

"It's not that. I—"

"So?" He smiled and brought his lips to hers, pressing her back on the bed. She started to struggle when she felt him lowering his briefs. This wasn't making love, she thought; this was being raped.

"Drake!"

He didn't hear her, or if he did, he didn't want to pay any attention. His hand was under her skirt again, pulling her panties down so hard that he scratched the side of her leg with his fingernail. She cried out, but he acted as though she was crying in ecstasy.

"The door," she pleaded. "It's still open . . . Stuart . . ."

"Forget about him. He's asleep." Drake lifted her legs and tugged her panties down over her ankles. Then he hovered over her, the look in his eyes more frightening than romantic. He looked as though he hadn't made love in months, maybe years. She recalled a movie she had seen in which a man who had been a convict for nearly fifteen years escaped and came upon a young girl. Drake had the same violent, hungry look. He pressed himself to her. She gasped when she felt how quickly and roughly he entered her. Then he lifted her and drove her back on the bed. She nearly lost consciousness. Never had he ever been this rough and demanding. It took her breath away. He spent himself quickly and rolled over, panting like a satiated dog.

"Drake, what's come over you?" she asked between breaths.

"Nothing. What do you mean? Didn't you enjoy it?"

"No."

He smirked.

"You know I like it when you're gentle," she said.

"Sometimes it feels good to just let go, let the animal in you run free. You should try it, Cynthia."

"I don't need any animals running free. We've got enough troubles."

She rose from the bed and went to the bathroom. Her face and her neck were red. She saw where Drake's fingers had chafed her chest and breasts. She wanted to cry but soaked her face in warm water and caressed her bosom with lotion. Then she prepared for bed, deciding to check on Debbie one more time. While she did so Drake went to the bathroom.

Debbie was still fast asleep. Her face felt a bit cooler. Perhaps it was only the twenty-four-hour flu, and in the morning she would be hungry and energetic again. When Cynthia returned to the bedroom she found Drake under the blanket, his eyes closed, a gleeful smile on his face.

"You should be ashamed of yourself, Drake Edwards," she said, putting out the lights and crawling in beside him. "Attacking me that way."

"I couldn't help it," he said, sounding surprised about it himself. He followed it with a giggle. "Fact is," he said, turning to her, "I'm in the mood again."

"Drake! You're not."

"Oh, yes, I am," he said, grappling with her as he tried to place his palms over her breasts. She felt as if she were on a date with an overzealous teenager.

"Stop it, or I'll sleep on the couch. Will you stop it?" she cried when he didn't relent.

"All right," he said, pulling back. She sensed he was sulking.

"You're acting so weird. You didn't even ask about Stuart, and he was so upset that he had to go to sleep before you returned. He wanted to be sure we were going to chaperon his dance. He's so proud of being class president. And Drake, you should have seen him prepare dinner tonight. It was good, too!"

Drake continued to stare up at the dark ceiling.

"Didn't you hear what I said? Stuart made dinner for me. He was so grown up. His new responsibilities are making him mature quickly."

"We can't chaperon his dance," Drake said dryly, and he turned over.

"What? Why not?"

"I won't be back from the workshop until Sunday. I've got to stay overnight."

"Why? Where is it being held?" she asked. He didn't reply. "Drake?"

"Florida," he said.

"Florida? You mean the state?" she asked. There was a Florida, New York, not far from them.

"Uh-huh. We're flying out at ten on a private jet. The car will be by early to pick me up."

"Florida!" She sat up on her elbows. He remained on his side, his back to her. "Why Florida?"

"That's where Mr. Leon lives, and that's where it's being held," he said nonchalantly. She stared down at him, still amazed. Suddenly he turned back to her, smiling. "So you see," he said, "I'll be far away." He reached up and ran the palm of his right hand over her breast. "I could be in a plane crash. Don't you want to make love as if it was for the last time?"

"Drake!" She pushed his hand away. "What a horrible thing to say."

"Just kidding."

"You know I don't like that kind of joke."

"All right, all right. What do you say?" he asked, reaching up again.

"Drake . . . you're scaring me. What's come over you?"

"Nothing," he said defensively. "Jesus, you show your wife some desire, and she thinks something's come over you. No wonder people treat marriage like something they get stuck in."

"That's not fair, Drake," she cried, and she fell back on the pillow.

They were both quiet for a moment.

"Okay," he said, "I'm sorry. I'm just a little hyped up from the day." He leaned over and kissed her softly on the cheek. "Am I forgiven?"

"Of course," she said. She kissed him on the forehead, and he started to nibble at her neck. "Drake."

"Right. Time to sleep." He turned over again.

"Oh, Drake. Stuart's going to be so disappointed. He's so excited about his party."

"He'll get over it. If he's maturing, he has to learn how to deal with disappointment, just like the rest of us," he mumbled into the pillow.

"But—"

"And another thing, Cynthia," he said, turning back for a moment, "we've got to start living a bit more for ourselves and not dote on the kids so much. It's not healthy for them, and it's certainly not healthy for us."

She didn't reply. He turned his back to her again. It was as if something had shattered the rose-colored, delicate glass world they had lived in. She could actually hear the tinkle. Her heart pounded.

Cynthia didn't sleep well, waking every so often, imagining she had heard Debbie cry out. Close to three A.M. her eyes popped opened once again, and she discovered Drake had gotten up. She thought he had gone to Debbie's room, but when she went there to look for him she found Debbie fast asleep and alone. Her face was a lot cooler.

Reassured she had Debbie's sickness under control, she went searching for Drake. A thumping and then rattling caught her attention. It was coming from outside on the driveway. It was a recognizable sound, but it was so out of place this time of night that it frightened her. Her heartbeat quickened as she opened the front door and peered out. The light above the garage door was on. Insects were bathing in the illumination, but what shocked her was the sight of Drake in his briefs, barefoot, tossing a basketball, retrieving it, and then dribbling madly, as if he were playing against some invisible opponent. He went up for another shot, moving with amazing grace and power. The ball cut through the hoop so neatly it barely disturbed the netting. He landed on his feet, something that would normally send him reeling with the pain around his bad knee.

"Drake!"

He stopped and turned her way. Caught in the driveway light, hugging the ball to his chest, he looked more like Stuart than Drake.

"What?"

"What are you doing? It's after three in the morning."

"I couldn't sleep. Too restless, so I thought I'd tire myself out." He straightened up. "I didn't want to wake you, and I didn't feel like taking a cold shower," he added, his implication clear.

"You're going to be exhausted in the morning," she said. "And you said you had to get up early." She didn't know what else to say.

"It's all right. Go back to sleep. I won't be much longer." He turned back toward the basket and backboard.

"But your knee," she cried. He didn't hear her. He had started dribbling again and charged forward. She watched him reach up and lay the ball perfectly against the backboard. He came down and turned to get his own rebound, and then he started dribbling again. It tired her out just to watch him. She shook her head in disbelief and went back to bed.

It was almost an hour later when he joined her. She heard him crawl in between the sheets and then heard him sigh. Shortly after, she knew from his regular breathing that he was asleep.

Everything that had happened seemed like a nightmare. Drake's ravenous eyes flashed before her, and that image of him in the driveway—his hair wild, his eyes catching the floodlight and looking like jade, his mouth twisted up so his teeth gleamed, making him look like an angry dog. He was dribbling that basketball viciously, and his feet pounded the driveway with an intensity that made him appear absolutely furious, vexed. This wasn't any sort of enjoyment for him; this was . . . violent.

Something was wrong; something was terribly wrong, but she didn't know how to express it. What would she say, her husband was too sexy or too energetic? Would she complain about his excitement over his new job?

There was nothing to do but swallow her fears. Maybe she was overreacting. She shut the door on the voices of warning that called to her from some deep, instinctive place in her heart and then crawled into the surrounding silence and darkness to find relief in sleep.

—— 6 ——

In the morning Drake was up before Cynthia was, dressed and having breakfast. Cynthia was so tired from the night before she hadn't heard him rise. But her eyes jerked open when she heard Stuart crying in her doorway. He stood there leaning against the jamb, his shoulders heaving and his hands clenched into little fists against his cheeks. She sat up quickly.

"What is it, Stuart? Don't you feel well?" she asked, assuming he had contracted Debbie's flu.

"Daddy . . . Daddy says he can't chaperon the dance and he doesn't care," Stuart moaned.

"Oh, honey." She got out of bed and went to him. "Of course he cares. He can't help it because of his new job. Didn't he tell you that?"

"He can help it. I promised everyone you and Daddy would be there. He can help it; he can," Stuart insisted, breaking out of her embrace. "He just doesn't care," he repeated, and he retreated quickly to his own room, slamming the door.

Cynthia flinched at the sharp echo and took a deep breath. She slipped into her robe and went to check on Debbie, who had thrown off her blankets during the night and now lay on top of them. But her legs felt cool.

Her eyes flickered open when Cynthia placed her hand on her forehead.

"How do you feel, Debbie?"

Debbie blinked and closed her eyes. Then she opened them again and moaned.

"Don't you feel better, honey?" Cynthia asked. Debbie shook her head. "Why not? Your fever's down, I'm sure."

"My stomach," she said, "still feels ugly."

"It's probably just sore from your being sick, honey. I'll get you some tea and a piece of toast with jelly."

"I don't want toast. I want Daddy," she demanded, and she groaned as she rubbed her tummy.

"All right. I'll send him right in." Maybe Drake can get her to eat something, Cynthia thought. "Be right back."

She found him seated at the kitchen table, reading the business section of the paper and drinking coffee.

"Good morning," he said, his eyes bright and fresh. Where was the fatigued look she expected because he had been up so much during the night? And was that a dream, or had she found him playing basketball at three in the morning? He was so chipper, while she felt as if she had been hit by a Mack truck.

"I didn't even hear you get up," she said. He nodded and sipped some coffee.

"I was going to wake you," he replied, winking and smiling salaciously, "but I figured you'd be mad as hell, and it wouldn't be good."

"Drake, is that all you think about lately?" His smile wilted. "Debbie wants to see you," she said. He nodded without moving. Why did he still seem so different to her? It was almost as if he were someone else, as if someone or something had possessed him.

And it wasn't just because he had used the Youth Hold cream, which admittedly made his skin young and shiny-looking. There was an altogether different look in his eyes, a nervous excitement, an energy that didn't seem natural.

"I'm starting a whole new regimen of living today, Cyn. Notice what I'm eating," he said, indicating his breakfast. "No sweet roll this morning, coffee without cream, and six ounces of Fiber Wonder." He patted his belly. "Got to look slim and trim."

"You were never really overindulgent before, Drake, and we always watched what we ate."

"And do you know what Paul told me, Cyn?" he said, ignoring her response. "People who become salesmen for Leon Enterprises are healthier as a rule because they keep themselves fit and eat well. The truth is, if you don't look good and feel good, they can't use you. The reasons are obvious. So one extra benefit is good health. Is this a helluva job or isn't it?" he asked, sitting back and smiling.

She couldn't argue with that logic.

"Debbie feels cool, but she's still complaining about her stomach. I'll make some tea, but we've got to get her to try to eat something . . . some toast. If she can't hold anything down, I'll run her over to the doctor."

"Okay." He folded his paper and slipped it into the black leather briefcase. "I hate to have to leave you with this mess," he said, closing the case, "but Paul and the limousine should be here any minute. Later this morning someone will drop off my car." He snapped the fasteners shut and glanced at his watch.

She felt a chill move through her body with electric speed.

"Drake, aren't you going to go up to see her? She's crying for you."

"Oh, sure." He rose from his chair.

"And what did you say to Stuart this morning? He's so upset."

"I told him I had other responsibilities," Drake replied, his face tightening. How dramatically his expressions changed lately, she thought. Fed by instant anger, his eyes burned so brightly they looked as though they could singe whatever they gazed upon. She didn't like the ugly new way his mouth turned up in the corner, showing teeth.

"But Drake, you have to understand that he's heart-broken. You did promise, and he told his class. Now he's—"

"He's got to understand the world doesn't revolve around him and his needs," Drake snapped. "I tried to explain it to him, and he started to whine and sulk. If he wants to be a class leader, he should show leadership. He has a crisis, he has to solve it. It's as simple as that, Cynthia," Drake lectured coldly.

"It's our fault he's the way he is," he added, softening his voice some. "We babied him."

"Babied him? When did we ever baby him? He always had his chores to do and did them. Few boys his age take as good care of their rooms and their things as he does, Drake. You told me that yourself as recently as last week. And you never have to ask him twice to do something around the house. He lives in your shadow, practically worships the ground you walk on."

"I know, I know," he relented, "but things are different now. We're on the verge of a major breakthrough in our lives, and his responsibilities have grown as well. I just don't have time this morning to cater to temperament," he concluded. "And besides," he recited, "there's nothing that ages and sickens people as much as aggravation. Paul Stoddard says avoiding things that irritate us and learning how to handle vexation is part of what we are taught at the Leon Enterprises workshop. I told you," he added as if they were in the middle of an argument, "there is a distinct advantage and a good sales reason to remain healthy and young-looking. I don't know why you can't understand this."

She was about to protest when the phone rang. It was Ellen Brenner.

"Cynthia, it works!" she exclaimed as soon as Cynthia had said hello.

"What?".

"Oh, I'm sorry to call so early. You probably think

I'm crazy, but I woke up and looked at myself in the mirror and just grabbed the phone. That stuff I used yesterday at the diner. It's a miracle cream. Is Drake there?"

"Oh," she said, realizing. "Yes, he's here." She held the receiver out to him. "It's Ellen Brenner. I let her dab her finger into the Youth Hold and smear it on her temples yesterday after the movie matinee, and she's impressed with the results."

Drake smiled widely and nodded. He pulled his shoulders back as if he were going to be filmed or televised speaking to her and took the receiver.

"Good morning, Ellen," he said cheerfully. He listened and winked at Cynthia. "Of course," he said. "You can be my first regular customer. Sure. I'll drop by your home next week. Well, I would appreciate that. Thank you. See you soon," he added, and he hung up.

"She's pretty excited about the results," he said. "She's going to tell some of her friends, who are bound to want Youth Hold, too. See?" he said, clenching his right hand in a fist and shaking it beside his face as he leaned toward her. "As Leon Enterprises believes, nothing works better than word of mouth. If the product does what it claims to do, you don't need expensive advertising campaigns," he said, his voice dripping with pride.

Cynthia stared at him. It was as if he had been working for the company for years, or as if he were the owner. He had never demonstrated as much self-esteem working for Burke-Thompson, she thought. Why couldn't she get excited about this, too? she wondered sadly.

They both turned at the sound of a car horn.

"That's Paul," he proclaimed happily. "The limo's here." His eyes burned with a new kind of fire, one kindled by excitement. He seized his briefcase and small suitcase and charged toward the front door.

"But Drake," she cried, surprised he was leaving without going to see Debbie or kissing her good-bye, "what about Debbie?"

"Oh, you explain I had to rush off, honey. I'll call you," he added as he opened the door quickly.

"Drake!"

He closed the door behind him and was gone. She ran to the window that looked out on the driveway and saw him hurrying toward the stretch limousine. His look of excitement turned into an expression of glee. The chauffeur stepped out to open the door for him. She couldn't see the man already seated within, but she did see his hand reach forward for Drake to shake it. He did so and then disappeared into the vehicle as though he were being pulled into a black hole.

The driver, a light-haired man who didn't look to be older than his late twenties, closed the door and looked toward the house—looked directly at her, she thought. It made her self-conscious, as if she had been caught snooping or something. She dropped the curtain and pulled back, her heart racing.

She gazed out again as the limousine backed out of the driveway and sped off. Then she stepped away from the window.

"Daddy!" Debbie cried from the top of the stairway.

Cynthia felt stunned by the morning's events. For a moment she just stood there, indecisive, overwhelmed, not sure where to go or what to do.

"Daddy!" Debbie called again.

"I'm coming, honey," she replied.

"I want Daddy," Debbie cried.

"I know," she muttered, and she turned to go to her. Suddenly she stopped in her tracks and spun around, realizing the most shocking thing of all.

Drake had left for the weekend with his daughter sick and his son upset. And he hadn't even told her where he would be!

Cynthia heard the musical sound of Richie's jeep horn and she sighed with relief. He had a knack for arriving at the appropriate time, Cynthia thought.

Richie had the kind of easygoing, happy-go-lucky personality that made him a welcome guest no matter when he arrived. He took after their father's side of the family: tall, with light brown hair he kept in a straight wave over his forehead. He had a slim build, muscular and athletic. He was quiet and shy, but much less so when it came to his niece and nephew. Actually, Richie had always gotten along better with children than he had with other adults.

If there was such a thing as chemistry, it flowed between her son and her brother, Cynthia thought.

She used to fear that Drake would become jealous of Stuart's affection for Richie, but he seemed to get just as much a kick out of it as she did. Sometimes the three of them, with Debbie sitting on the sidelines watching, would practice baseball or basketball, each giving Stuart the benefit of his experience.

Debbie had withdrawn into a dismal sulk when Cynthia had told her Drake had to leave before coming in to see her. She wouldn't eat; she even refused the tea at first, drinking it only when Cynthia threatened to take her to the doctor and maybe the hospital. Stuart remained in his room, refusing to come out for breakfast. He lay in his bed, his face pressed against the pillow, and continued to brood. The morning had hardly begun, and Cynthia already felt exhausted.

When she gazed at herself in the mirror she saw that the slight wrinkles and lines that had disappeared after her Youth Hold treatment were returning. So much for the wonder of that, she thought. Drake had been right: There was no protection against the consequences of aggravation. It sped up the aging process. Maybe she should have joined him at his workshop.

Anyway, reinforcements had arrived, she thought, and she went to greet her brother, expecting Stuart to be right behind her. But her son's depression and disappointment was deeply set. He remained in his room.

"What's doin'?" Richie asked as she stood waiting in the doorway. He moved in his casual gait, his nonchalance and innocence welcome. He saw the way her eyes watered and stopped. "Something wrong?"

"Oh, Richie," she said, and then she couldn't help herself. She burst into tears.

Any show of emotion embarrassed her brother. He looked away as if he had been distracted by something and waited for her to get hold of herself. She sucked in her breath and wiped her eyes.

"What happened?" Richie asked. She knew he already regretted having stopped by, but if there was anyone she would confide in, it would be Richie, even before she would call her mother or father. Both her parents hated to see anyone cry and had no tolerance for it even if their own children were doing the crying.

Cynthia and her brother had been brought up to believe that emotions were personal; family problems were not to be shared and displayed. This infatuation America was having with exposure, spouting forth your most intimate difficulties on television talk shows or revealing all in magazine interviews, was obscene as far as Cynthia's parents were concerned. Cynthia recalled having a difficult time getting her mother to discuss intimate female questions. Sex was something that you discovered and learned about through some kind of osmosis or instinct. In fact, her mother was a devout believer in the power of instinct. She had a favorite response when Cynthia did ask intimate questions and pursued her stubbornly for an answer.

"You'll know," she would finally say. "You'll just know."

Richie wore their mother's expression of fear. What was she about to lay on him?

"It's Drake," she finally said. "Something's wrong with him."

"Oh." He looked relieved. "Did he go to the doctor?"

"No. It's not that kind of wrong. He's acting peculiar." Richie started to smile. Then she spilled it all in a staccato manner: "He quit his job, took a new position with a completely different kind of firm, met new people, went to dinner in New York last night and didn't come home until late, and left this morning to go to a weekend workshop without telling me where he would be. And Debbie's sick," she added. That seemed to be the only thing Richie heard.

"Debbie's sick?"

"She has stomach flu. He didn't even say good-bye to her, and she won't eat anything, not even a piece of toast."

Richie nodded. This was something he could deal with.

"I'll go see her, see what I can do. Where's Stuart?"

"In his room, sulking because we can't chaperone his party tomorrow night."

"Party?" Richie smirked. "He's having a party?"

"His class. Remember he's class president?"

"Oh, yeah." He laughed. "Drake and I were kidding him about that."

"Well, he's not laughing now," she said, folding her arms under her bosom. "Did you hear the other stuff? Drake quit his job with Burke-Thompson."

"Who's he with now?"

"A cosmetics company, Leon Enterprises. He sells skin cream," she said disparagingly. Richie's eyes widened. He nodded slowly.

"Better pay?"

"Yes. A lot better," she confessed.

"Well, he often complained about his old firm, about not getting the promotions he thought he deserved," Richie reminded her.

"I know, but—"

"What's this workshop?"

"I don't know," she said, grabbing onto that. "It's in Florida. He's flying down there on the company's private jet."

"No kidding?" Richie looked impressed. This wasn't what she had intended, she thought.

"He rushed out of here without telling me exactly where he's going!"

"He's probably just excited. He'll realize he didn't tell you and call you later. He'll call to see about Debbie anyway, right?"

"I hope so," she said. "At least he said he would."

"So?"

She looked at her brother. He had the same laugh lines around his eyes that had made their father so handsome. And just like their father, Richie had a way of making what seemed to be a large crisis insignificant in moments. She racked her brain to find reasons why this wasn't insignificant. She looked up at the basketball net.

"Drake couldn't sleep last night. I woke up at three in the morning and heard him out here. Do you know what he was doing? He was playing basketball! At three in the morning!"

"Really?" Richie's smile widened. "What did he say?"

"He was restless and couldn't sleep."

Richie shrugged.

"I've gotten up and watched television. Once I took a fast walk around the block. Things get you riled up," he explained without hinting at what those things could be. Cynthia surmised quickly that it had to do with his sex life. Her brother had been hurt badly by his first serious relationship. He had been going with a girl from his high school days, and they were at the point where they were talking marriage when he found out she had been unfaithful. And more than once!

The result was that he became even more timid and very cynical. He had dates, but when they started to become serious he usually backtracked. She thought some of the girls he drove away would have made him fine wives.

"He's different, Richie," she insisted. "He's just diffcrent."

"Hey, it's not easy to quit a job you've had for so long and start somewhere new, even if you're going to make a helluva lot more money. He's probably very nervous and just doing weird things because of that.

Every time I get disgusted with what I'm doing and think about doing something new I get the shakes," he admitted. She looked at him with interest. "So forget about it," he advised quickly. "After a while, when he gets used to what he's doing, he'll be his old self. Let me see Debbie," he added quickly, and he moved toward the stairs.

Maybe he was right, she thought. Richie was shy, and Richie was set in his ways, but he was strong, too, and very calming. She gazed down the road in the direction Drake had gone and nodded. Richie was right, she concluded. Drake will settle down, and things will get back on track. When you're as deeply in love and as committed to each other and family as she and Drake were, things had to work out.

Drake took his seat next to Paul Stoddard in the Learjet and fastened his seat belt. When he heard the engines start he looked about the otherwise empty plane with surprise.

"Are we the only ones going?"

"What?" Paul looked up as if he had just noticed that they were on a plane that was preparing for a takeoff. "Oh, yes. No one else this trip."

A stewardess who looked barely twenty, if that, approached them. She had a vibrant, bright smile and radiant hazel eyes set in a fair-skinned, freckled face. Her auburn hair was brushed neatly down around her shoulders. She had a freshness about her that made him envision a cool, clear spring.

"Good morning," she said. "Can I get you both a cup of coffee?"

"Just black for me," Paul said quickly.

"Me, too." Drake hadn't gotten used to drinking coffee black yet, but he was working on it.

The stewardess directed her buoyant smile only at him, and he felt himself warm under the glow. He watched her move back down the aisle, her light blue uniform clinging so tightly to her hips that he could actually see the muscles in her buttocks flex and relax as she took her steps. The sexual energy he had woken with that morning was revived. It quickened his breath and brought a flush to his face. He hadn't felt so vigorous since he was . . . sixteen, he thought.

Just after the plane took off and the pilot reached his cruising altitude she brought them their coffee.

"Nice-looking girl," Drake remarked when she returned to her station up front.

Paul winked.

"She'll be at the compound. Layover," he added, smiling slyly.

"I'm a happily married man," Drake said, although he still smiled and watched the stewardess move about.

"I was happily married, too," Paul replied, but so sharply Drake had to turn to him.

"I'm sorry; I forgot."

Paul shrugged.

"Nothing to be sorry about. You learn to go on with your life. What's the other choice?" he asked rhetorically. Drake nodded. Paul's hedonistic smile returned. "Let's just concentrate on what awaits us at the compound."

It wasn't until they landed and were driven to the compound in another stretch limousine that Drake understood why Paul referred to it as a compound. Mr. Leon's property was located a dozen or so miles off I-95. They headed away from the ocean and traveled through Everglades country. Suddenly they came to a clear field. Drake knew they had reached the Leon property because a sign on a fence clearly warned intruders that the fence was electrified. The chain-link barricade topped with strands of barbed wire seemed to run on for miles.

"That's the factory where Youth Hold is made." Paul pointed to a long gray stone building. A macadam roadway snaked around the building that looked to Drake like a long bomb shelter. There were no windows in the building. There was an entry on the side, and apparently a loading dock in the rear.

About a thousand yards from the gray building, however, were a dozen or so small cottages constructed in a half circle. They were all quaint little structures in white stucco with red tile roofs. The grounds bloomed with colorful flowers and hedges and palm trees. Every half dozen yards or so there was another fountain spouting crystal-clear water that glittered in the noonday sun.

"What are those cottages?" Drake asked.

"Guest houses," Paul replied dryly. "But you will be staying in the mansion."

And mansion it was, Drake thought as they drew closer to the main gate. The sprawling hacienda could be classified as nothing less. It seemed to go on forever, with porticos and patios and atriums. At least ten men worked the grounds, weeding and feeding the plants and flowers.

"It looks like a small castle."

Paul nodded. Drake just caught a glimpse of the pool and patio behind the house, but off to the left were the tennis courts, a large gazebo, and what looked like a miniature botanical garden. As the limousine continued Drake spotted the armed guards and Dobermans patrolling in pairs. In such a pretty, colorful, and peaceful setting they were conspicuous and looked incongruous.

The limousine wound around the highway and turned into the long driveway before stopping at the main gate. The security guard shot out of the booth. The driver lowered his window, and the guard gazed in at him and then moved down the length of the car to look at Drake and Paul. Paul lowered his window.

"Hello, Mr. Stoddard," the guard said. "Is this your guest?"

"Yes," Paul said. Drake thought he looked nervous, as if there was a chance they wouldn't be admitted or something. The guard stared intently at Drake for a moment. He smiled back, but the guard's expression remained intense; his eyes, although clear, were a cold

green, scrutinizing. Drake thought the man looked seasoned beyond his years. There was a toughness that
didn't go with the light hair and fair skin.

The guard nodded and turned toward the gate. It
opened, and the limousine continued on.

"Why all the security?" Drake asked.

Paul laughed.

"Can't you just imagine how many other companies
would like to get their hands on our formula? Industrial
espionage is worse than political espionage," he added.

"Oh." Drake nodded. That made sense, especially in
light of the value of Youth Hold. As soon as they
reached the front of the hacienda another security guard
appeared in the doorway. When Drake and Paul stepped
out, however, there was a third suddenly behind them.

"Excuse me, sir," the guard said.

"Oh, yes." Paul turned and nodded to Drake, who
turned to face the guard. He waved the metal detector
at them and ran it the lengths of their bodies. Then he
nodded to the guard at the door, who stepped aside to
permit a servant to rush out for their suitcases.

"Right this way," Paul instructed, and the two of
them followed the servant into the great house.

In the long, wide foyer Paul introduced Drake to Gerald Dorian. Or, as Drake thought, turned him over; for
immediately after the introduction Paul excused himself,
and Gerald took Drake down a corridor to his suite, the
opulence of which took his breath away: plush white
carpet, gold-lined drapes, an oversized heavy oak bed
with a hand-carved headboard, a tiled bathroom as big
as his bedroom at home. In it were a Jacuzzi tub and a
shower stall that looked half as large as his kitchen.

"Mr. Leon is tied up with some business at the
moment," Gerald explained. "He wants you to make
yourself at home. His house is your house, and that
includes everything in it. Actually," Gerald continued,
smiling, "your time is pretty tightly scheduled. There
are people, advisers, experts we want you to meet. You
have a full orientation ahead of you. So," he said, going

to the drapes, "until we come looking for you, enjoy." He pulled the cord to open the drapes. When he did so, he revealed the swimming pool.

The windows were so thick and tight Drake couldn't hear the laughter and the conversations without, but he could certainly see. Gerald turned and smiled licentiously. Drake looked stunned. A half dozen barebreasted young women were frolicking in the water, each one as beautiful as the next.

"Feel free to take a swim," Gerald suggested.

"Swim? Who—"

"Those are some of Mr. Leon's long-term guests," Gerald explained. "They stay at the cottages. But as I said, Mr. Leon wants you to know his house is your house, and"—Gerald gazed out the window—"that includes everything in it."

— 7 —

Cynthia's brother cheered up her children. Debbie ate her toast and held it down and then asked for something more. Cynthia made her some hot oatmeal with honey, and she ate that in front of the television set while she watched a stream of Saturday morning cartoons. Stuart got dressed, ate his breakfast, and went for a ride with Richie to get some toggle screws.

A little more than a week ago she and Drake had decided to put up some shelves in the family room. Cynthia had gone to the home improvement center and bought some nice do-it-yourself shelves with brackets, but Richie pointed out she had bought the wrong nuts and bolts. So he went off with Stuart to get the right ones and then return to put up the shelves.

"Guess what!" Stuart exclaimed when he and Richie returned. He came charging through the door, his face lit up. Cynthia turned off the vacuum cleaner.

"What?"

"Uncle Richie's gonna chaperon my dance tonight."

"He is?" She smiled with surprise as Richie followed Stuart in. "You are?"

Richie shrugged.

"I got drafted."

93

"And he's bringing his date," Stuart revealed, eyes wide.

"Date?"

"Her name's Sheila, and she's an aerobics instructor," Stuart disclosed.

"Is that right? How come you know so much?"

"Richie and I tell each other secret stuff," Stuart confessed with characteristic male bravado. He even had a bit of the swagger. She kept herself from laughing.

"Is that so? And what secret stuff did you tell him?"

"I can't tell you that," he said indignantly. "It's man-to-man."

"Oh, excuse me. Sheila, huh?" She turned to Richie. "So how long have you been seeing Sheila?" she asked.

"On and off, a few months," he said.

"What's she like?"

"She's about Mom's height, all legs, with coal-black hair and hazel eyes. I can beat her in a sprint, but she can outlast me on the long runs."

Cynthia laughed.

"Where did you meet her?"

"On a pole."

"What?"

"I was working on a telephone pole up in Hasbrouck, and she came around the bend on a bike. She hit some gravel on the turn and took a spin. I worked the bucket over to her to see if she was all right, and she thought that was the most hysterical thing she had seen in a long time."

"You came down in a bucket, and you wonder why she thought that was funny?"

He shrugged. "It was the fastest way to check on her."

"How old is she?"

"Twenty-five, but she looks like nineteen. Proper diet and proper exercise," he added, smiling. "She says it will keep you young forever."

"It doesn't hurt," she replied, but a shadow drifted

over her heart. "Everyone worries about staying young forever nowadays," she said, more to herself.

"She's like you, too," Richie said. "She likes to read and drives me nuts with going to the movies, and she's a great cook, a gourmet cook. She can make an ordinary salad seem like—like steak and potatoes," he concluded.

Cynthia laughed.

"On and off for a few months, huh? Sounds to me like you've been seeing more of her than you want to admit to."

"Don't make a big deal of it," he warned, checking his own enthusiasm.

"Why not? You've been a bachelor too long. And besides, you're doing something very serious with her tonight by chaperoning a seventh-grade party. That's the same as getting engaged," she kidded.

Richie glanced at Stuart. "You're responsible if I get married because I took Sheila to your party tonight, champ."

Stuart's mouth dropped open.

"You're getting married?"

"I didn't say that."

"Uncle Richie's getting married," he cried, and he ran off to tell Debbie.

"Oh, man."

Cynthia laughed. She hugged her brother.

"I'm so glad you came around today, Richie. So glad."

After Richie finished putting up the shelves he took Stuart to Taco Charlie's for lunch. Shortly after sitting down to have her own lunch Cynthia heard a car drive up and gazed out the window to see Larry Thompson get out of his Mercedes sedan and approach the front door. She had met both of Drake's former bosses on a number of occasions, including Christmas and New Year's parties at Larry Thompson's home, and she had always liked the six-feet-two-inch, distinguished-looking fifty-four-year-old man and his wife Janet. They had money, but they were very down-to-earth people.

She heard the doorbell and got up to greet him.

"Hello, Cynthia. Sorry to bother you people on a Saturday, especially on a day as pretty as this one."

"It's no bother. Come in, Larry."

"Thank you. When I drove up," he said, stepping in, "I was admiring your rhododendrons. We always have so much trouble with them at our house. Drake told me you do most of your own gardening. Green thumb, eh?"

"I don't know. Lucky, I guess. I like planting and taking care of flowers and bushes. My therapy. Sort of like golf to some people," she kidded. Drake had told her how well Larry played.

"Don't let anyone tell you golf is therapy. It's an addiction and should be a controlled substance." He looked around. "I was here for Drake's thirtieth birthday party, right?"

"Yes." She stared at him, sensing that their small talk had ended.

"Drake's not home?"

"No, he's . . . he's away."

Larry Thompson nodded, pressing his lower lip over his upper. His eyes were filled with concern, but she sensed his hesitation.

"Oh, too bad. I was hoping to have an informal chat. Thought if I came over on a weekend and just shot the breeze a bit . . ."

"Please, sit down, Larry," she said, indicating the couch. The way their home was designed, the living room appeared abruptly on the right at the end of the foyer. He entered the living room and sat on the couch. She followed and sat on the high-back cushioned chair across from him.

"Needless to say," Larry Thompson began, "we were taken by surprise at Drake's abrupt departure. He hadn't given us any indication he was considering such a move. In fact, Gordon and I were talking only last week about how successful Drake has been for us and how much we wanted to make him a part of our enterprise, so when he turned down the partnership and—"

"Partnership? Drake turned down a partnership?" She leaned forward, practically on the edge of the chair.

"Well, yes, I . . . he didn't tell you about our offer?"

"He said he thought you were going to make him a vice-president."

"That's true, but in this case the vice-presidency included a percentage of our business. My father-in-law's getting along in years; it's not going to be much longer before he retires. Of course," Larry said, smiling, "he'll go down swinging, fighting it all the way, but my mother-in-law's determined, and he realizes the time's come. So when Dad and I went over our personnel, we naturally considered Drake. I know he's been frustrated, waiting for something big, but there was just so much we could offer. Until now, that is.

"Coincidentally, I sent for him at the same time he was coming in to resign. I made the offer, but he wouldn't even give me the opportunity to explain anything. I had never seen him so charged up, and if I hadn't known him for years, I would have thought he was on some kind of drug. Anyway, I let a day or so go by and thought now that the smoke's settled, maybe I could talk to him. Do you expect him soon or later today? I've got a client up here I want to see, and—"

"No, Larry. He won't be home until tomorrow. He's in Florida."

"Florida?"

"At a workshop for his new company."

"That's this Leon Enterprises he mentioned?" She nodded. "I've got the name right?"

"Yes, why?"

"Well . . . it bugged me, I have to admit. The kind of money Drake claimed he was offered, the product . . . I . . ."

"What is it, Larry?"

"No one I know seems to have heard of the company. I asked some friends to do some checking so I could let you and Drake know more about it, but so far I haven't learned much."

"I know they have an office in Manhattan. Drake was there yesterday."

"Leon Enterprises? You're sure that's the name they go by?"

"Of course. Wait a minute," she said, and she went upstairs to get the Youth Hold. She returned with the tin and showed it to him. He shook his head.

"I don't understand it. Anyway, I came here to tell Drake I thought he was making a mistake. He's a damn good insurance salesman, and we've got a very successful business. I am willing to make him a full partner after a few years. That's how much confidence I have in him and in our business."

He looked at the tin of cream.

"They might suck him in with an attractive offer, but in time, after the polish is gone . . ."

"I know. I have the same fears."

"I'll see what else I can find out about them. Well," Thompson said, standing, "I had to come up here anyway, and I thought while I was here . . ."

"Of course. I appreciate it, Larry, and when Drake returns I'm going to have him drop by to speak with you."

"I'd like that. As I said, I didn't get much of a chance to talk to him. The way he burst in and resigned"— Larry shook his head—"it wasn't the Drake I know."

Cynthia looked up sharply when he said that.

"What do you mean?"

"He looked . . . like he was under some kind of spell . . . hypnotized. Oh, it can happen to any of us, I suppose. Especially when you start getting into middle age and think it's all passed you by, and you wonder about the things you might have done. Even I have had those feelings." He smiled. "I once had ambitions of becoming a professional golfer. My father-in-law might even have staked me, but . . . I settled for beating the pants off my buddies on weekends. Regardless of what Drake decides to do, Cynthia, best of luck."

"Thank you, Larry, and regards to Janet."

"Bye," he said, and he was gone. She watched him get into his car and drive off, and then she turned and looked at the tin of Youth Hold on the coffee table in the living room. The way it reflected the sunlight coming through the window, it was as if it had its own glow.

It was ridiculous to ascribe an evil force to an inanimate object, Cynthia thought. She knew that, but she couldn't help scooping it up and rushing upstairs to bury it in a bottom dresser drawer under her nightgowns.

Sitting before the bank of monitors in his office, Mr. Leon observed Drake entering the hacienda. He pressed a button and had the camera zoom in for a close-up. Yes, he thought, this was a good candidate. Look at the way he gazes at everything, the innocence and awe in his eyes. Another lump of clay to mold.

He glanced down at the Edwards résumé in a folder on his dark oak desk. It was a history and description of Drake's family. And what a perfect little family it was, Mr. Leon concluded disdainfully—hardworking, devoted, loving. Lawns and toys and Thanksgiving dinners, pride in the children, Brownie troop leader and Little League coach. He could envision the way they stood at the start of "The Star-Spangled Banner." He could see them sitting before their television set and crying during the Jerry Lewis telethon. They took vitamins and brought their children to the dentist for regular check-ups. It was all there, detailed in the folder, all of it demonstrating a confidence in the marriage, a faith in the sanctity of the family.

It disgusted him and at the same time made him envious, although he wouldn't admit that, even to himself. He had had a family once, hadn't he? He looked up and gazed at his reflection in the wall mirror. Was it he or someone else in his body? As the years ticked by, how many times had he died and been reborn? And each time, wasn't he reborn as someone else? He dreamt of a parade of souls, each stopping for sixty or seventy years in his carcass and then moving on to . . . to hell.

It had been hundreds of years since he had had a family. He had had children, but he certainly couldn't keep track of the progeny—not as prolific as he was. There was a line of children that flowed back so far, it boggled his mind. His memories bounced back and forth in sealed chambers until they became distorted and turned into nightmares.

But there were children he would never forget, his Indian children. They had gathered one night to kill him. Funny, he thought, so much was lost in time, confused, diluted, forgotten, but the images of them approaching, three dark heads silhouetted in the moonlight, never ceased being as vivid as it had been that fateful night.

He had anticipated it, seen the blazing hate in their eyes, the thirst for revenge on their lips. They came in swiftly, as quietly as the night breeze, and drove their knives into the stuffed blanket, so compelled with anger and the need for vengeance that they didn't pause and realize they were stabbing cushions.

When he lit the lamp they froze in the glow. Maybe they thought he was already a ghost. "The god from the sea who had killed death." He killed each of them quickly, feeling nothing more than he felt stepping down on an insect. Children, family.

He looked up sharply at the monitors again and caught Drake Edwards moving about his suite, impressed with the luxury. Mr. Leon smiled. He would be just like the others—just like him, in fact. In the end Drake would step down on whatever was necessary to be like the "god from the sea who killed death." His family would become as insignificant as insects.

He widened his smile, thinking about it, and turned his chair to gaze at another monitor, one that revealed a Harvey Leland, a two-year disciple, making love to his new bride. It had been Mr. Leon's ingenious idea to have Harvey enjoy his honeymoon there, to feast, enjoy all the facilities, and then . . . bored with the ways his disciples had carried out his commands in the past, Mr. Leon had decided to have famous murders, fictional or otherwise, reenacted. Harvey would perform Othello. He was black, wasn't he? he thought, chuckling softly. It was almost time.

Harvey's wife, an attractive caramel-skinned Jamaican girl, sprawled on her back on the king-size bed and threw her arms out in crucifixion style, inviting Harvey to enjoy her body. Appropriate, Mr. Leon thought. Harvey stepped into the picture wearing that wonderful caftan Gerald had acquired from a costume agency. It was meant to be worn by an actor performing Othello. An authentic touch. Mr. Leon loved it.

Harvey stood there stupidly gazing down at his bride. "It's the moment of decision, Harvey," Mr. Leon said to the screen. As if he had heard Mr. Leon, Harvey looked up in the direction of the camera. Then he pulled his arm out from under the caftan, his hand clutching a small pillow. His new bride looked up with surprise. Harvey began to recite the lines, accusing her of infidelity. Mr. Leon had rehearsed him himself in the office. After all, he had seen Othello performed a hundred times.

Look at the expression of shock on her face, Mr. Leon thought, shaking his head. She was a beautiful girl, as beautiful as Desdemona, and for a moment he toyed with the idea of keeping her himself. But the delight he expected from watching someone murder the one he loved overrode his own amorous desires. Besides, he had a number of girls who were just as attractive.

Harvey moved quickly, shoving the pillow over her face and pressing down on her with all his weight.

It wasn't much of a struggle—rather pathetic, Mr. Leon concluded with disappointment. Harvey was too strong, and after it was over she looked like she was pretending to be dead. There was no blood, no visible sign of murder. It looked like a poorly staged television soap opera. There was very little satisfaction there, even watching poor Harvey cry.

He reached over and shut off the monitor, disgusted. He should have had him strangle her with piano wire.

At least there would have been blood, and he could have watched her eyes bulge. Reruns. So much of life was reruns. He had to find more originality.

Mr. Leon spun around in time to see Drake Edwards slide open his patio door and step gingerly out to the patio. The young women stopped talking and splashing each other and turned to him. Obviously he didn't know where to go or what to do. He waved and moved awkwardly to a lounge chair.

But the girls knew what to do. They gathered around him, two sitting at his feet, the others sitting on lounges beside him. Mr. Leon could just imagine the turmoil going on in Drake Edwards—this harem of beautiful girls, the pain of conscience, the pleasure of their beautiful bodies, the visions of betrayal and infidelity.

Another happy home began to crumble before Mr. Leon's eyes. This was more like it. He pulled himself closer to the monitor as one of the girls produced a bottle of ginseng oil and another produced a sponge.

Oh, Christ, Mr. Leon thought, this was going to be good. Drake looked so confused. The girls were urging him to lie back on the lounge. His confusion made his resistance look silly. Finally he succumbed, and they were all over him, one taking down his swim trunks while the others caressed and kissed him.

They began the erotic massage. Now this had the makings of something, Mr. Leon decided. It stimulated him as well, and he stayed with the monitor until Drake was brought to an orgasm. Having spent him, the girls left Drake naked on the lounge, stunned by pleasure.

Mr. Leon chuckled at the sight, but he realized it took much more to entertain and satisfy him these days. He had to keep reaching out for new and creative ideas. He turned away from the monitor to consider what he would design for Drake Edwards. He looked down the list of fictional and nonfictional murders he had thought interesting.

Daniel Taylor, a nineteenth-century psychotic, smothered his wife by painting tar over her body and clogging her pores. The police first thought she was some kind of sculpture.

What about the Hitchcock film where the husband poisoned the wife slowly? That took time, but there was a certain pleasure in the anticipation.

Here was a good one: Kaye Samuels, a turn-of-the-century murderess in Georgia, stabbed her husband to death and then cut up his body and baked it away slowly in the stove, serving some of him to a visiting policeman assigned to locate the missing man.

There certainly was no lack of ideas, Mr. Leon thought. Oh, well, he didn't have to make his decision right now. There was a lot of work to be done to bring Drake into the fold.

He looked back at the monitor. Drake had retreated to his room. Probably feeling guilty as hell, Mr. Leon thought. He rang for Gerald.

"Sir?"

"Let Mr. Edwards know I'll see him in fifteen minutes, Gerald."

"Very good, sir."

"The girls were rather good. Did you see any of it?"

"No, sir. I was filling Mr. Stoddard in on what you had planned for Mr. Leland."

"You could have done that later, Gerald." He switched off, annoyed. He sensed that Gerald was starting to fray at the edges. He wasn't wearing life well anymore, and it was beginning to be depressing. One thing Mr. Leon would not tolerate around him was depression.

Perhaps it was time for a new personal assistant, one who wasn't as serious. Gerald hadn't been much of a challenge to win over; he was eager to do what had to be done, to perform the most abominable acts. But that was nearly one hundred and twenty years ago. He had kept his handsome face and fine figure, but he had lost his sense of humor.

Yes, replacing him was something to think about. Maybe he would design a contest, see who was most deserving. Paul Stoddard, Harvey Leland, one of the women perhaps; maybe even this Drake Edwards. Who would gladly perform the most loathsome and repulsive acts in order to become his favorite? He might even give Gerald a chance to compete and keep his position. Wouldn't that be interesting?

He slapped his hands together. He was kind of excited. Coming up with the idea reassured him he would never grow bored.

Cynthia sat near the telephone in the living room waiting for Drake to call. The television droned on, but she didn't see or hear anything. Debbie was curled up beside her, her head on Cynthia's lap. Cynthia twirled some of Debbie's hair around her forefinger gently and then straightened the strands. She wasn't even aware she was doing it until Debbie groaned.

"Want to go to sleep now, honey?"

"Uh-uh. I want to wait for Daddy's call," she insisted despite her heavy eyelids.

Damn him, Cynthia thought. Didn't he know the child would lie awake waiting?

"You go up to bed, and as soon as he calls I'll call you to the phone in my room, okay?"

"Okay," she said, struggling to sit up. She had to be carried up the stairs.

"Remember, call me when he calls," Debbie cried as Cynthia started out.

Bruised, angry-looking clouds had been gathering throughout the late afternoon and early evening, and as Cynthia started to descend she heard the first raindrops tap against the windowpanes. It added another layer of depression and foreboding to the blanket of despair that had covered her most of the day after Drake's departure. For a few moments she stood by the living room window staring out at the rain. Then she returned to the couch in the living room to watch television and wait.

Occasionally, when the canned laughter was turned up, she snapped out of her reverie and concentrated on the sitcom. Then something would remind her of Drake, and she would look down at the phone again. She felt a tightening in her chest as her frustration built. Surely by now he would have realized that he hadn't told her where he would be. Surely by now he would be concerned about her and the children.

After a while she began to despise the phone, hate it for its dumbness. Twice she imagined it had rung and reached for the receiver only to freeze her fingers around it and wait in desperation for a second ring to confirm the first. It didn't come; it never came. The early evening passed away, and before she knew it she heard Richie driving up with his girlfriend Sheila and Stuart.

Cynthia had been pleasant when Richie had first arrived with Sheila, but her mind was so occupied with thoughts and concerns over Drake that she didn't give the girl the kind of welcome she should have. She liked the girl, too. There was a sincerity, a fresh honesty about her. She reminded Cynthia of the wholesome girl-next-door character in forties and fifties films, with her black hair tied in a ponytail. As Richie had said, she didn't look more than nineteen, if that. She had dressed in a light blue cotton skirt, matching socks, and white L.A. Gear sneakers. Under the dark blue wool jacket she wore a pretty white and blue blouse with pearl buttons.

Cynthia got up quickly and went to the door as Richie and Stuart burst in out of the rain without Sheila.

"Hi, how was your party, honey?"

"It was great, Mom," Stuart said. "Right, Richie?"

"Ten times better than any school party I can remember. Except for the food fight in the corner."

"Food fight? Not you, Stuart?" She grimaced.

"Of course not, Mom," he said with indignation.

"Good. Well, why don't you wash up and get ready for bed?"

"Did Daddy call?" he asked.

"No, not yet."

"Not yet! Well, when's he going to call? It's very

late, isn't it?'' Stuart said with his hands on his waist. Having her twelve-year-old son snap at her nearly pushed her over the edge.

"Just get ready for bed, Stuart," she commanded more firmly.

"Don't you want to hear about the party?" he asked in a more pleasant tone.

"It's late. You can tell me all about it tomorrow."

"I wanted to tell Daddy, too," he complained.

"Go on, champ. Get some sleep," Richie said, and he ran his hand through Stuart's hair. "Before I tell your mother about all those girls chasin' after you."

"They weren't."

"Go on," Richie said, and Stuart headed for the stairs.

"Where's Sheila?"

"Oh, she's waiting in the car. She didn't think you wanted company this late, so—"

"Oh please, Richie. Ask her to come in for a cup of coffee or something."

He stared at her.

"I can't understand Drake's not phoning. I can't," she moaned. "I need some company for a while. Really," she emphasized.

Cynthia was far more pleasant and outgoing this time. In fact, she found herself rattling on and on, practically babbling. She realized she was clinging to their company like a woman overboard clinging to some driftwood. With the children asleep the house would be terrifyingly quiet. She would be waiting even more intently for Drake's belated call.

Finally she caught the looks between Richie and Sheila and realized she was keeping them away from each other.

"Oh, I'm sorry I've been talking your ear off, Sheila."

"It's all right," she said. "You make up for Richie. Sometimes I feel like I'm drilling for oil trying to get a word out of him."

Cynthia laughed.

"All right," Richie said quickly. "We're not going to hear any 'that reminds me of Richie' stories. We gotta go. The rain's stopped."

"Of course. Thanks, both of you, for coming to the rescue and chaperoning the party."

Cynthia walked them to the door.

"Maybe you'd like to go for a jog with me one weekend," Sheila suggested. "I do Morningside Park on Sundays, late afternoon."

"Maybe she can join you tomorrow," Richie said.

"No," Cynthia said quickly. "I mean, I'd like to, but I've got to wait for Drake."

"He may not be home until the evening, Cyn," Richie said softly. "I mean, it's not like he's down the road a piece."

"But it's so unlike him not to call. We haven't been apart from each other overnight that often," she said. Richie glanced quickly at Sheila.

"I'm sure it'll be all right. As you said earlier, he's just overwhelmed with all the new responsibilities," Sheila said.

"Yes. I guess you're right. Well, thanks again."

She watched them leave and then turned slowly to the living room to continue her vigil near the phone. That was where she finally fell asleep and didn't awaken until she felt Stuart shaking her in the morning.

"Huh?" She sat up slowly. "Did the phone ring?" she asked, looking around.

"No. How come you're all dressed but still asleep?" Stuart asked.

"What?" She looked down at herself and then realized what had happened. "Oh. I must have dozed off and"—she scrubbed her cheeks with her palms and ran them through her hair—"is Debbie up yet?"

"Yes, but she won't get out of bed because she's mad at you for not calling her to the phone last night when Daddy called."

"Daddy called? No," she said, answering herself. "He

didn't call. This is ridiculous. *Debbie!''* she screamed. "Go tell your sister that if she's not out of bed and dressed in ten minutes, she will be punished," she said. "Go do it!" she snapped when Stuart hadn't moved. He flinched as if she had slapped him and backed away.

"Why do I have to put up with everyone's temperament?" she demanded, getting up. But as soon as Stuart left she regretted her tone and behavior. Why take it out on the children? she asked herself. Damn. Damn, damn.

She stripped off her clothing and went into the bathroom to take a quick but hopefully reviving shower.

Early in the afternoon Richie called, and she had to tell him Drake had not phoned. For the first time she heard concern in his voice, too.

"Not this morning either?"

"No, Richie. It's just not like him."

"Maybe I should come over and check your phone. Have you had any other calls?"

"Yes, Mom called, and Steffi Klein. I didn't say anything to Mom. She doesn't like to hear me complain about anything anyway. Steffi was really calling to speak to Drake. She saw Ellen Brenner and was impressed with the effect Youth Hold had had on her face."

"Youth Hold?"

"Drake's miracle product."

"Oh, yeah. Okay, so the phone's working. Well, maybe he didn't call because he wants to surprise you."

"With what? Silence?" she said dryly. Richie was quiet. "It's all right. I'm all right," she said. "What I should do is go meet Sheila and run my frustrations off."

"You should."

"And what about you, big shot?"

"I told you, I can't keep up with her."

"What makes you think I could?" she asked mournfully. "All day I've been moping about and walking like a zombie. A stiff wind could knock me over. I'd be left in the dust."

"For you she would slow down," he said. "For me, no mercy," he added, and they laughed. It was the only time she had laughed all day, but when she hung up the phone she realized she wasn't laughing, she was crying. The quick transition back into sorrow frightened her. It was ominous, and what made it more ominous was not knowing exactly what made her feel that way.

8

A little after eight o'clock Cynthia heard a car pull into the driveway and looked out to see the same Leon Enterprises limousine that had picked up Drake Saturday morning. It was almost an exact replay, for after Drake stepped out he shook hands with the man inside, and again all that she saw was his arm and his hand in Drake's. The driver looked her way again, too. She heard Drake's laughter and then stepped away from the window to await his entrance. Behind her came the sound of the children pounding down the steps.

"Daddy's home!" Debbie cried, rushing by her as the front door was opened.

Drake paused in the entryway just long enough to set himself for Debbie's leap into his arms.

"Hey, hey, hey," he laughed. He kissed her cheeks and bounced her in his arms as though she were as light as a balloon. Debbie's enthusiastic vault didn't even make him flinch. He stood straight, firm, unaffected.

For a few moments, as Cynthia confronted him under the entryway light, she was so taken by the bright look in his eyes and the energy they radiated, it was as though she were back in college greeting him at her apartment door. Despite her anger, she couldn't prevent her heart from skipping a beat the way it had when his smile first charmed her. He looked just as beguiling, just as enchanting.

Drake seemed to know it, too, for she detected that youthful confidence, that look suggesting he could conquer the world. He held his shoulders back firmly, his head straight. He appeared inches taller, and even though he had been in Florida less than a full day he had a smooth, even tan that gave his face a healthy, robust radiance and accentuated his eyes, which had a bright rust glow. When he turned to her she was held in his gaze, seized and bound by the look that stirred her sexual inclinations, even though it was the last thing in the world she expected would happen when she first confronted him.

She couldn't help her confusion. Drake, who had been handsome and attractive to her, of course, looked exceptionally so at the moment. He looked like a movie star, the man with Rudolf Valentino eyes or Paul Newman eyes—bewitching. She was tempted to fling herself into his arms so he would embrace her and press his lips to hers in a kiss like Clark Gable's and Vivien Leigh's in *Gone With the Wind*. A variety of such fantasies flashed across her mind.

"Hi, honey," he said. He looked down at Stuart, who had edged up beside her. He, too, wanted to be angry but was unable to fight off the urge to rush into his father's arms. "Hey, buddy. How's it going? How was your party?" Drake asked, scrubbing his son's head quickly.

"It was good."

"Just good?"

"It was great," Stuart corrected, smiling.

"That's what I expected from an Edwards," Drake said, and he turned back to Cynthia. He held his smile, but when his eyes had shifted to Stuart she had been able to slip out of his hold and recall her dissatisfaction.

"Where were you, Drake? Why didn't you call us?" she demanded.

"Honey," he said, shaking his head, "I've never been so consumed and absorbed. I mean, time lost all meaning. You can't understand, I know, but to me it seems as though I was away an hour."

"It's been more like a day and a half," she said dryly. He nodded and lowered Debbie to the floor.

"I'll tell you all about it," he said, "but first . . ." He snapped open his suitcase and produced a doll with a face that had been created with such detail and singularity it looked more like a work of art. The doll's hair looked like real hair, too. The eyes shifted from side to side as if the doll had come to life and was inspecting her new home.

Debbie's mouth dropped as she gazed covetously at the toy.

"From France," he said, extending it to her. "You squeeze it at different places to have it do different things. See," he said, "when I squeeze it here, she moves her eyes; when I squeeze it here . . ." The doll turned its head toward Debbie, who squealed with delight. "You can have fun discovering all the different things it does," he said, handing her the doll. She took it gingerly and stared at it in awe.

"Now, Mister Edwards, Junior," he said, "who has become an executive of sorts, will need something like this," he added, pulling out a pocket computer. "Not only does it work as a calculator, but it has a built-in clock and can store dozens of telephone numbers or notes. Here are the instructions, Stuart," he said, extending the computer in one hand and the little booklet in the other.

"Thanks, Dad. Wow!" Stuart turned and began to read.

Drake turned his attention to Cynthia and smiled in such a way that she felt he had come to his third child and was about to produce her placating gift. He reached into his inside jacket pocket and produced a small, narrow box.

"What is it, Drake?" she said as he held it out to her. She didn't reach for it.

"I couldn't resist, honey. I kept seeing it around your neck and thinking that's where it belonged, that was its destined home."

"Drake," she said, still not reaching for the box, "don't you understand that I was sitting here on pins and needles waiting for you to call? You never told me where you would be or how to reach you should anything happen."

"Did anything happen?" he asked with the arrogance of someone who already knew the answer.

"That's not the point."

"Debbie looks fully recuperated," he said, gazing at her. She had already retreated to a chair in the living room and was experimenting with her doll.

"But you didn't know that for sure," she protested.

"Oh, I knew she would be all right. Besides, I have great faith in you, honey. I knew you could handle it."

"That's not the point," she repeated more insistently. His smile didn't diminish, nor did the glow in his eyes dim. He looked unflappable.

"And the party . . . Stuart. We were just lucky Richie decided he would chaperon with Sheila."

"Sheila?"

"His new girlfriend."

"Oh. So," he said holding his arms out, "you see? Everything went well. Very well," he added, and he leaned toward her, his eyes widening and his smile deepening. With his empty hand he dug into his inside pocket again and this time produced an envelope.

"What's that?" she asked.

"First paycheck."

"Paycheck? But . . . I don't understand. All you did was go to a seminar or something, right?"

"Uh-huh, but employees of Leon Enterprises get paid for all their time, no matter what they do for the company or in the company's name."

She looked from the small gift box to the check, not

knowing which to reach for first. Impatient with her indecision, he opened the gift box and held out its contents
for her to inspect. It nearly took her breath away. She
actually backed up a step. The diamonds came to life
and glittered proudly under the entryway light.

"What is that?"

He laughed.

"What's it look like? A diamond necklace."

"But they're so big! They're not real diamonds, are
they?" she asked incredulously.

"Of course they are." He laughed again and then took
them out of the box and dangled them before her.
Slowly she took the necklace and fingered the stones.

"Let's see what it looks like," he said, taking the
necklace back and stepping behind her. He brought it
around her neck and fastened it. Then he turned her to
the hallway mirror.

She started to bring her hand to the necklace, gazing
at it with skeptical eyes, looking as though she didn't
believe it was really there and had to touch it to confirm
its existence. Drake brought his lips to her neck and
whispered, "You can't appreciate it like this." His
hands moved from her shoulders to her blouse, and he
began to unfasten the buttons slowly. "You've got to
see it against your skin," he said softly, and gently he
pulled her blouse apart so the necklace would lay just
at and under her collarbone. His fingers continued to
pull her blouse back, however, exposing more and more
of her bosom and cleavage. The diamonds, his fingers,
his warm breath on her neck and the soft, wet touch of
his lips against her made her heart pound and sent the
resulting pulsating thump through her veins with an electric speed. It was as if she had stopped breathing and
then had the air rush into her lungs with thrust and
impact. She thought she might explode with excitement.

The tips of his fingers caressed the crest of her bosom.

"Beautiful," he said.

"Drake . . . how much did this cost?" she asked
breathlessly.

"Cost? Or how much is it worth?"

She touched the diamonds.

"How much is it worth?" This time she did hold her breath waiting for the answer.

"It's worth fifty . . . thousand . . . dollars."

"Drake!"

"Yes," he said laughing. "It really is."

"But how—how could we afford this?"

"It's part of the story of my time in Florida—the people I met, things I did and learned. I'll tell you all of it after I get settled and we're both relaxed. In bed," he added.

"But Drake," she said with much less angry fervor, "you didn't call, and I waited and worried."

"I know, but before I had realized it I was on the plane coming home, and Paul thought I might as well just arrive. We'd be here that soon. So," he said stepping away from her, "the house is still in one piece, Debbie's better, Stuart's happy, and I'm back. Oh," he said, remembering the envelope. He brought it out again. "Deposit this in our account tomorrow, will you?" he said with obvious nonchalance. He plucked the check out with his forefinger and thumb as if it were something detestable. She took it from him and gasped again when she saw the figure.

"Five thousand dollars!"

"Starting salary," he said, shrugging. "It'll get better soon."

"Better? Is this for every two weeks?"

"Every week, honey. Please. I'm not starting that low."

"Five thousand dollars a week!" she said. He gathered his things without replying and headed for the stairway.

"A hot shower," he called back.

"But Drake . . ."

She stood there dumbly, staring at the check. Then she turned back to the mirror to admire the necklace. The diamonds looked virtually on fire.

"Mommy!" Debbie cried, running up to her. *"Look!"* She squeezed her new doll at the thighs, and a smile formed across its face—but it was a strange smile for a doll, a coy, licentious smile, Cynthia thought.

"Let me see that," she said, and she took the doll into her hands. The hair was soft, real. The doll's skin was so much like human skin it was eerie; but the thing that surprised her the most was the doll's bosom. Unlike other toy dolls, this doll's bosom was made of silicone and felt like tiny real breasts.

She squeezed the doll at the thighs to reproduce that prurient expression again. Was it just her imagination, the projection of her own sexual feelings, now heightened, or did the creators of the doll intend for it to look promiscuous?

"Isn't she beautiful?" Debbie asked, impatient with Cynthia's clinical examination of her gift.

"What? Oh, yes, honey. This is the most unique doll I have ever seen."

Debbie took the doll back, satisfied with Cynthia's words, and returned to the living room to play.

Alone, Cynthia felt drained by Drake's dramatic entrance. Confusion returned. She was caught in a struggle of emotions. Her annoyance and disappointment with his aloofness and neglect of the family had not entirely dissipated, but her sense of pleasure and excitement over the gifts and the money and Drake's attractive appearance flowed in like water to put out the fires of anger. The earlier feelings smoldered, but the new feelings were quickly building strength.

She shook her head. He said he had an explanation for it all. At least, she told her stern, critical self, I can listen and give him the benefit of the doubt. She smiled again at her diamond-bedecked image in the mirror. Wait until Ellen sees this. Wait until Steffi sees it!

She shook her head and went after Drake, her thoughts homing in on what it was going to be like lying next to him in bed.

*   *   *

Dressed in a new black silk robe, Drake emerged from the bathroom.

"Where did you get that?" Cynthia asked, unable to stop herself from smiling appreciatively at the sexy figure he cut. Never had his shoulders looked as broad or his waist as trim. She attributed it to the effect black had on him. The robe was open at the chest.

"I found it in my room at the Leon hacienda. Gerald told me it was mine to keep. Just another gift from the boss," he said, tossing it off as if it were something he was accustomed to.

"Gerald?"

"Gerald Dorian. Mr. Leon's personal assistant. Very nice young man who has an uncanny knack for anticipating the needs of all the guests," Drake said with a twinkle in his eyes that Cynthia couldn't interpret accurately.

"All the guests? How many were there?"

"It seems there are always a half dozen or so. It's so big you could probably arrive and remain for weeks without attracting much attention. Unless you went near Mr. Leon's personal quarters or the factory," he added thoughtfully.

"Why is that?"

"Security. It's very tight. Industrial espionage," he whispered, shifting his eyes to the door dramatically. It brought a laugh to her lips. "No, I'm serious. The place is an armed camp: electric fences, electric-eye alarms, guard dogs, a small army of guards. Look," he said explaining quickly, "Mr. Leon's got a product that has the capability of changing the face of the world. You know how people feel about losing their youthful appearance."

He approached her and took her shoulders in his hands.

"I'm sorry," he said, "about running off the way I did and forgetting to check in. They had something for me to do every waking hour, and I was just overwhelmed. There is no other explanation. It certainly wasn't because I've stopped loving you or caring for my children." He shook his head, his eyes fixed on hers. "I was just like a little kid in a candy store: limousines, personal jet planes, servants waiting on me hand and foot, gifts, a suite that rivals the best in any hotel, and a parade of brilliant and interesting people, not to mention Mr. Leon himself." He kissed her softly and then took her hand and led her to the bed. She hadn't undressed. It was too early. The kids were still awake and occupied with what Drake had brought them. But Drake seemed oblivious to this. He started to kiss her on the neck.

"Drake . . . we've got to wait." She looked to the doorway. "Stuart and Debbie will be coming up any moment."

"They're too busy with their things," he declared, and he kissed her on the neck again.

"Drake. Tell me about Mr. Leon. What's he like? And tell me what you did there," she requested. She felt like a teenage girl trying to distract her boyfriend until her parents left the house.

Drake fell back against the pillow, his hands behind his head.

First he described the trip, how he had to do a quick study of some updated facts about Youth Hold. Then he described the Leon estate, the elaborate security and the grounds. He told her about the house and mentioned the pool and tennis courts but claimed he never had a moment free to enjoy them.

"Mr. Leon promised you and I would be flown down to holiday there," he added.

"Did you like him?"

"Like him?" Drake paused as if the question had never occurred to him. "Yeah, he's . . . different . . . he's the most unique man I've ever met. He's tall, not particularly good-looking, but charming. He has such a strong grip. You know," Drake said, smiling, "Dad always used to say you could tell a great deal about a man by the way he shakes hands. Confident men hold on tightly and aren't afraid to put a little squeeze into it. Men who are unsure of themselves let you do the squeezing and simply offer their fingers and palm. Warm men, friendly men, hold on a bit longer. Selfish men, or men who aren't really all that interested in you personally, give you that perfunctory shake, slipping their hands in and out of yours so quickly you don't really feel it. I never appreciated Dad's wisdom," he added, his look far off.

"So? What was Mr. Leon like? Did he squeeze your hand firmly?" she asked with a smile.

"Don't ridicule me, honey," he said sharply. Cynthia felt a needle pass through her heart. Drake's warm, sensuous look had turned cold and hateful.

"I was just kidding. I wasn't ridiculing you," she protested, and she straightened up.

His eyelids flickered, and his warm expression returned.

"I know. Anyway, Mr. Leon is a very confident man. He doesn't look his age. Obviously, he uses his product, but you can see the wisdom and the experience in his eyes, and he's not just another businessman. He has a deep, resonant voice that seems to be drawn up from the deepest part of him. You feel the man's knowledge. He just overwhelms you with his intensity, and when you leave him you're juiced up, ready to sell. I felt like I was really with someone great—a president, a great philosopher—someone people are going to remember for a long time. And here I was, a part of it all," he added softly, reverently, looking like someone who was still in awe of his good fortune.

Cynthia was silent. While Drake was describing Mr. Leon, he looked away from her, but she could see from the way his eyes narrowed and his pupils sharpened that he had called the man's image up vividly before him. He must have been impressive, she thought.

But the manner in which Drake spoke and the expression in his eyes made Cynthia uneasy. Of course, people idolized other people; they had their sports heroes, adored their film and television stars, and sometimes went crazy when they were in the presence of celebrities, but there was a light and enjoyable excitement to it, she thought.

This was different. Drake was acting like a man who had already sacrificed his soul to win the favor of his hero. She sensed he would not tolerate the smallest criticism or negative thought about Mr. Leon or Leon Enterprises.

"How old is he?"

"Fifty-four. I asked Gerald. But he doesn't look it. He's got boundless energy. You have to trot to keep up with him. He whips a tennis ball something fierce," Drake added. "I can vouch for that."

"I thought you said you hadn't had a chance to enjoy the facilities," Cynthia said.

Drake looked at her, that strange new blinking occurring again.

"Well, I really didn't enjoy the facilities. I . . . Mr. Leon likes to challenge his guests to something, and I thought I stood a chance with tennis. I'm not the greatest swimmer, and I've never played racquetball."

"But your leg—"

"What about it?"

"Your knee," she said, pulling herself back. Was this Drake, or some clone that hadn't been programmed completely? He looked as if he didn't have the faintest idea of what she was referring to.

"Oh, I don't know. My leg hasn't bothered me for a few days now. It's weird. It just stopped giving me trouble. Maybe whatever was there finally disappeared. Anyway, I couldn't get out of at least one game of tennis. He killed me."

She stared at him a moment.

"Next time I'll challenge him to one-on-one basketball. I don't think he's that good at hoops."

"Well, what sort of things did you do with the rest of your time, Drake?" she asked, still annoyed that he had had time for a tennis match, but not time to call.

"Seminars in selling, sessions with psychologists who train you in what to look for in a customer, when to know you're going to succeed and when to change strategies. Stuff like that," he said, summarizing and waving it off. "But when I had a chance to think—" he said, reaching for her hand.

"Let me get the kids to sleep first, honey," she said. "I don't want to be interrupted."

"Right," he said, winking. "Neither do I. So," he said, leaning back again, "Richie has a new girlfriend, huh? What's she like?"

"She's very nice, down to earth, just his type. I think he's getting serious about her."

"No kidding. I was beginning to think he'd found something he liked better than sex."

"Now, Drake, you know that's not fair. Richie's a sensitive person. He's had some bad experiences, and—"

"I know, I know."

"He put up those shelves."

"Oh, yeah." Cynthia could see that nothing about the house would interest him.

"We had a visitor," she said, remembering Larry Thompson. "Actually, he came here to see you."

"Really? Who?"

"Larry Thompson. Drake, why didn't you tell me they were offering you a percentage of their business?"

"Big deal, a percentage of their business."

"He said you wouldn't even listen to his proposal. He thought there was something wrong with you."

"Why? Because I didn't want to be part of his mediocre firm?"

"No. He thought you were just too hyped up. He had his business manager check up on Leon Enterprises, and—"

"He did what?" Drake sat up.

"He was only concerned for you and your future. He didn't want you to start something that didn't have any promise, Drake," she said quickly. "Anyway, he said neither he nor his other business friends had ever heard of Leon Enterprises. He wanted us to know he would see what he could learn."

"Who asked him to check up on me? He has a lot of nerve driving all the way up here to upset you."

"He wasn't checking up on you, honey. After all the years you spent at his family firm—"

"Sneaky son of a bitch," Drake said, shaking his head. "He probably found out I was going to be away and came up."

"Oh, Drake, how could he know that? And why would he do it anyway?"

"To screw things up so I would have to go back to him and beg for my job again. Then he would give me even less of a raise," Drake replied. She shook her head. "Oh, yes, I know the way he thinks."

"Drake, you're wrong. Really, he was very nice."

"See," Drake said. "It almost worked. Look how you reacted."

He got up abruptly, his shoulders hoisted. When he turned his back to her he looked like a bird of prey about to pounce.

"He just wanted to have one more talk with you, Drake. That's all."

Drake was silent for a moment, and then his shoulders relaxed.

"Forget about him." He turned around and smiled. "I'll see about moving the kids along," he said. "Tomorrow is a school day," he sang, and he headed out of the bedroom. He paused in the doorway and turned back to her. "Better prepare yourself for your new man," he said lasciviously.

He was kidding, of course, but she felt a foreboding that was growing uncomfortably familiar.

9

After seeing that the children had gone to bed Cynthia returned to her bedroom expecting to find Drake waiting eagerly for her, but he wasn't there. She was surprised, because he had practically bribed the children to go to sleep early, gazing at her suggestively all the while. Curious about his absence, she descended the stairs and heard him speaking in a low voice on the telephone in the den. She started for the den to see why he was speaking so softly, but he hung up just as she reached the doorway.

"Hi," he said, looking up at her. "Kids asleep?"

"Yes. Who was that?"

"Oh, I was just talking to Paul Stoddard. I had to check out one thing for tomorrow." He rose from his desk chair. "Ready for bed?"

"I'll be right up. I just want to get some milk."

He grimaced.

"Milk?" He shook his head.

"Yes. You know I like a little warm milk before bed sometimes, and—"

"You don't want milk tonight. Tonight we ought to be drinking champagne. Sure," he said, clapping his hands together. "You go up, and I'll bring it, okay? For our delayed private celebration," he added, winking.

"Well . . ."

"Come on, loosen up. Milk?" He shook his head disparagingly again. "You're behaving like an old married woman with kids."

"I am a married woman with kids."

"Not old, though. Not old," he sang, waving his forefinger as he went for the champagne. She took a deep breath and laughed after him. Actually, why shouldn't he want to celebrate? she thought. He had a lot to be happy about. And considering the money he had brought home, and the diamond necklace, so did she.

She returned to the bedroom and waited. He entered with the bottle of champagne and two glasses. He handed her a glass and poured the champagne into it. Then he poured some into his glass and stood back, holding it up. The bubbly liquid caught the light and looked dazzling.

"To us," Drake said, smiling brightly. "To our new life. To remaining young, healthy, and happy forever."

They touched glasses and drank. Drake finished his in a single gulp.

"I thought you were supposed to sip champagne," she said, laughing.

"Don't worry. There's more," he replied, and he poured himself another glass, emptying that one in a single gulp, too.

"Drake!"

"I've got more." He laughed maddeningly and poured a third glass.

"Drake, you're going to give yourself a hangover, and you're supposed to be off selling in the morning."

"Me? A hangover?"

"You always get a hangover from too much wine and champagne," she warned. He took a long sip on his third glass as if in defiance.

"Drink up," he coached. "We'll finish this bottle, which, if you'll notice, just happens to be a bottle of Cristal," he said, turning the bottle's label to her.

"Where did we get it? I don't remember that."

"It was a gift from Mr. Leon. He gave it to me as I was leaving."

"What else did he give you?" she asked.

"Why?" The sharp, cold look in his eyes surprised her.

"It just seems . . . like he gave you so much," she said. "That's all."

"Oh. Yeah, well, he did. He's a very generous and giving person who enjoys sharing his good fortune. Especially when he's found himself another crackerjack salesman," Drake said, swelling up with pride. "Don't worry,' he concluded. "I'll be giving him plenty, too, before this is over." He downed the remainder of his third glass and poured her some more champagne as well as a fourth glass for himself. "Almost there," he said, holding up the bottle.

Why was it so important that he drink it all up? she wondered. His appetites were so much greater these days, practically insatiable.

He looked at her hungrily, a smile building around his sexy eyes. Her heartbeat quickened. It didn't take more than a glass or two to get her blood boiling and make her pleasantly dizzy. She started to giggle and clamped her hand over her mouth when Drake moved his tongue over his lips licentiously. His obvious and dramatic gesture looked more like low comedy. Despite his bright and youthful appearance, he reminded her of a caricature of a dirty old man.

"Hey, what's this? I thought you missed me."

"Yes," she said, but when she removed her hand from her mouth it was as if she literally wiped the smile from her face. "However, I'm still mad about you not calling." She downed the remainder of her champagne abruptly to demonstrate her displeasure.

"Aw . . ." He put the bottle down with his glass and leaned over her legs so he could look up at her. "What can I do to get you to forgive me, since diamond necklaces are obviously not enough?"

She pretended to think of some penance.

"Promise it will never happen again, for starters," she said.

"I promise," he said quickly. He ran his forefinger up the inside of her thigh, parting her robe as he did so. She placed her glass on the night table and turned back to him to weave her fingers through his hair. It felt soft and looked so much darker.

"Drake?"

"Yes, honey?" He was kissing the inside of her thigh now. She giggled again and tightened her grip on his hair to pull his face from her skin.

"Ouch. What?" he asked, a note of annoyance slipping in.

"Your hair . . . are you coloring it with one of those things that takes gray out?"

"What? Oh." He raised his eyes and stared at her as though he didn't know the answer to the question. "Yes, I've been trying something. How's it look?"

"I didn't notice before. I guess I was a little too angry to notice anything," she added. Then she considered. "But . . . I don't know," she said. "I sort of liked that middle-aged, distinguished look you got with the gray."

"Who the hell wants to look middle-aged and distinguished?" he snapped. He smiled when she flinched. "When you can look young and vigorous. Huh?" He brought his lips back to her thigh and moved forward until his head touched the small of her stomach.

"Drake," she said. She lost her breath when he pressed his face into her crotch and she felt the hot tip of his tongue move like some small animal to find its way between the elastic of her panties and her skin.

"Relax," he said. "Just relax." His hands were up to her hips, his fingers hooking the waist of her panties. He brought it down slowly, lifting her gently to get them over her buttocks. He slipped them down her legs and over her feet. Then he leaned over her, pausing and leering. The look in his eyes unnerved her.

"Drake, why are you looking at me like that?"

"I feel like I can make love forever," he said. He

started to lower himself to kiss her and then stopped. "Wait. Where did you put"—he looked over at her vanity table—"ah."

He got off the bed to fetch the new diamond necklace.

"I want to put the ice on the heat," he said, returning with it.

"Drake, really."

"No. There's something about diamonds lying on a woman's naked skin."

"How would you know about such things, Drake Edwards?"

"Just instinct," he said as he fastened it around her neck and smoothed it out over her collarbone. He slid his fingers off the stones and down through her cleavage, peeling her robe away as he descended her body. She closed her eyes and moaned, lifting herself softly to make it easier for him to take off her robe.

But after he started to slip it over her shoulders and down her arms he stopped. She snapped her eyes open to see him smiling down at her again, that same strange leer in his eyes.

"Drake?"

Suddenly he seized the belt of her robe and wrapped it quickly around her left wrist.

"Drake! What are you doing?"

"You'll see," he said, twisting her left arm back so he could wrap the other end of the belt around that wrist. She started to resist, but he pressed his torso over her, forcing her back. In moments he had her arms tied behind her back.

"Drake, I don't like this," she said, struggling to free herself. He sat back on her legs and gazed down at her, running his right forefinger over the necklace again.

"Sure you do. All women do," he said with a sneer. "Relax and enjoy."

She started to twist out from under him, but he pinned her shoulders back. Because her arms were under her a sharp pain knifed up her shoulders to her neck, forcing her to cry out. He didn't retreat.

"Drake, please." She felt the tears coming into her eyes.

"Will you relax?" he said angrily. She looked into his eyes and saw a new vehemence. "I thought you missed me."

"I did, but this isn't—"

"Then act like you did," he said, and he brought his lips down on hers firmly, pressing his tongue so quickly against hers that she gagged. He pulled back and laughed. Then he lowered himself slowly, kissing his way down over her breasts, pausing at each nipple to nibble and torment her with his tongue.

"This isn't fair, Drake," she cried. "I don't like it. Stop."

"Don't you like feeling helpless?" he asked, moving his forefinger along the nearly invisible line of hair from her belly button down. "Doesn't it heighten everything for you?" he asked.

"No," she said. "It doesn't." She squirmed under his touch. "Please, Drake."

He stared at her a moment and then sat back with a look of confusion.

"We don't need to do these things, Drake. We never did before. Please. Untie me. Please," she pleaded.

He grunted and reached around to untie her wrists. As soon as he did she brought her arms forward and rubbed each wrist.

"Sorry," he said. "I thought you would enjoy it."

He groped over the bed to locate his glass and the remainder of the champagne. He poured it and drank it quickly.

"Where did you get the idea that I'd like that, Drake?" He tipped the bottle to finish the last drops of the champagne. "I want to make love with you, Drake, but the way we usually do—lovingly. And especially not the way we did the other night."

"All right, all right," he said with annoyance. "Let me just lie here a while. You've taken some of the fire out of me."

"If that's what the fire does to you, I don't mind taking it out," she replied. "You frightened me."

"All right," he said.

"Well, you did," she insisted. "You made me feel cheap, made me feel like . . . like a whore. I hated it, Drake, hated every moment of it," she said, feeling the blood of anger rush into her face. He saw it, too.

"All right," he said in a softer tone. "I'm sorry."

"It was disgusting."

"Okay. I'm sorry," he repeated. His look of sincere remorse began to mollify her.

He took off his black silk robe and lay back beside her. He kept his eyes closed, squeezing the lids shut tightly as if he wanted to shut away some horrible sight.

She fingered the diamond necklace.

"Drake?" He didn't reply for a long moment.

"What?"

"You were going to tell me about this necklace. Is it really worth fifty thousand dollars?"

"Of course it is. Can't you see the quality and size of those diamonds? Can't you see their clarity?"

"Yes, I can, but how did you get it?"

"Mr. Leon has a client who is in diamonds, and he was so appreciative of what Mr. Leon did for him, he presented him with a number of fine gifts. Mr. Leon wanted you to have this one."

"But why? I never met him."

"I told you: It's his way to be generous."

"But—"

"Why do you keep saying 'but'?" Drake snapped. "Why aren't you just grateful, like any other woman would be?"

"I am grateful. I'm just surprised," she explained. "What did Mr. Leon do for this man to make him so appreciative?"

"I didn't ask a thousand questions, Cynthia. He offered the gift, briefly explained how he had gotten it as well as other things, and that was that. His exact words," Drake said, turning to her and bracing himself on his elbow, "were 'Please give this to Cynthia for me, and tell her beautiful things belong on beautiful people.' "

"He said that?"

"Yes," Drake said, smiling like someone recalling a great moment. "He did."

"Why didn't you tell me that before?"

"I forgot." He shifted his eyes to her. "Not really. I was a little jealous of the way he said it. I wished I had thought of it. I was going to filch the line and say it to you myself, pretending I had thought of it."

"But Drake, he doesn't know me. I never met him. He doesn't know what I look like, whether I'm pretty or plain. Why should you be jealous? It was just something to say, probably a remark he had heard a thousand times before."

"Yes," Drake said softly, "a thousand times before."

"Did you ever find out who Harris Levy was?"

"Who?"

"The man who recommended you for all this in the first place."

"Oh. No. To tell you the truth, I forgot all about it, and no one mentioned him. Why?"

"I just wondered."

"Um. I'll ask Paul one day."

"Drake," she said, shaking her head and fingering the necklace, "what sort of a man gives away a fifty-thousand-dollar necklace?"

He shrugged and smiled impishly.

"Want me to bring it back? Say you can't accept it?"

"No."

He laughed and kissed her on the cheek.

"You're so sweet," he said. "And so delightfully innocent. I'm sorry I frightened you before, and I'm sorry I was rough with you the other night."

"It's all right," she said. When Drake was soft and gentle and loving she couldn't resist him; and now, looking so virile, healthy, and happy, he was even more irresistible.

They kissed, and they did make love the way they

always had: passionately, but considerately. Afterward he fell asleep. His eyelids fluttered when she kissed his forehead but didn't open. She slipped off the diamond necklace and put it back in the jewelry case. Then she snuggled up beside Drake and fell asleep herself, never feeling more content.

Drake was up before she was. She was surprised she had been sleeping so soundly that she didn't hear him get out of bed, shower, and dress, but there he was when she descended the stairs—dressed and having his breakfast.

"Boy, you got up early," she said.

"I've got to get on the road. I'm going to start at the end of my territory and work my way back. I already have a few stops to make nearby late today as well," he added, and he emptied his coffee cup in a gulp.

"Did I tell you Steffi called? She had seen Ellen and was so impressed with how she looks now, she wants to get some Youth Hold, too."

"That's the way it spreads," he said. "See why it's not necessary to advertise and put it into stores?"

She poured herself some coffee and nodded. It appeared that everything Drake had told her was coming true.

"You get one woman to take it and before you know it, all her friends want it, too."

"Only women?" she asked quickly.

"Well . . . women are more sensitive about facial wrinkles, so we concentrate our attack on them, but men buy Youth Hold as well. They're just not as obvious about it. What they really do," he continued, leaning over the table to whisper as if it were a big trade secret, "is use their wife's or girlfriend's Youth Hold, and then naturally she needs more faster." He sat back, grinning. "That's why they tell us to try to sell to married women."

"It does sound like a great deal of research has been put into this."

"Of course," he said. "That's why they had me meet

with those psychologists and marketing analysts." He folded the newspaper. "It's getting late. I've got to get on the road."

"Gee, I hate to wake the kids so early, but they'll be upset to find you already gone."

"It's all right. I'll see them tonight." He got up and put on his suit jacket. "How do I look?"

She considered him. He looked fresh, new, eager, as green as an inexperienced young man about to begin his first important job. But behind those amazingly bright eyes there was a hint of age, a sense of seasoning. The strange hybrid of youth and age, innocence and wisdom made him interesting, attractive, even a bit mysterious.

"Well? Is that a difficult question?"

"I was just thinking how handsome you look, honey."

"Oh. Thanks." He scooped up his briefcase. "Kiss for good luck?"

"Of course."

He held her to him a moment longer than usual. She sensed a hesitation, a glimmer of indecision in his eyes, as if there were another, second Drake behind this surface one, the old Drake being carried along against his will.

"Are you all right?" she asked. His eyelids flickered, an uncharacteristic gesture Cynthia noticed more often lately. Then his confident smile returned.

"Sure," he sang. "I'm off."

Cynthia walked to the front window to watch him back out of the driveway. He started away, but as she began to turn from the window he suddenly stopped the car and looked back at the house as if he had forgotten something. She waved to him, but he turned around and shot off abruptly. In moments he was gone, and she realized that for all practical purposes their new life had begun.

Over the next week Drake was always up before she was, no matter how hard she tried to rise before him and make his breakfast. But not only did he rise and leave exceptionally early every morning, he didn't return until early evening. Their dinner hour had to be moved back an hour, sometimes an hour and a half. It was harder on the kids, who got hungry early, but who wanted to eat with Drake. She made them little snacks, but she could foresee that eventually she would have to make two dinners—one for them and one for Drake and herself. She couldn't even get him to commit himself to coming home early one night during that first week so she could make a dinner for Richie and his new girlfriend, and he was very indecisive about the immediate future.

"Remember we have the party at Paul Stoddard's Saturday night," he reminded her.

"What about Sunday, then?"

"We better wait to see my schedule."

"But you don't have to work Sunday nights, do you?"

"I don't know what I have to do yet," he said cryptically.

"But I wanted you to meet her," she complained.

"I will." Then he thought for a moment. "How old is she? Maybe she would be interested in some Youth Hold," he said.

"She looks barely nineteen as it is. I don't think so."

"Yeah, but it's something she might want to keep in mind for later on in life."

"I don't like not being able to plan any social events, Drake," she said. "Now we can afford to do things, but we're not."

"It's only going to be this way until I get my routes established," he promised. "Then we can plan things out more sensibly and return to our pattern of life. Not that being so regular and organized was so good," he emphasized. "Sometimes you need spontaneity. It keeps you youthful."

Youthful, she thought. He gets younger and more vigorous every day, and I'm getting older faster.

Much of her failure to keep up with him in the morning could be blamed on their passionate nights. Drake's sexual needs appeared unquenchable. They made love

133

every night that week, voraciously, and on Wednesday night, a few hours after they had fallen asleep, she felt him nudge her. When she opened her eyes there he was, eager to make love again.

She told him she was so tired she couldn't move, but he was undaunted.

"You don't have to move," he said. "I'll do all the work for both of us."

She groaned, but he was at her, and to her it felt more like a dream. She kept her eyes closed and her hands at her sides while he slipped himself between her legs and lifted her. She was thankful he reached his orgasm quickly and rolled over. In moments he was asleep, but she, exhausted as she was, was so disturbed and riled up, she couldn't fall asleep again for hours.

The next morning she slept so late he was already gone by the time she rose from bed. It was the children who woke her, and she had to rush to get them breakfast and organize them for school. They just managed to make the school bus, for which she was grateful. Otherwise she would have had to drive them, and that particular morning her head was pounding so, she had to take aspirin.

My newly invigorated husband, she thought while she gazed at her drawn face in the mirror, is killing me. She ran her fingers along her eyes to feel the small puffs of skin that had produced tiny but discernible wrinkles, and there were definite bags under her eyes. She thought about it for a moment and then searched for that tin of Youth Hold.

"If it works, why not?" she mumbled. But when she went to where she thought she had put it, it was gone. She searched about to no avail and finally gave up. Even Drake didn't have any in his cabinet. She shrugged and thought she would ask him for some when he returned in the evening.

She was really too tired to meet her girlfriends for their Thursday afternoon get-together and lunch, but she forced herself to go.

Cynthia hadn't seen Ellen Brenner since Ellen had begun using Youth Hold. She noticed the difference immediately. Ellen's face glowed, and her complexion rivaled Steffi's. All the little wrinkles around her eyes were gone. She had lightened her hair and had it teased. Despite the fact that she was still overweight, she wore a tighter skirt and a more revealing blouse, the neckline of which dipped well into her cleavage. It was as if she had had herself remade. And all because of Youth Hold.

Steffi glared enviously at her rejuvenated friend. Cynthia thought it was because she couldn't lord it over her anymore. The more self-assured Ellen Brenner did not sit back like a wallflower in Steffi Klein's shadow. She batted her eyelashes, turned her shoulders, laughed loudly, eyed young men coquettishly. In short, she had begun to appropriate all of Steffi's mannerisms, despite Steffi's obvious unhappiness about it.

Both her friends were overwhelmed at the sight of Cynthia's new diamond necklace. Steffi, who knew the value of such jewelry, was very impressed.

"I have nothing that compares," Steffi confessed sadly. It got them into a conversation about clothing and jewelry, and instead of going to a movie matinee they decided to go shopping, because Ellen needed to revamp her wardrobe.

"What are you trying to do, dress like a teenager?" Steffi snapped when Ellen was drawn to a pair of jeans and an oversized sweatshirt. "That will look ridiculous on you. Where will you go dressed like that? George won't like it."

Ellen laughed.

"You should go with how you feel, not with what other people think you should wear," Ellen advised. "Even if it's your own husband. You know who told me that?" she said, turning to Cynthia. "Drake."

"Drake?"

"Uh-huh. We had a nice discussion the other day when he brought me my Youth Hold. I can't get over how good he looks. This new job is doing wonders for his disposition," Ellen said. "You must be very, very happy."

"Well, I am, but it's a little hard for us right now. Drake has to work so many hours to establish his routes."

"Is that why you look so tired?" Steffi asked. She couldn't pick on Ellen, so she's turning her attention to me, Cynthia thought.

"No," Ellen said, answering for her knowingly, "I don't think that's why." She flashed a coy look at Steffi.

"Oh? What's going on?" Steffi asked, turning back to Cynthia.

"Don't you recognize that look?" Ellen pursued. "Newlyweds have it when they emerge from their honeymoon suites after a few days of living on love," she explained, not disguising her note of envy.

"Really?" Steffi waited for Cynthia's reaction.

"What makes you say such a thing?" Cynthia asked, wondering how Ellen could know. Was she right—did she look like a love-fatigued newlywed?

"Oh, I know. A birdie whispered in my ear," Ellen teased.

"Come on," Steffi said.

Ellen considered Cynthia for a moment.

"It was just something Drake said, that's all. I assumed—"

"What did he say?" Cynthia asked quickly.

"He said he was feeling like a teenager again, energetic, sexy. I'm sure he meant he was falling in love with you all over again. I thought it was very nice," she added, patting Cynthia on the arm. But Cynthia wasn't sure she appreciated Drake's discussing his sex life with Ellen Brenner. "Didn't he seem that way to you?" Ellen asked Steffi.

Steffi glanced quickly at Cynthia. "I was more interested in the cream," she said. "Although I always thought Drake was a nice-looking man." Before Cynthia could respond Steffi suddenly grew interested in a blouse.

"Sorry if I embarrassed you," Ellen said.

"No, you didn't embarrass me." Cynthia hesitated to say anything else, and Ellen went to pay for her jeans, so it wasn't until lunch that Cynthia confessed that what Ellen had said had some truth to it.

"You sound like you're complaining," Ellen remarked. "I've got to dress up like the ninth hole at the country club golf course before George will remember what that thing dangling between his legs was meant to do."

"Oh, God," Steffi said.

"Well, it's true, I'm sorry to say," Ellen complained. She turned sternly to Cynthia. "You don't know how lucky you are to have a man as handsome as Drake interested in you as passionately as Drake's interested in you, Cynthia."

"I never said I wasn't. It's just that . . ." What? she wondered. How does she express it to make any sense? "I've got to get used to how Drake's new work is changing our lives. That's all."

Yes, she thought, that's all. She nodded and looked at Steffi, who was gazing at her in the strangest way. When Cynthia widened her eyes inquisitively Steffi turned to the menu.

"I'm not that hungry," Steffi said, peering over the menu at Ellen, "but as usual, I don't suppose you want to share anything."

"Oh, yes I do." She ran her hands down the sides of her body. "I've got to get the body to match this complexion," Ellen said, and then she beamed at Cynthia.

"Isn't it wonderful, Cynthia, how much of an effect your husband has already had on me?"

It was the first time she had returned from an afternoon with Ellen and Steffi and felt so unhappy. Usually the two of them were so entertaining. But the way Ellen spoke about Drake and her inability to express her unhappiness sensibly to her closest friends made Cynthia uneasy.

To top it off, the children were unusually hyper when

they returned from school. It was as if they had been kept caged like wild animals and then suddenly released. They were loud and active—Debbie shrieking as Stuart chased her through the house. Finally Cynthia lost her temper and confined them both to their rooms.

"I wish Daddy was home," Debbie moaned after Cynthia escorted her to her room. "He's never grouchy."

"I'm not grouchy, I'm just tired. And anyway, don't get smart with me, Debbie."

She pouted, pursed her lips, and went to her new doll. Cynthia was about to turn away and go downstairs to prepare supper when something near the doll caught her eye. She reentered the room. Debbie looked up at her, surprised.

"What . . . where did you get that? And what are you doing with it?" Cynthia asked, pointing to the tin of Youth Hold.

"Daddy told me I could have it. He told me to put it on my doll and it would never get old."

"What? That's ridiculous." She seized the tin and opened it. Most of the cream was gone. "You've actually been putting this on your doll?"

"Daddy told me to," she said. "He said I had to do it every day."

"Let me see your doll," Cynthia demanded. Debbie handed it to her obediently.

Cynthia studied the doll's face again. It looked remarkably like real skin. The possibility sickened her; she felt a churning in her stomach and quickly handed the doll back to Debbie.

"Don't you like my new doll, Mommy?" Debbie asked.

"I like your old dolls better," Cynthia said, and she hurried out, the tin of Youth Hold in her hand.

Later she felt ridiculous about how she had acted with Debbie. That couldn't be real skin kept smooth and young with Youth Hold. The whole idea was absurd. Drake was just letting Debbie pretend. She had no right to terrify the child that way. She decided to make it up to her, and to Stuart as well, by calling them both down to help prepare the dinner and help her make an apple pie.

A little after seven Drake called to tell her not to hold dinner for him.

"I'm behind, and I'll be late. I'll just grab something on the road," he said.

"Maybe you're working too hard, Drake."

"Me?" He laughed. He didn't sound tired.

"Rome wasn't built in a day."

"I know, but that's because I wasn't around," he said. "I'm just going to tie up some unfinished business and head home."

"I made an apple pie."

"All right. Save me a big piece, and a big piece of you as well," he added.

"Oh, Drake."

"Love ya," he said, and he hung up. She stood there with the receiver in her hands until she heard the dial tone. The children were standing behind her. They had heard the conversation.

"Might as well sit down and eat right now," she told them.

"Daddy promised to help me with my homework tonight," Stuart said. "What time's he going to be home?"

"I don't know for sure, Stuart. I'll try to help you."

"Daddy knows how to do it," Stuart said.

"I said I'd try to help you, Stuart," she snapped. "Now let's eat."

"I hate Daddy's new job," Debbie said.

"So do I," Cynthia mumbled under her breath. "So do I."

— 10 —

Larry Thompson turned his Mercedes onto his street. He had deliberately left the office later than usual to avoid rush hour, and he was pleased with the time he had made. They still hadn't replaced Drake Edwards at the firm, so he had picked up some of what had been Drake's responsibilities and had to remain at the office somewhat later anyway. Janet wasn't happy about it, but the work had to be done.

At first Larry had been shocked and angry about Drake Edwards. They hadn't treated him badly. If he had only been a little more patient, they would have rewarded him with the promotions and salary raises he had deserved. Then he thought about the way the man looked when he had come into his office to resign and felt sorry for him. That was really why he had stopped at Drake's home. Seeing Cynthia confirmed his belief that he was right to sympathize. She was obviously very upset by Drake's actions, and even somewhat frightened. Well, he couldn't lie to her. Whatever those people had promised Drake, they were full of crap. From all he could learn, it was some sort of scam, and Drake had been sucked into it. The poor schnook.

He was sorry Cynthia couldn't get Drake at least to

phone him. Maybe he could have talked him into reconsidering and returning. Larry's father-in-law hadn't been aware of his attempt to get Drake back, but he would have agreed if Larry had insisted. He felt sure of that, but now there was nothing more to do about it.

As always, Larry decided to put all those problems behind him as soon as he turned off the Major Deegan Expressway. New York City and the firm were to be forgotten. Fortunately, Janet wasn't one of those wives who asked their husbands dozens of questions about their work. Occasionally she wanted to know if everything was going all right for them financially, but other than that, nitty-gritty details of the day-to-day business held no fascination for her. If anything, whenever her father and Larry's mother-in-law visited, Janet would force them to stop talking about the firm. Thankfully.

Larry was not in love with the insurance business. In a real sense, he had backed into it. His father-in-law had always assumed that whoever married Janet would become part of his firm. Larry had harbored dreams of becoming a sports commentator, if not a professional golfer. In high school and college he had always worked on the school newspaper writing the sports news. His senior year at college he was sports editor and had his first taste of commentary when he worked on the school's television station.

But he met and courted Janet Burke that year, too, and his story became a familiar one. When they started to get serious she invited him to meet her family; her father, seeing the writing on the wall, took him aside and made proposals. He had to confess he was attracted by the obvious success, and Janet was used to living well. He wanted to keep her in that style, if he could.

Larry knew he was glib and personable. Selling insurance would not be hard, and starting out immediately on top would not be too hard to take. His father-in-law was a bit of a conniver, too, Larry recalled. He had told the old man of his dream to be a professional golfer, and the old man had made it seem as though that would be no problem. In fact, he would get all the financial backing he needed.

He did get to enter the Bud Open up at Grossingers Hotel in the Catskills and he won, but he was unable to enter the Palm Beach PGA Open after he had paid his entry fee and booked tickets. The old man suffered a mild heart attack, and Larry had to remain in New York at the firm.

Sometimes Larry wondered if the old man hadn't staged his own heart attack and subsequent prolonged recovery just to get him firmly anchored to the business. It was even difficult for him to get onto a golf course on weekends those days, and sports, any sport, was really for the young when it came to doing it professionally. Age chipped away at his timing, and the longer the periods between playing a round of golf became, the harder it was to get himself back into the swing, especially as he grew older and the layoffs grew more frequent.

He watched his dreams drift away like smoke in the wind and, like so many other people, transferred those dreams to other things or to his children. He hoped his son would do what he had been unable to do. At fourteen he was already the top golfer in his high school club. There was something to be said for genetics, he thought. Come to think of it, wasn't there a tournament the coming weekend? The prospect of watching his son play and their spending most of the weekend talking golf cheered him. The day's fatigue slipped away as he looked ahead to the evening with his family.

They had one of the finer homes in one of the finest sections of Yonkers. His two-story brick colonial with its gardens and fountains and free-form pool was the envy of everyone, even men who made more money. One of the things that made his house even more desirable was its location at the end of a cul-de-sac. It had been a good place for the children to grow up—safe, roomy, luxurious.

The lighted windows of his home loomed before him, warm and inviting. All the box lanterns in the mauve tile circular driveway were on, and he could see that the lights were on in his and Janet's bedroom, too. She was dressing for dinner or meditating with those mood tapes Nancy Statler had gotten her. That was amusing, he thought. There was no one like Janet when it came to the latest fads. All she had to hear was "Everyone's doing it," and she wanted to do it, too. Everything except cook.

Oh, well, their new cook was fabulous. Larry's mouth watered in anticipation of one of those Cajun dishes.

Yes, he had a great deal to be thankful for, despite his frustrations and disappointments. He was wealthy, respected, and healthy. Why, there was even some talk about his running for a seat on the city council. Maybe, he thought. If he could get the firm running smoothly again.

He turned into the cul-de-sac and then slowed down as he leaned over to peer through the windshield.

"What the hell . . ."

One of their garbage cans had rolled into the street. He pulled into the driveway and stopped before the garage door, shifting the car into park, but leaving it to idle. Then he got out and headed down the driveway to the street.

Because the other car was black and because its lights were off he never saw it parked on the other side of the cul-de-sac, parked on the wrong side of the road. Larry heard a car engine and turned just as the black car shot toward him.

"What the—"

Still without its headlights on, it bore down on him. Larry held the garbage can up and froze for a moment. Then, realizing the car was not going to swerve away, he dropped the can and started to run, but the driver anticipated his move and turned abruptly, bouncing onto the sidewalk and coming off to catch him squarely at the center of its grille. The impact of the automobile was enough to lift him off his feet and toss him a dozen feet ahead. His buttocks smacked the pavement first, snapping his torso back as if he were a giant rag doll, and slamming the back of his head sharply on the macadam. He bounced and rolled over on his stomach, where he lay facedown, perfectly still, the blood trickling out of his ears and nose and mouth.

The black car idled nearby, panting like an excited animal. Then it moved off slowly, its headlights turned on again as it disappeared down the street.

No one in the Thompson house heard the garbage can clang to the road or heard the black car strike Larry. Downstairs the children had the volume on the television set up because something they all liked had come on MTV. Upstairs Janet Thompson was listening to that sensitizing tape of ocean sounds that was meant to relax her before dinner. And in the kitchen the cook had the radio on.

Finally Janet checked the time and then went to the window, annoyed that Larry was so late. She saw his car with the lights on idling in the driveway. Then her gaze drifted to the garbage can, and finally she shifted her eyes to the left and saw Larry sprawled on the street, clearly illuminated by their new incandescent lights.

Ironically, her children didn't hear her screaming until she finally descended the steps, pointing madly at the front door.

A parade of three cars entering the driveway brought Cynthia and the children to the living room windows. They gazed out curiously as Drake's car led the other two up to the house. Drake pulled his car into the garage.

"Who's with Daddy?" Stuart asked. Cynthia shook her head. The second and third car were identical late-model black Cadillac Eldorados. Drake emerged from the garage quickly, and the driver of the first Cadillac stepped out and handed him the keys. They shook hands, and the driver got into the third car. It was backed out. Drake waved and watched it disappear down the street. Then he walked over to the remaining Cadillac, ran his hand over the roof appreciatively, and turned to come into the house through the garage. Cynthia and the children were there to greet him.

"Hey, everybody's still up," he cried, scooping Debbie into his arm. "Hi, Peanut."

"Whose car is that, Dad?" Stuart asked quickly.

Drake laughed and ran his hand through Stuart's hair.

"Still got my piece of pie ready?" he asked Cynthia without replying to the question.

"Of course, but who were those people, and why did they leave a car in our driveway, Drake?"

"Surprise," he said. "It's a company car that has been turned over to me for my use."

Cynthia was more surprised at how nonchalantly he explained it.

"Everyone do his homework?" Drake questioned.

"That's really your car now?" Stuart asked.

"Uh-huh."

"Wow. Can I go look at it? Can I?"

Drake laughed. "Sure, but did you do all your homework?"

"Most of it," Stuart admitted. "Mom tried to help me with the math, but there were some problems."

"Okay, I'll look at it before you go up to sleep. And the Peanut?"

"Can I go look at the car with Stuart, Daddy?"

"Sure, go ahead," he said, lowering her to the floor.

"Put on your jackets. It's chilly tonight," Cynthia called after them. The two rushed to the hallway closet. Smiling widely, with his hands on his hips, Drake stood watching them.

"That's very generous, giving you a car to use," Cynthia remarked as she went to warm the coffee and cut him a piece of the apple pie.

"Now that they see I can do it, they're doing everything they can to make me happy," he replied confidently.

It was coming to him; he had expected it, she thought, despite his pretense of surprise.

"Where did you have supper?"

"Oh, I caught something on the road, but I didn't have any dessert, thinking about your pie."

"You had a good day, then?"

"Sure. How could I help it?" he said arrogantly. "With what I have to sell." He pulled out a chair and sat down.

Cynthia moved about the kitchen mechanically, clanging dishes and banging pots a little more sharply than was necessary.

"Why do you sound so testy?" Drake asked. "Something else go wrong today?"

"No," she said turning to him, her arms folded just under her bosom. "Nothing went wrong. I saw Ellen today. She, Steffi, and I went shopping and had lunch."

"She looks great, huh?"

"Yes," Cynthia said reluctantly. Drake heard her hesitation.

"So? Isn't that wonderful? The product works, and I'm selling it exclusively in this territory."

"Drake, how much time do you spend with these women when you go to sell them Youth Hold?" she asked directly, her eyes fixed on him.

"What's that supposed to mean?" he asked, smiling cautiously.

"Apparently you spent a great deal of time talking to Ellen."

He thought a moment, pressed his lower lip over his upper, and shook his head.

"No, not an inordinate amount of time. She was already sold on the product. I had to explain to her that it was company policy that I could sell only two tins at a time." He smiled. "She intends to get George to use it."

"From what she told me, your conversation wasn't so much about Youth Hold as it was about your sex life."

146

"What? Nonsense. She wanted to know what it was like for me to change jobs after being with Burke-Thompson so long, but I didn't discuss our sex life."

"I didn't say *our*"—the microwave buzzed—"I said *your*."

She took out the cup of coffee and the warmed pie and served it to Drake.

"This smells great and looks great. Honest," he said, looking up at her before digging his fork into the pie. "I don't know what you're talking about. She said I talked about sex?"

"Well . . . you told her you were full of energy or something, and—"

"Oh, and she interpreted that to mean sexual energy?"

"I don't remember exactly how she put it," Cynthia replied. She was getting confused, and the reasons for her being annoyed seemed gray and vague. What was her point? "The kids have been complaining about seeing so little of you these days," she said, skipping to something more tangible.

"This is good," he said, chewing. "Have they? Well, after next week things should slow down. Besides, I haven't been away all that much more than I used to be, if you consider the time I wasted commuting."

"You're leaving even earlier and coming home later."

"I told you, it's just temporary. Come on," he suddenly pleaded, his voice softer, his eyes more loving, "everything's going so well for us. Why look for problems? Relax, enjoy. This weekend we'll be driving around in a new Cadillac."

Cynthia softened. Was he right? Was she manufacturing problems and blowing things out of proportion?

"I'm sorry," she said. "I'm just tired, I guess."

"Tired? Oh." He smiled. "I'll leave you alone tonight," he said, raising his hand as if he were taking an oath. Then he devoured the pie, eating with a ravenous appetite. His big bites and gulps made her laugh.

"There's more, Drake, and no one's looking over your shoulder."

"Huh? Oh," he said, laughing, "I didn't even realize. Sometimes lately I just find myself wanting to consume, seize and consume with an unquenchable lust. I feel like a kid just starting out—idealistic, optimistic, eager to meet any challenge, eager to blaze a trail."

His fervent expression took Cynthia's breath away. Actually, she was envious. How lucky he had been to find something that would restore those feelings, she thought. Drake's face literally glowed, and it didn't seem to matter what time of day or night it was.

"I looked for the Youth Hold you had given me," she confessed. "I thought I had put it in my dresser drawer, but it wasn't there. Today I needed some."

"Ah, you don't look so bad. You should have seen some of the women I visited. They're going to need more than just a couple of tins."

"But what happened to the tin I had?" she pursued. "Was that the one you gave to Debbie? For her doll?"

"Oh, yeah. She came in with her doll, and I remembered Mr. Leon told me to have her use the Youth Hold on it frequently."

"But why?"

He shrugged. "Keeps it looking nice, I guess. Don't look so concerned. There's plenty more for us. I'll dig out another tin for you."

"I'm not worried about that. Drake, that doll, it's such an unusual doll. The way it smiles . . . the details in the face. Did you see the doll's breasts and feel its hair? It's almost human."

"Unique, I know. Everything Mr. Leon gives his people is unique. I liked it because it reminded me a little of you."

"Me?" The idea gave her the chills. It was as if it were some voodoo doll.

"Yeah, didn't you notice it has the same color hair as you do? And there's something about the look in its eyes. Well," he said, pushing the plate away and gulping down the remainder of his coffee, "I think I'll go up, take a shower, and get into some comfortable clothes."

"I'd better get the kids. They'll play in that car all night if we let them."

Drake laughed.

"Okay. Where's Stuart's math?" he asked, starting away.

"In his room on the desk,' she said, and she brought his emptied coffee cup and dish to the sink.

"Hey," he said, pausing. "Don't look so glum."

"I'll be all right," she said. "After a good night's rest," she said pointedly. He smiled coyly and came back to embrace her.

"I can have a little welcome-home kiss, can't I?" he asked.

"Of course. As long as it stops at that," she warned.

"No problem." He kissed her in a short, perfunctory manner, which surprised her. "I need a quick shower," he repeated, and he started away again. She watched him go, but something caught her attention, something that lingered in the air around her.

A scent.

It was a pleasant one, a familiar one. She could almost feel her brain searching, tracking, scrutinizing moments and events.

Finally it stopped and centered in.

That scent—it was Steffi's perfume.

Drake lived up to his promise. After he had helped Stuart with his math he went right to sleep. She was still wondering why she smelled the scent of Steffi Klein's perfume on Drake, but she decided not to bring it up after asking those questions about Ellen. He would surely think she had become a paranoid, jealous wife overnight.

As he had said, he didn't have to rise as early as he had been. In fact, he was still in bed when the children got up for school. They were so happy about it that she had to chase after them continually to wash, dress, and eat their breakfast. Debbie wanted to bounce around with him in bed, and Stuart wanted to take advantage of his audience to tell him about all the other class activities he was planning.

"I'll be home early tonight," he promised them when Cynthia insisted they leave him and continue to prepare for school. "That's a promise."

Cynthia had just finished packing them off for the school bus when the telephone rang. Drake was descending the stairs and had just entered the kitchen when she lifted the receiver.

"Hello? Oh, hi, Marty," she said. Drake paused at the coffeepot and raised his eyebrows. "It's Marty Collins," she mouthed. He smirked. She knew Marty Collins had been one of his co-workers at Burke-Thompson and imagined that was the reason for his reaction. She listened a moment longer and then extended the receiver toward him.

"He wants to speak to you," she said. "He says he has bad news."

"Oh. Maybe they fired him and he wants me to get him a job with Leon Enterprises. They don't hire just anybody," he added, taking the receiver and pulling his shoulders back.

Drake was never this arrogant, she thought.

"Hi, Marty. What got you up so early? Shouldn't you be plodding along on the commuter assembly line?" He listened. "You're kidding." His eyes widened, and he turned to Cynthia.

"What is it?" she demanded. He held up his hand to indicate she should be patient.

"When did this happen? Jesus," he said. "Right in front of the house? Sure. Sure. Yeah, I appreciate your calling. No, no, everything's been great—better than I had anticipated, in fact. Well, okay. Maybe I'll see you there. Thanks again, and tell everyone at the firm how sorry I am."

"What is it, Drake?" she repeated. He lowered the receiver slowly and shook his head.

"Larry Thompson's dead," he said.

"What? How?"

"Hit-and-run driver last night. It happened in front of his house."

"My God!" Cynthia pressed her palms against her chest and sat down slowly. "He was just here," she added. "We had such a nice talk. Poor Janet, the children . . . how could such a thing happen, Drake?"

"I don't know," he said, his eyes taking a far-off look.

"Well, you know, they don't exactly live on a major thoroughfare," Cynthia said. She and Drake had been to Larry Thompson's beautiful house. "People don't go speeding by. So what do they think? Could it have been deliberate?"

Drake looked up sharply.

"Maybe." He shrugged.

"Who would want to kill Larry Thompson?"

"How would I know? Maybe a dissatisfied client, maybe he was into something," Drake said sharply. "I worked for the guy, but I don't know what went on in his personal life."

Why does Drake sound so defensive? Cynthia wondered.

"But murder."

"Well, there's nothing we can do about it."

"When's the funeral?"

"Monday."

"We'll go, of course."

"I don't know," Drake said, returning to the coffeepot.

"What do you mean you don't know, Drake?"

"I mean I don't know," he repeated with annoyance.

"But Drake . . . you were there all those years. How can we not attend Larry Thompson's funeral?"

"I got a big day Monday. A lot of traveling, people expecting me."

"But Drake—"

"We'll see. Let's not talk about it right now. I don't like being depressed before I start out. Depression and unhappiness age you," he added.

"What?"

"You have to learn to slip past problems, not let difficulties and tragedies dig too deeply into your psyche." He smiled. "It's part of what I learned at the compound in Florida. Positive thinking," he said, pointing to his temple with his forefinger. "Always look at the bright side," he advised.

"Drake, this isn't exactly a minor event, something we can ignore. The man was just here, hoping to win you back."

"I know," he said sharply. "Please," he added. "I don't want to talk about it." His ordinarily bright eyes darkened angrily. There it was again, she thought—those abrupt emotional and personality changes.

"Well, I don't care if you're going or not," she said defiantly. "I'm going."

"Fine. In fact, maybe that's the best solution. You go as my representative."

"I'll be going for myself," she retorted. "I liked Larry, and I have my own identity, Drake."

"Oh, boy," he said. "All right, all right. Let me just eat my breakfast in peace, will you?" He went for the oat bran and then buried himself in the business section of the newspaper as if the morning had begun just like any other.

After Drake drove off in his new company car Cynthia sat in the living room, unable to stop herself from trembling. It took her nearly the entire morning to do the simple chores, make the beds and straighten up the children's rooms. A hot shower didn't revive her or settle her down as much as she hoped it would, either.

When her brother Richie pulled into the driveway in his telephone company bucket truck she had never been so happy to see him.

"I was working in your neighborhood and thought I'd drop by to see what you had for lunch," he explained.

"I'm so glad," she said. "It's been one of those roller-coaster mornings."

"Oh?"

"Sit down, I'll make you a turkey sandwich."

"Thanks. So what's with the morning?"

"First Drake's company delivers a car for his use—a brand-new Cadillac."

"No kidding! This was a good move for him, huh?" She just looked up.

"Oh, Richie . . ." She swallowed her tears and took a breath. "We got a call . . . Larry Thompson, Drake's old boss, was killed in front of his house."

"Killed? How?"

She shook her head and leaned back against the counter. Richie moved to embrace her.

"Hey, take it easy. What happened?"

"He had just been here," she said. "He came to see if he could talk Drake into coming back. He said all sorts of things about Drake . . . how wild he looked the day he resigned . . ." She caught her breath. "Anyway, it seems he was the victim of a hit-and-run driver."

"In front of his home?"

"Yes, and the Thompsons live on a cul-de-sac, not a thoroughfare. The police are investigating further."

"That does seem like a suspicious death," Richie concluded.

"I'm so upset with Drake. He won't go to the funeral. He was never this insensitive."

"No, that doesn't sound like Drake." Richie's face took on a look of concern.

"He's very different," Cynthia said. She continued to prepare the sandwich and then poured him a cold beer.

"Thanks."

She sat across from him.

"Not eating?" Richie asked.

"No, I'm not hungry yet."

"Sorry I wasn't around to see Drake earlier, but we've been busy as hell. They had to send some of our guys upstate to help restore service after that bad storm in the Utica area. Everybody's bitchin'."

"I was going to invite you and Sheila for dinner this weekend, but we have a party at Drake's manager's home in Westchester Saturday night, and Drake didn't want to commit to any other night just yet."

"Just as well," Richie said. "I'm going to be working in Westchester County all next week anyway. In fact," he said, blushing slightly, "Sheila's coming down next weekend."

"Good," she said. "I like her. Things are getting serious between you two, huh?" He tilted his head.

"They gave him a brand new Cadillac?" Richie said, obviously eager to change the subject. "Must be a very wealthy company."

"I don't know what it is, Richie. When Larry Thompson came here he said he couldn't find out that much about Leon Enterprises. He thought that it was some fly-by-night outfit and that Drake would end up being hurt."

"But you said they paid him for attending the workshops, and it was a whopping salary check."

"I know. I don't know what to think," she said.

"And the owner, from what you've described, must be a very wealthy man. That diamond necklace you told me he gave Drake to give you—"

"I know, I know," she said, unable to hide her annoyance. "I should be happy. Drake's so happy. Drake looks so good," she added. Her bitterness puzzled her brother.

"What's wrong with that?"

"He's changing, Richie. He's . . . arrogant. He's like a teenager, boasting, bragging. Suddenly all our old friends are no longer good enough. This house is now a dump. I know you're going to think I'm crazy, but there's just a strangeness about him, and I get these bad vibes. It's hard to explain."

"Have you tried talking to him about it?"

"Yes . . . and no. He doesn't want to hear anything critical."

"Maybe after a while . . ."

Her face suddenly brightened with a thought.

"There is something I want you to see. Another gift

Drake brought home from the Leon compound in Florida. Something for Debbie."

"What?"

"Wait here," she said, getting up. "I'll bring it down."

She went upstairs to Debbie's room, realizing that when she had straightened it up that morning she hadn't seen the doll. She imagined Debbie had put it with her other dolls in the toy chest her parents had bought her for her last birthday. Cynthia knelt down and lifted the lid.

When Richie first heard her he thought she was just calling for him, but the second time she screamed he realized something was wrong. He jumped up out of his chair and ran up the stairs, taking them two at a time. He found her on the floor next to the toy chest with her hands over her mouth.

"What? What's wrong?" Richie cried.

Cynthia pulled back on her haunches and pointed to the toy chest, gagging. Then, with her hand still over her mouth, she got up quickly and ran out of the room and to the bathroom.

Richie watched her in confusion and then turned his attention to the chest. He walked to it and slowly lifted the lid. The stench hit him immediately. It wasn't an unfamiliar putrid odor; he had smelled it whenever he passed a dead animal on the highway or came across one while working on telephone lines.

He held his breath and looked down into the trunk to see what it was—dead mouse, rat, something Stuart had brought in to tease his sister with? What?

There on the floor of the chest were the remains of what looked like a doll. The hair was still intact, but the face looked like a tiny, rotted human skeleton.

Richie slammed down the lid and went out to look for Cynthia. He heard her getting sick in the bathroom.

"Cyn, are you all right?"

After a moment she stopped gagging. He heard her turn on the water.

"I'm okay," she said. He waited in the hallway. Finally she emerged, looking pale, holding her hands on her stomach.

"What was that?"

"That," she said slowly, "was the doll Drake brought home for Debbie."

— 11 —

That is totally absurd," Drake said. "A doll made of human skin that needs Youth Hold to keep from degenerating?" He shook his head and laughed. "Come on, Cynthia. What do you think it was, a shrunken body? It wasn't a voodoo doll from Haiti."

"Richie said it smelled like decaying flesh."

"Ridiculous. It was probably just some material that went bad. I can't believe how hysterical you're getting over this. You've even gotten the Peanut shaking upstairs in her room right now," he added angrily.

"Well, you didn't smell how bad it was, Drake," she protested. "After Richie got the thing out of the toy chest and into the garbage I cleaned the room for hours trying to get the odor out. I couldn't have the child sleeping in there the way it stank. Go stick your head into the garbage can and take a good whiff if you don't believe me," she added.

"I didn't say I didn't believe you," Drake replied more calmly. "All right, it's over and done with."

"Easy for you to say," she mumbled. She didn't want to let go. Finally she had found something negative associated with Mr. Leon and the whole business, and she

157

wanted to beat it to death, if for no other reason than to bring Drake back down to earth.

But he went through one of those instant and radical emotional changes. The anger lifted off his face, revealing a calm, soft smile. She knew immediately what it meant; she knew what he was doing. He had described it to her a number of times before—the avoidance of any frustration and conflict in order to prevent unnecessary aging. He would simply shut out the unpleasantness, take a moment to compose himself, and go on to something else.

"Okay," he sang, "I'll go up and see what I can do to cheer up the Peanut."

Cynthia watched him bound up the stairs. Just watching him wore her out these days. He never had a low moment, never collapsed in her arms on the couch the way he used to when he returned home from the city. His old knee injury was just a distant memory. He hadn't brought it up in days, nor did he gripe about any other aches or pains. With his hair darker, his skin softer, smoother, he looked as if he was getting younger with each passing day.

Cynthia flopped into the deep-cushioned easy chair and closed her eyes. Was she going mad complaining about these things? Was she simply jealous? Richie hadn't known what to make of the incident with the doll, but at least he looked at her with more sympathy when she complained about the changes in Drake. He promised to return after dinner to see for himself. At least she would have another opinion.

She must have dozed off, for twenty minutes later her eyes snapped open at the sound of Drake and the children coming down the stairs. He had Debbie in his arms, and Stuart stood at his side, the three gazing in at her as if she were the one who had become weird.

"I must have fallen asleep. I don't know what happened," she said, her face flushed.

"Don't get up," Drake said, holding out his hand.

"The children and I will get supper on the table and call you. You've had a tough day. Right, kids?"

She sat forward and began to protest, but the children were excited; they were finally doing something with their father. Perhaps she should let them get supper served, she thought, relenting. A few minutes later Drake sent Debbie to fetch her. She curtsied in the doorway.

"Daddy says I should announce that dinner is ready and being served in the main dining room."

Cynthia laughed. Debbie took her hand to escort her as Drake had instructed. She didn't know what Drake had promised Debbie as a replacement for her doll, but whatever he had done, it had turned her sad, sour face into the rosy face of a cherub once again.

And once again there was excited conversation around the dinner table. Stuart talked about his school activities, eager to take advantage of his father's interest.

The one difference Cynthia noticed was the way Drake continually pumped him up, encouraging him to be more forceful, more of a leader. Stuart was far from an arrogant boy, despite his successes at school, and she was afraid that Drake would spoil him with his talk about "an Edwards being better," "an Edwards having superior instincts." What superior instincts? Drake's brother was certainly no ball of fire, she thought.

"Okay," Drake said when dinner ended. "Let's clean up for Mom and then go out and shoot some hoops."

"Great!" Stuart cried.

"Don't you have any homework, Stuart?" Cynthia asked. Stuart glared at her.

"He'll get it done later," Drake said, running his hand through Stuart's hair as he always did. "He's got plenty of energy at his age. Right, boy?"

"Uh-huh."

"Just as long as he gets it done," Cynthia warned. She wanted to help clean up, but Drake insisted she go relax. Afterward Debbie came to her with one of her reading assignments, and she sat beside her on the couch and worked with her while Stuart and Drake went out to the driveway to play basketball.

Richie arrived just as he had promised. When she heard him pull in Cynthia rose from the couch and watched how Drake greeted him. He pumped his hand vigorously and patted him on the back. Then he tossed him the basketball, and Richie was pulled into the game.

But something new did happen. Instead of the two of them coaching Stuart the way they usually did, they broke into a one-on-one game themselves. Despite Drake's work being more sedentary and Richie's being more physical, it seemed that there wasn't all that much difference between them. Drake moved just as quickly and was just as agile. Halfway through their contest Richie was puffing harder and missing shots. A number of times Drake blocked his shot so vigorously, he nearly pounded the ball back into Richie's face.

Her brother was not one to lose his temper easily, but she could see him clearly in the driveway lights and saw he had a determined, angry look. The politeness and timidity that he usually evinced when he and Drake played ball against each other was gone. It was as if he were involved in an age-old school rivalry, and all restraint had been tossed aside. Drake's new attitude had done it; the gloves were off. When it had come to sports in high school, Richie had been a sharp competitor.

Once in a while Richie cast a glance at Stuart, whose attention and admiration had become the prize. He clapped when each made a shot or did something spectacular. She could hear Drake turning to him each time he did something well and saying, "Not bad for an old man, huh, Stuart?"

"You ain't so old," Richie finally snapped.

"Not anymore, buddy." He tossed the ball back to Richie with a challenge in his eyes, and Richie dribbled toward the basket and went up for a lay-up shot. Drake, a little overanxious, chopped down on him, cutting into his arm just below the elbow.

"Foul!" Stuart cried, unable to avoid sympathizing

with his favorite uncle. Richie fell to the driveway, clutching his arm.

"Sorry," Drake said, but when he turned to the house and saw Cynthia and Debbie watching them he smiled arrogantly, holding his chest out.

Richie rubbed his arm.

"You okay?" Drake asked, holding his hand out to help him. Richie stared up at him.

"Yeah," Richie said quickly, "but that was definitely a foul." He avoided Drake's hand and got to his feet himself.

"Sorry," Drake repeated. "Got a little too enthusiastic. For a moment there"—his eyes took a far-off look— "for a moment I thought I was back in high school." Drake realized everyone was staring at him and snapped out of his reverie. "Come on. Let's get a cold drink. Stuart's got to start on his homework anyway, or Cynthia will have my head," he said, looking her way pointedly. She stepped back from the window as the three of them entered the house.

"Are you all right, Richie?" she asked him.

"Yeah, sure. Wasn't the first time I was fouled," he said with surprising sharpness.

"Ho, ho, ho," Drake said. "Sounds like sour grapes."

Richie was piqued but looked away quickly.

"Wasn't that a great game?" Stuart cried.

"Yes. Now go up and do your homework before I do have your father's head."

"Go ahead, Stuart," Drake commanded, and Stuart snapped to obedient attention and ran off. "Come on, Richie, I'll get you something cold. A beer?"

"Okay," Richie said. He looked at Cynthia, and she read the thoughts in his eyes. "I'm beginning to understand what you meant," he muttered. "He's changed . . . arrogant. You want me to say something to him?" he asked, looking Drake's way.

"I don't want to start any fights between you."

"Don't worry. I'll be subtle."

He nodded and followed Drake into the kitchen. Cynthia remained with Debbie and left them alone. She was worried over how long they remained in the kitchen, but neither of them raised his voice. Later she learned that Drake had turned the conversation on Richie after he had asked him about Sheila.

"Your brother's so naïve when it comes to women," Drake explained after Richie had left and they were alone.

"Since when did you become an expert about women, Drake?"

"I don't claim to be an expert, but I've learned a great deal about psychology recently. So many women today give the impression they want to be totally in charge of their lives; they want this independence they claim men have had since Adam and Eve. You know, their own identity—separate bank accounts, separate homes, their own space," he added disdainfully.

"And you don't agree?"

"Naw. They really want to be dependent. Deep down they're all seeking a take-charge guy," Drake told her. "I told Richie not to be afraid of being firm with this new girl. Don't make everything a democratic decision. In the long run she's going to appreciate him more."

"And what did Richie say?"

"He just listened, but I think I got to him."

"Did you discuss anything else?" she asked, fishing. Richie had shaken his head just before he had left, indicating the conversation hadn't gone the way he had intended.

"I gave him some advice about investing his money, too. You know, he's making good money with his overtime and all, only he's not too sophisticated when it comes to stocks and bonds."

"Since when did you become a financial wizard, Drake?"

"Oh, I've learned a lot from Paul Stoddard and some of the other Leon Enterprises employees these past few days. We take care of each other. The company's very concerned that everyone do well in every way," he added. "You'll see when you meet some of them this weekend."

She hadn't forgotten about the party at Paul Stoddard's; on the contrary, she had begun to dread it. Not a night passed without Drake's talking about it and building it up in her mind. According to him, the people she would meet were all very sophisticated and worldly. If he was right in his characterizations, she would seem like a country bumpkin. And he never stopped emphasizing how important it was that they—meaning she, mostly—make a good impression on everyone.

Drake insisted she buy a new dress. Even though she had some very pretty dresses, according to him, nothing that predated his employment at Leon Enterprises would do. Of course, she would be wearing the diamond necklace, so he wanted her to buy something that showed a great deal of neck, shoulders, and bosom.

"Buy something daring," he advised. "Be sexy, glamorous. Every other woman there will be, I assure you."

"But how do you know, Drake? You haven't met them all, have you?" she wondered.

"I just know," he said, nodding confidently. "Believe me. I know."

Ellen and Steffi went dress hunting with her. Actually, it was Steffi who directed her; Ellen just came along for the ride. They finally found one Steffi thought fit the bill. It was a strapless black chiffon with an embroidered, deeply cut V-neck. The dress cinched her waist so that it made her bosom inflate even more. But Cynthia wasn't comfortable in it because it wasn't her kind of dress. It was almost like getting into something from Frederick's of Hollywood.

"All I need," she said, gazing at herself in the mirror, "is a whip and chain."

"Oh, don't be silly," Steffi said. "This is just what Drake meant."

"How do you know?" she asked quickly. Ellen's eyebrows rose as she turned to Steffi, too.

ANDREW NEIDERMAN

"Oh, I just know the way men think," Steffi said, and she followed it with a thin laugh, but she blushed. "If you don't want it, don't buy it," she said, regaining her composure. "But I think you look terrific."

"Ellen?"

"I hope this dieting gets me your figure," Ellen said covetously. "You're going to stand out," she added with a serious face, "and if that's what Drake wants you to do, this dress will help you do it."

Cynthia nodded. In the end she bought the dress, and when she tried it on and modeled it for Drake his eyes lit up.

"How did you do it?" he said. "That's perfect. I'm not going to be able to keep my hands off you."

"I had help," she said dryly. "Steffi," she added, scrutinizing his face for his reaction.

"Oh." His expression changed, becoming serious. "Well, it's perfect."

"I guess she was right," Cynthia said. She had harbored suspicious thoughts since the night she smelled what she was certain had been Steffi's perfume on Drake. But he didn't show any nervousness or guilt. Instead he became thoughtful.

"She's been buying clothes a lot longer and more frequently than you have, honey," he said, "but that's changing. You're going to pass her up."

"I don't care about passing up Steffi Klein, Drake. I care about us being happy."

"Me, too," he said, holding out his arms. "That's all that really matters."

"I have a wonderful surprise for you," Paul Stoddard said when he opened the front door of his sprawling, brick-faced, five-bedroom home. Cynthia had just taken in the beautifully manicured lawn, the enormous driveway, and the flagstone walkway. She and Drake stepped up to the tiled patio and pushed the buzzer on the thick, dark oak door. It was opened so quickly, Cynthia had

164

the impression Paul Stoddard had been standing right behind it the whole time, just waiting for them to arrive.

"In just about an hour," he continued, obviously very excited about his surprise, "Mr. Leon is going to be beamed in via satellite to speak to us over the large-screen set in my den."

Cynthia stood staring at Drake's district manager, a man who looked younger than Drake. He had rich light brown hair styled in waves and the bluest eyes she could recall, eyes that gleamed so brightly with exhilaration that they stimulated her own excitement. His happiness was indeed contagious.

Cynthia hadn't expected such a greeting, not after what Drake had revealed on the way over. He told her Paul Stoddard's wife had disappeared weeks ago. How could he have a party? Cynthia had wondered aloud, and Drake had replied that he wasn't having the party for himself; he was having it for the company.

"And when it comes to the company," he added, "we all try to make sacrifices, no matter how painful or difficult they might be."

These days Drake talked about the company the way someone else might talk about the country. He was devoted to it with the same fervor evinced by a patriot. It annoyed her, but she tried not to criticize because he would either act surprised or grow angry and then avoid her, as if avoiding her avoided his being angry.

"That does sound exciting, Paul. Paul, this is my wife Cynthia," Drake said. Paul Stoddard nodded perfunctorily, as if he had known her for years and years.

"Pleased to meet you," he said. "Come on in. Everyone else has arrived."

"Thank you," Drake said, indicating that Cynthia should enter. Light music played over a stereo, providing soft background to the chatter she heard coming from the sunken living room where the guests milled about the modern furniture set in an Art Deco motif. The tiled floor of the entryway gave way to a thick black rug. All of the furniture—the cubed tables and chairs, the leather settees and couches—were done in black and white. There were Jackson Pollock and Andy Warhol prints everywhere with arty lighting beneath or above them. The chandeliers that hung from the ceilings and the pole lamps that hung over the couches and chairs were all different—some made of crystal, some with shades made of milk glass, and Tiffany with brass or cast-iron stems.

"I just redecorated the house," Paul explained. "I decided to try some more up-to-date things, but," he added with a laugh, "I can see I will grow bored with this shortly and redo it all again. What of it?" he said, holding out his arms. "It's just money."

Drake laughed with him.

Just money? Cynthia thought. She panned the room. The dozen or so people looked their way, all smiling, bright, young, vibrant-looking people. A waiter and a waitress moved about the room, the waiter carrying a tray filled with glasses of pink champagne, the waitress carrying a tray of hors d'oeuvres: caviar on crackers, cheeses, and varieties of meat wrapped in crêpes.

In the adjoining den Paul Stoddard had a white marble-faced bar behind which a bartender prepared mixed drinks. The bar stools were covered with what looked to be mink. Just to the right of the bar was a matching marble fireplace and mantel. There were two circular black leather couches in front of it with a long rectangular table of marble and glass. The floor was black and white checkered tile except for the large white wool rug in front of the fireplace. Above the fireplace, set in the wall, was an enormous television screen. The wall adjacent to the fireplace consisted of shelves of books. The shelves were built in and blended with the creamy white paneling on the other walls.

The rooms were certainly large, airy, and bright, Cynthia thought.

"Let me take your shawl," Paul said, but Cynthia, still self-conscious about her revealing dress, peeled her shawl off her shoulders slowly. Paul's eyes twinkled.

He glanced at Drake and then back at Cynthia, his smile widening appreciatively. "I love your dress."

"Thank you," Cynthia said. When she looked at the other women in the room, however, she saw that her dress was not unusual. Drake had been right. One woman had worn a dress that was cut away at the sides. It was backless as well, cut just above her buttocks so that the beginning of the cleavage was visible. The bodice of the dress was nothing more than the top of a two-piece bathing suit connected to the remainder of the dress by a slim piece of material that opened at her belly button and then joined with the skirt.

There were two women with dresses similar to the one Cynthia wore, and one woman who wore a dress so sheer, the outline of her breasts so emphatic, she was only a step away from complete nudity.

The men, on the other hand, were dressed like Drake—colorful, sporty jackets and slacks, gold chains showing on their necks and dangling within their opened shirts, fingers filled with rings, wrists holding Rolex watches or similar expensive timepieces.

"Let me introduce you guys to everyone," Paul said. Patricia Stanley, Estelle Brown, and Brad Peters were standing together on the right. "You people have already met Drake Edwards," Paul said. "Now meet his wife, Cynthia."

"Hi," Brad said quickly, extending his hand to take Cynthia's. He beamed at Drake. "What have you done, bathed her in Youth Hold?" Estelle and Patricia laughed. For a moment Cynthia wasn't sure she was happy about it.

"Didn't have to," Drake said. "Cynthia's always looked ten years younger than she is."

"How lucky for you," Estelle said. "A day doesn't pass that I don't work at holding back time."

"Ditto for me," Patricia chirped.

"Neither of you looks the worse for it," Cynthia said. "You're all salespeople?"

The three laughed.

"Wouldn't do anything else," Brad said. "The three of us do all of Long Island now."

"I'll bring her right back," Paul promised. "I want to introduce her around so she meets everyone before Mr. Leon comes on."

After Paul had presented Cynthia and Drake to everyone, Cynthia realized that she and Drake were the only married couple present.

"Aren't any of these other people married?" she asked him.

"Some are."

"Where are their wives and husbands?"

"I don't know," he said. "Maybe they couldn't make it."

"All of them?"

"I don't know, Cynthia. I'm meeting most of these people for the first time, too," he claimed. He handed her a glass of champagne, and she took a small dish of hors d'oeuvres. When Paul pulled Drake aside to talk about business she wandered back to the den.

The woman in the sheer dress was at the bar and turned just as Cynthia approached.

"I'm sorry," she said. "Paul introduced you so quickly back there that I missed your name."

"Cynthia. You're Adrian?"

"Yes. I see you have a better memory than I do, but then I never had a good memory. I wasn't much of a student," she said, leaning close to Cynthia. She put her hand on her wrist when she spoke and kept it there. "Not that it ever mattered very much," she added, laughing. "Men always remembered my name, even if I forgot theirs."

"You sell Youth Hold, too?" Cynthia asked. It seemed incredible that this woman could do anything serious.

"Uh-huh. I have Bronxville, Yonkers, and most of the rest of Westchester."

"Yonkers?" Adrian nodded and sipped her drink.

"Did you know a Larry Thompson?" Adrian thought for a moment and then shook her head.

"Should I?"

"He lived in Yonkers."

"Oh, so many people do and did," Adrian said. She started to laugh again. She was punctuating everything she said with a giggle, just like a teenager, Cynthia thought.

"I thought you might have known him or heard of him. He was my husband's ex-boss."

"Oh?"

"Yes, but he was killed recently, hit and run. The police suspect foul play."

"Oh, dear, how dreadful. I don't even read the newspapers anymore. I hate all the bad news. You should avoid distasteful events, Cynthia," she said, pressing on her wrist again. "They only depress you, and depression is one of the worst causes of aging."

Cynthia stared at her for a moment. It shouldn't surprise me that she says the same things Drake does, Cynthia thought; she probably had the same training.

"Do you live by yourself, Adrian?" Cynthia didn't think it was chic nowadays to ask a woman if she were married.

"Now I do, which is another sad story."

"Oh, I'm sorry."

"I'll tell you what happened, but I don't like to dwell on it." She took a deep breath, closed her eyes, and recited, "I lost my husband in a freak accident. He electrocuted himself in the bathtub. The radio he was listening to fell in."

"Oh, my God!"

Adrian opened her eyes.

"See why I don't like to talk about it?" She downed the remainder of her drink and smirked. "Now I need another one of these," she said, and she turned back to the bar.

"Cynthia, hi," Brad Peters said, tapping her on the shoulder before she had a chance to react any further to Adrian's story. "Drake left you alone so he could talk business with Paul, I see."

"Yes."

He shook his head. "My wife used to hate that. It got so I would have to swear on a stack of Bibles I wouldn't let it happen at another company party, or she wouldn't attend with me. Can I get you another drink?" he asked, nodding toward the bar.

"No, this is fine. You look too young to be married," she said.

He smiled softly and tipped his head to the side shyly. "We were sort of high school sweethearts, but we didn't get married until I graduated from college."

Cynthia smiled.

"That's nice," she said. "How long have you been working for Leon Enterprises?"

"Oh, a long time. I got the job right out of college, which was lucky for me. I didn't have very much money. My dad owned a small hardware store in Burlington, Vermont. I had to borrow the money for school. No easy grants and loans for college kids back then."

"Back then?" He made it sound like ages ago.

He smiled and reached out to take another glass of champagne off the tray when the waiter drew close and handed it to Cynthia.

"Thank you. Your wife couldn't come tonight, or she didn't believe your promise?" Cynthia said, starting to smile.

"No. She . . . died in a horrible accident some time ago. She was pregnant at the time, too."

Adrian's peal of laughter took her attention for a moment. A man was pressing himself up against her rather suggestively, and the bartender was smiling. Cynthia turned back to Brad.

"She was pregnant, you said?"

"We had a wonderful old house in Vermont with a great circular stairway. She was coming down one afternoon, and the railing just gave way."

"Didn't anyone realize it was loose?"

"Nope." He took a long sip of his drink.

"Did you have any other children?"

"No. Never remarried either," he said. "I guess I will soon, though. Mr. Leon likes his employees to have families."

"What?"

"Anyhow, I'll go tell Drake that he's taking a rather big chance leaving you all alone."

Cynthia watched him walk away. Mr. Leon likes his employees to have families? What a strange reason for him to want to get married again, she thought. And wasn't it a strange coincidence that the first two people she had spoken to had both lost their spouses in accidents? She shook her head. It had all given her a chill. Maybe she should have a stiff drink, she thought, and she went to the bar to order a scotch and soda.

"How you doing?" Patricia Stanley asked, coming up beside her.

"It's a nice party," Cynthia replied in an even tone of voice. Patricia nodded knowingly.

"It's always hard for someone outside the company to appreciate these get-togethers. Inevitably the talk winds around to business or common experiences. But I won't mention a word about Youth Hold, except to say everything I've heard about Drake has been wonderful. I thought he would be successful when I first met him at dinner in New York. He's very personable."

"Oh, you had dinner with him that night?"

"Me and Estelle and Brad. And Paul, of course. So tell me about yourself. Where did you two meet? How long have you been married?"

At least I've found someone I can talk to, Cynthia thought, and she proceeded to describe her and Drake's courtship, their family and children. Patricia listened attentively and didn't interrupt her with tales of similar experiences.

"You sound like you have a wonderful marriage," Patricia said, not hiding her envy.

"I think so. Hope so," Cynthia said.

"And it can only get better now that Drake works for Leon Enterprises. You'll see."

"You're not married, I take it?"

"No. For a long time I took care of my mother and avoided relationships, but she died this past fall."

"Oh, I'm sorry."

"She lived into her nineties."

"Oh, well, that's certainly a ripe old age," Cynthia said. "I'm sure you gave her a great deal of happiness."

Patricia's smile evaporated, and she took on a strange, far-off look.

"Sorry I stole your husband away," Paul Stoddard said, coming up between them with Drake at his side. "I apologize."

"It's all right. It gave me an opportunity to meet some people," Cynthia replied.

"I bet you would like me to show you the house," Paul said.

"Why, yes—yes, I would."

Paul extended his arm for Cynthia.

"First tour is starting now. Drake?"

"That's all right. I've seen the house," Drake said. "I'll wait at the bar." He smiled at Patricia, who settled back beside him.

"If we're not back after an hour or so, you'll know why," Paul kidded.

"There's only about fifteen minutes before Mr. Leon is on the television screen," Patricia said in what Cynthia thought was a voice of panic.

"I'm just kidding," Paul said. "We'll only be a few minutes, and everything is set for Mr. Leon's appearance. Don't worry." He smiled at Cynthia and led her away.

He showed her the kitchen first. It was nearly twice as large as her own, with an island in the center containing a Jenn-Air grill, a built-in Mixmaster, and a salad sink. There were two cooks busy preparing dinner.

Paul showed her the guest bedrooms, each with its own large bathroom and each bathroom with its own whirlpool tub; a sitting room with another marble fire-place, and another large bathroom. He walked past what she imagined was the closed door of the master bedroom and took her directly to his office. She saw a chart on the wall behind his desk and happened to notice Drake's name.

"What is that?" she inquired.

"Oh, that's our sales to date this year. I'm the head of Mr. Leon's northeast sector, so I have to keep track of all this," he said, not hiding his pride. "As you can see from the chart, Drake has had an impressive start."

Cynthia stepped closer and looked at the chart and the names. Everyone she had met so far was up there. She couldn't believe Adrian's success, but just before she turned away a name above Drake's caught her attention: Harris Levy, Weston, Connecticut.

"Oh, is that the Harris Levy who recommended Drake to you?" she asked.

"What's that?" Paul smiled and stepped forward. "Oh, yes, yes."

"Drake couldn't recall from where or when he knew him," she said.

"Not unexpected. Harris has an amazing memory, though, and recalled your husband when he was quite young. I guess he knew his father, too."

"His father? But then . . ." She turned back to the chart.

"It's time, Paul," Brad Peters said from the office doorway.

"Right. I'm afraid we'll have to get back to the living room and the den, Cynthia. Mr. Leon will be beamed in in a moment."

She looked back once and followed him out. All the guests were gathered in the den, their eyes glued to the blank screen. Drake was at the front. He smiled at her but quickly turned to the screen again as if he were afraid he would miss something. She came up beside him and was about to tell him about the chart and Harris

Levy, but as soon as she began to speak he seized her arm firmly and told her to be still.

The screen exploded with light, and suddenly the face of Mr. Leon appeared. For a moment he just stared into the camera, and his audience just stared at the screen. Cynthia looked around slowly at their faces and saw how intent everyone was. No one stirred; some looked as still as statues. Giddy Adrian had immediately sobered.

Cynthia turned back to the screen. The man certainly didn't look like a movie star. He wasn't ugly, but he was far from handsome. He had a lean face with a sharp jaw and a thin nose. She didn't like the way the line of his lips curved up at the corners. It was almost as though he was sneering. Finally his face softened.

"Good evening, everyone," he said. "Of course, I'm sorry I'm not there with you, but we thought this might be best. First, I want to congratulate you all on this month's sales report. Some of you have surpassed our expectations."

Cynthia sensed a movement through the guests, who were now closing the small distances between them as though it were important they all be touching. She noticed how Drake and Patricia leaned toward each other so that their shoulders grazed.

"I can happily report that we are getting the same sort of results from all other sectors of the country, and even from our overseas offices. In short, Leon Enterprises is expanding at an accelerated rate. You can rest assured that your investment in the company will pay off forever and forever," he said.

There was a distinct murmur of pleasure, a sound that emanated with such synchronism from the group, it was almost like a ritualistic chant. Once again Cynthia observed the faces of the guests, noting their religious intensity. They looked ecstatic. She turned back to the screen. Was she missing something? What did this rather plain-looking man have that she didn't see?

"We'll make no changes in our methods and take our time expanding into other areas," he continued.

"Remember the lessons of supply and demand. We want to remain unique.

"Now," he said, smiling more warmly, "I want to take this opportunity to welcome our newest member to the company. From what Paul Stoddard has told me, he has already had an auspicious beginning. Drake Edwards," he said, raising his voice and deepening his tone as if he were playing God or some high prophet calling from a mountain. "Drake Edwards," he repeated in the same tone, "welcome to our family, and congratulations on your initial success."

The audience broke out in applause. Drake turned to them, beaming. He glanced down at her quickly and then back at the screen.

"I would also like to extend my congratulations to Drake's wife, Cynthia," Mr. Leon, turning his head slightly in her direction.

But how could he do that? she wondered. He can't see through the camera into this room. His selective gaze sent a chill through her breasts. She felt everyone's eyes on her as well, and Drake smiled at her weirdly. It was more like he was a proud father than a proud husband.

"Now, don't let me take up any more of your party time," Mr. Leon said. "Enjoy, enjoy. Soon I will be inviting you to my home." He turned slightly toward her again. "Especially you, Cynthia," he added, and then the screen popped off as though it had blown a tube, and he was gone.

With the loss of his picture the guests groaned. Even Drake expressed disappointment. Cynthia looked about in confusion. Why were they so despondent? Did they want to listen to Mr. Leon all night? What was he saying anyway?

People came over to congratulate Drake. Some of the men looked very jealous, she thought. They shook his hand and glared with envy. The women, however, gazed at him as though he were some national hero. She could see that he was enjoying the adulation.

"Time to eat, everyone," Paul announced, and the group moved off toward the dining room, where tables of lobster, shrimp, roast beef, pasta salads, breads, and a variety of quiches were set out.

"Drake," she said, taking his arm as they began to follow the others.

"Yes?" He spoke to her, but his attention was elsewhere as he nodded and smiled at the others who nodded and smiled at him.

"That Harris Levy . . ."

"Yes?"

"It was the same Harris Levy, the man who worked with your father. I saw Paul's chart in his office, and his name was on it, so I asked."

"So?"

"But Drake . . . you said Levy would have to be a hundred or so."

"What's the difference, Cynthia? Look at all we have and all we're going to have. And another thing," he added, his expression changing quickly to one of anger, "it's not appropriate for you to be so nosy."

"Not appropriate, but—"

"Oh, man, look at all this food," he said, pulling away. The moment he did so the other women drew close to him, as if he were some celebrity.

— 12 —

The chill in the air greeted Cynthia as soon as she and Drake stepped out of Paul's house. The sky was overcast and the air was so humid, she could taste the rain. She wrapped her shawl around herself tightly, regretting more than ever that she had succumbed and bought the ridiculous dress. She hadn't felt comfortable in it all night and didn't enjoy the way some of the men had ogled her. She couldn't understand why Drake had wanted her to look like that.

"Wasn't that just about the best party you've ever been to?" Drake asked as soon as they drove out of Paul Stoddard's driveway. Her silence didn't discourage him from continuing his rave review. "All that food, those interesting people. And Mr. Leon being beamed in via satellite!" This time her silence drew a reaction. He turned her way. "Didn't you enjoy yourself?"

"Honestly?"

"Of course, honestly."

She took a deep breath and said, "I hated every moment and couldn't wait to leave."

"What?" he took his foot off the accelerator and slowed down. "Why? I don't understand how you could hate that party."

"First," she began, "except for one or two people, everyone was snobby, cliquish. I certainly didn't feel like I was a member of one big family," she added, using his words.

"That's not true," he whined. "I saw people talking to you."

"Sure, if I bothered to talk to them, but for the most part that was like pulling teeth. I don't think those people are half as sophisticated as you think, Drake. Some of them are . . . are very common."

"I can't believe you're saying that. You just didn't give them a chance," he said, nodding with satisfaction at his own conclusion.

"A chance to do what, Drake, maul me? Did you see the way some of those men were gaping at me in this ridiculous dress? I felt as though I were naked. And did you see the dress that Adrian Blake was wearing? You saw it," she replied quickly, recalling the way Drake had fixed his eyes on her as well as some of the other women. Actually, one of the things that annoyed her the most was the way Drake had floated around the party, touching base with every female, their conversation and demeanor seemingly so intimate, it was as though he had already slept with each woman.

"I'm sure it's in style if Adrian was wearing it," he said in her defense.

"She wouldn't know one style from another. If ever I met an airhead . . ." She turned to him. "I can't believe she is a successful saleswoman for Leon Enterprises. She must be fronting for someone else who actually does the work. If I ever had such a person come to my door to sell me anything, I would burst out laughing."

"Adrian happens to be a very intelligent woman, Cynthia."

"Very intelligent. She never went to college and told me herself that she can't remember anything, especially men's names. Dynamite salesperson," Cynthia quipped.

"Well, she does do well for the company," he insisted. "Paul told me so."

"Maybe he's sleeping with her."

"Oh no, he's—"

"In mourning over his disappeared wife, I know. He looked it," she said dryly. "And that's another thing, Drake."

"What is?"

"I spoke to Adrian, and she told me her husband died in a freak bathroom accident."

"So?"

"Then Brad Peters told me his wife was killed in a freak household accident. While she was pregnant! She fell off a stairway when the railing gave way."

"I never knew that. He never said a word."

"Why should he? He would break the code—never discuss or dwell on sad and depressing things because they tend to age you, right?"

"Maybe you drank too much," Drake said, sounding annoyed.

"Maybe I didn't drink enough. Think about it, Drake. Paul's wife is off babbling someplace, these two lost their spouses. I think it's a rather depressing group of people. Why, even Patricia Stanley, with whom I had a halfway decent conversation, just lost her mother. Even though her mother was in her nineties, I was afraid to ask how she had died."

"These things happen. Why make a big deal out of it?" He started to drive faster.

"And then the way they all behaved when Mr. Leon came on the television. He didn't look like any old-fashioned gentleman to me. He doesn't look more than forty, and yet you'd think he was some guru and they were all his disciples, or they were idealistic and enamored campaign workers listening to their man. Even you. You should have seen your face when he was speaking."

"We all respect Mr. Leon and what he has accomplished. I'm sorry you can't appreciate that. Believe me, it's your loss," he said in a controlled voice. She ignored his subtle reprimand.

"It was almost funny," she said. "I did all that I could to keep from laughing."

"I'm glad," he said, not hiding the underlying tone of threat in his voice.

"Drake, really."

"Really nothing, Cynthia. I'm disappointed in you, terribly disappointed. Here I bring you to meet these people, all of them very successful, and you ridicule them. And the party—when did you go to a house party with such elaborate food? Not even Steffi and Sheldon Klein put out such a spread. And weren't you impressed with Paul's house? It made the Klein's colonial look like a dump."

"Yes, but—"

"And you ridicule Mr. Leon? After he's already given us so much?" He shook his head. "Your father used to be afraid I wouldn't be able to support you and a family on a salesman's salary and commission. I guess we can put that to rest. But are you grateful? No," he snapped.

"Drake—"

"I don't want to talk about it."

"But—"

"*I don't want to talk about it!*" he screamed. In the flash of an oncoming car's headlights she saw his face—his mouth twisted and ugly, his eyes wide with anger.

She sat back, her heart pounding, and they drove all the way home in silence.

Things returned to normal for the remainder of the weekend. When her friends called to see how the party had gone Cynthia pretended to have enjoyed it. Steffi wanted to know how people had reacted to her dress. She told her she was the center of attention, but Steffi didn't pick up on her sarcasm. Instead she replied that she had known it would go over well.

Drake decided they should take a ride to look at some house lots that were for sale. He was talking more seriously now about their selling their home and building a newer, bigger one. He told the children they would have a real basketball court as well as a pool and tennis court. It was difficult, if not impossible, for her to remain despondent in the face of all this optimism and promise. The one bleak moment came when she brought up Larry Thompson's funeral again. Drake was adamant about his not going.

"I've got too much to do. I can't start goofing off just as I'm getting under way for the company," he explained.

"It's not goofing off, Drake. How often do you have to go to your ex-boss's funeral? In light of how long you worked for them, I'm sure everyone at Leon Enterprises would understand."

"I can't do it," he insisted.

"You mean you won't," she replied, but he ignored her and went off to play a video game with Stuart and Debbie.

So after he left for work and the kids were off to school Cynthia dressed and drove down to Westchester to attend the funeral. A light drizzle made the ride depressing, and when she arrived at the church by herself it was embarrassing. All of Drake's old co-workers asked after him. She tried to excuse his absence by claiming he was out of town for his new company, but no one seemed to believe her.

After the church service Cynthia stood with some of the people she had known from Drake's office. They were talking about the investigation of Larry Thompson's death. The police had concluded it was a deliberate killing.

"Do they have any concrete leads?" she asked Marty Collins on the steps of the church. The rain had stopped and the sky had begun to clear.

"A few things. We heard a neighbor happened to be looking out of the window and heard the tires squealing, although he hadn't realized what had happened until much later on. Anyway, he saw what they are now pretty sure was the car."

"Oh?"

"It was a black Cadillac Eldorado," Marty said.

Cynthia's heart skipped a beat. She brought her hands to the base of her throat.

"Black Cadillac?"

"Uh-huh. Recent model, too. Are you going to the house?"

"What? Oh, no, I have to get back for the children."

"Drake's doing well, then?"

She nodded but looked away quickly so that Marty wouldn't see the worry in her eyes.

"You okay?"

"Yes. Thank you," she said, turning back and smiling. "I'd better be on my way. Good-bye, Marty. I hope when we meet again it's under better circumstances."

"Regards to Drake," Marty called as she started toward her car. She drove home in a daze. Surely this was just another coincidence, she thought.

She still had a good hour or so before the children returned from school, so she headed for Ellen Brenner's house. She needed to talk to someone, and Ellen was really her closest friend. She caught her just returning from one of her increasingly frequent shopping sprees.

With the success Ellen had had using Youth Hold she had become more motivated about her diet and had already lost enough weight to justify buying outfits. Her arms were loaded down with packages when Cynthia arrived. She turned with surprise as Cynthia pulled in behind her. Oddly, instead of looking happy about Cynthia's visit, Ellen looked concerned, almost disturbed.

"Hi," she said. "Something wrong?"

"I just returned from Westchester. Drake's ex-boss's funeral."

"Oh," Ellen said, a look of relief on her face. "Well, come on in. I want you to see this new outfit I got at The Dazzle House."

"The Dazzle House?" Cynthia stepped out of her car, smiling. The Dazzle House was almost an exclusively punk-rock clothing store—dresses with ornate sequins, leather and silver, hard rock T-shirts, and ornaments mostly worn by teenagers. The loud music had been enough to keep them out of the place before, Cynthia thought.

Ellen managed to get the front door open but then struggled to twist herself and her packages around to enter. Cynthia rushed up to help her by taking one of the boxes out of her hands. It was heavy.

"What's in here?"

"A great dress; it's got a silver embroidered top that makes me look like Madonna."

"You like that?" Cynthia asked, following her into the house. She turned into the living room and dropped the packages on the couch. Relieved, she stood up straight and smiled.

"Uh-huh. Especially how it looks on me," she said, straightening up and running her palms down her sides and over her hips. "George will flip out, of course, but . . . that's George. Just put that right here," she added, pointing to the space beside the pile of boxes. "I guess you want a drink or something after attending that funeral, huh?"

"No, no, I'm all right."

"I'll get something . . . some wine, at least. I have a bottle uncorked in the fridge. Sit down," she sang, and she went off to get the wine.

Is everyone crazy but me, or am I the crazy one these days? Cynthia wondered. Ellen returned quickly with two glasses of Zinfandel blush. She handed Cynthia one and sat down beside her acquisitions, patting the top box.

"I want your opinion of this blouse. It's cut a little low and is a bit shear, but I thought it might go great with my black leather pants."

"Black leather pants?"

"I couldn't resist. The snug way they hug my bottom . . . So it was a bad funeral I imagine, not that any could be good." She sipped her wine and peered at Cynthia over her glass.

"Very bad. The police have concluded he was murdered, hit by a new black Cadillac Eldorado."

"Oh, dear. Any leads?"

"Not yet. Ellen, I'm worried about Drake," she said, sitting back.

"Heavens, why?"

"He's so different these days, so into this new business. It's changing him. He wouldn't even give up the time from work today to attend the funeral. I had to go myself, and everyone saw through my lies. I hate to say the old cliché, but money's changing him. He's growing arrogant, and I don't know how to handle it. I know he's getting more and more annoyed with me, thinking I'm not growing along with him, but I don't want to grow that way."

Her friend nodded but just stared nonplussed.

"You didn't notice anything different about him when you last saw him?"

"I didn't, no. He looked healthier, happier, as I told you, and if anything, he was more so on Friday, but—"

"Friday? You saw him on Friday?"

"Oh." Ellen laughed. "I needed more Youth Hold. I've been overdoing it, I'm afraid. He had to come back with two more tins. I wanted to buy a whole case right out," she added, as if to explain away the need to see Drake so often, "but there is some sort of company rule about how much he can sell at a time. So the way I use it, I guess I'll see him quite often," she added.

"I see." Cynthia recalled what Drake had told her might happen. "George wouldn't be into it, too, by now, would he?"

"George? No way. I tried to get him to use it, but he absolutely refused. You know George. It's in the family genes. It took his father two years to use an indoor bathroom after it was built in their old house. He insisted the outhouse was just as good. Anyway, if anything, I think Drake is more personable. He gets better-looking with age, and I think he knows it, too," she added, shifting her eyes away quickly as if she had said too much.

Cynthia felt a tingling at the base of her spine. Ellen was acting almost guilty about her meeting with Drake. Cynthia recalled the way he had behaved at Paul Stoddard's party. He was something of a flirt, even though it had never been in his nature to be so. Could it be that he had come on to Ellen Brenner, too? Her friend looked embarrassed about discussing Drake.

"You want me to show you these things, or aren't you in the mood?" Ellen asked.

"Oh, no, please. I probably need something to take my mind off things," Cynthia said, and she sat back to watch Ellen giggle and squeal over her new clothes.

Drake knew Cynthia had gone to the funeral, but when he came home he didn't ask her about it. She attributed that to his excitement. The first thing he did when he entered the house was make a grand announcement: they had been invited to the Leon compound in Florida two weeks from Friday.

"We'll fly down on the private jet. Wait until you see that. There's nothing like having a plane all to yourself. With a stewardess, too!"

"That does sound wonderful, Drake. I'm happy for you."

"For us. We're both invited. That's the point."

"I meant for us."

"When you meet Mr. Leon you'll see that your negative feelings about all this have been unwarranted."

"I hope so, Drake. Don't you want me to tell you anything about the funeral?"

"What can you tell me?" he said, shrugging. "A funeral's a funeral. I imagine it was unpleasant and there were a great many people there."

"The church was full. Your friends were asking about you."

"It couldn't be helped," he said, almost snapping.

"The police have determined for sure that he was murdered, Drake."

"Oh?" That brought a pause. "Do they have suspects?"

"No, but they have a description of the car. It was a black Cadillac Eldorado. New," she added waiting for his reaction. He stared at her.

"Common enough car," he finally said. "No license plate numbers?"

"I don't know. That's all Marty Collins told me."

Drake nodded. Did he looked relieved, Cynthia wondered, or was it her imagination?

"I was at Ellen's today after the funeral. You've been back to see her already?"

"Got to satisfy my customers," he said, smiling. She didn't like what she thought she read in the grin. Her stomach tightened.

"Yes, your Youth Hold has had an amazing effect on her."

"She looks good, huh? It is amazing stuff."

"Not just her looks, Drake. Her entire personality. She's losing weight, buying silly clothes—"

"So? She's getting a kick out of life again. What's wrong with that? You sound like you're complaining about it."

"I don't know," she said, shaking her head. "It seems . . . unnatural."

"That's ridiculous, Cynthia. What the hell are you doing . . . talking to that born-again cousin of yours? What's her name?"

"Lori, but I haven't spoken to her in months."

"So relax, will you? Go out and buy some things to wear in Florida. Get a new bathing suit . . . one of those string bikinis," he suggested seriously.

Afterward he was more subdued than he had been recently, listening attentively to the children when they talked at dinner and spending time with Stuart on his homework. But she also noticed that he locked himself in the den and spoke on the phone for a good portion of the evening. Afterward, contrary to what she had come to expect, he went directly to bed and fell asleep.

Of course, Cynthia's mind went on overtime. Was he getting his sexual satisfaction someplace else? Is that why he smiled and told her he had to satisfy his customers? She lay awake for hours, thinking. Whenever she closed her eyes she saw Paul Stoddard's guests gazing with such reverence and adoration at the oversized television screen. They had all looked drugged—Drake included. What could she do? The money was terrific; her friends thought the new Drake was wonderful; every time she voiced a complaint, he managed to turn things in such a way that she looked stupid, foolish, or selfish.

But she had to do something, she thought, if for no other reason than to satisfy her own irritating doubts and end that persistent and annoying scratching inside her chest, the scratching of something that wanted desperately to be out in the open.

She decided she would take a ride the next day, its exact purpose unclear, even its exact destination unknown. She would go to Weston, Connecticut, which was just a two-hour drive, and see if she could find the mysterious Harris Levy, if only to see how someone so old could be so active.

Of course, she didn't want to give Drake any indication of what she planned to do. He didn't notice her excitement and nervousness the following morning. He was too wrapped up in his own plans for the day, describing the routes and the small towns he would visit. When she asked him how he knew where to go exactly, he replied cryptically that the company provided him with the targets.

"Targets?"

"That's just sales talk, honey," he said, laughing. He kissed her good-bye and was on his way in his new black Cadillac Eldorado. While the children ate breakfast Cynthia went upstairs to shower and dress. As soon as they boarded the school bus she got into her car and drove off, unable to recall a time in her life when she was more determined to do something.

She had the definite feeling she was fighting for the life of her family, yet she had no evidence as to why she should have that foreboding. Was it a mother's instinct, or the instinct to survive? Just asking the question chilled her and sent her flying off looking for some answers.

Cynthia had always loved that part of Connecticut. Most of the homes were rustic and quaint, set in picturesque wooded areas a good distance from the road. She had been there at least a half a dozen times before, twice with her own parents on a family outing. Her mother was often after her father to consider moving there, but he liked where he was, where he had grown up and established himself.

"Maybe you will live here someday, Cynthia, and I'll be able to come visit you," her mother told her with a sigh.

It was fun riding along those peaceful country roads looking at all the houses, some of which dated back to the late seventeen hundreds. They were marked as such so that a traveler would feel he or she was moving through history.

But there was nothing antiquated about the villages and towns. Malls, streams of modern stores, were spaced along the quiet, clean, wide streets. The area was close enough to New York City to be a bedroom community, but the city pace was left at the commuter stations. Here people moseyed along, seemingly without any pressure or tension

Cynthia pulled into one of the small malls and looked for a phone booth. She remembered once reading a mystery story in which an amateur detective located a suspect quickly by looking him up in the local phone book. Luckily, she found only one Harris Levy listed. Actually, his wife was listed with him: Harris and Selina Levy, 18 Seaton Way.

What proved to be much more difficult was locating the street. Apparently, there were so many newly created streets, some with only two or three houses on them, that even stopping at service stations and asking proved fruitless. Finally, she decided to do what the amateur sleuth in her mystery story had done. She went to the fire department.

A group of firemen were out in the front washing down one of the trucks when she pulled up. They all turned her way, but when she got out she chose a short, bald-headed man with a pleasant face who looked like a lifetime inhabitant. He was standing with his arms folded across his chest as though he were supervising the washing of the truck.

"Seaton Way? Yeah, used to be called Dunn's Drive when old man Dunn was the only one living there. But that was before those new houses were built and it became exclusive," he said, raising his bushy eyebrows. "Whatcha do is go down here to Lyon Plains Road and make a left, then take your first right. About a thousand yards in you'll see a road going off to the left. Take it in a hundred yards, and the street off to your right is Seaton Way."

She thanked him and drove off. His directions were perfect. The numbers on the homes had little to do with the way the houses were set up, however, which made her wonder if the inhabitants hadn't just picked the numbers they liked best. The first house was 7 Seaton Way, and the second was 10. The third house was 18 Seaton Way. She paused in the driveway and gazed at a beautifully restored turn-of-the-century farmhouse with a wonderful wraparound porch. The house was very pretty, but the grounds were all overgrown. Did that mean the inhabitants were gone?

She drove ahead very slowly and stopped in front of the garage. For a moment she waited in the car to see if anyone would come to the front door. She listened; sometimes people had dogs, and the dogs would begin to bark as soon as someone pulled in, but there was nothing but the wonderful wooded silence characteristic of this part of Connecticut. She thought she heard the faint murmur of water flowing, a stream behind the house.

In the bright late-spring sunshine, with the light filtering through the green leaves, the forest around the house took on a magical look. It was as though she had driven into a land peopled by fairies and nymphs. Even the birds sounded different, more melodic, ethereal. She took a deep breath. How peaceful; how wonderful this home cloistered in nature was. For a moment she longed for a simpler life—Drake having a decent job and not having to go out on the road and make thousands and thousands of dollars, driven by an almost ruthless ambition, Cynthia living here, planting a garden, reading on the porch.

Maybe the house was for sale, or soon would be, she speculated. Would Drake consider it instead of opting for that luxury home with a huge pool, tennis court, and full basketball court? They could put a tennis court here, she mused, off to the left there in a shady wooded setting. And they could put a modest-size pool in the rear of the house, she felt sure. Was this too much to hope for? Maybe Drake could be transferred to the Connecticut territory, and what her mother had wished for her years ago would come true.

She stepped out of the car and walked up the wooded steps to the front door. She gazed around the porch, at the rockers and the swinging settee. When she turned around and looked down the driveway and around the front yard she saw how secluded it was. Picture perfect, she thought, and she went to the door. There was a brass knocker in the shape of a hammer. She lifted it and let it tap. The hollowness of the sound within discouraged her, but she let it tap again, and once more she was met with the echo of the brass resonating inside.

She went to one of the panel windows in front and leaned down, shaded her eyes to gaze through it into what was obviously the living room, still fully furnished, all the pictures still on the fireplace mantel and on tables, knickknacks everywhere. Whoever lived there was certainly into antiques, she thought as she looked from the tables to the fireplace implements to the dark oak magazine rack.

Disappointed, Cynthia started off the porch when she heard the clap of a loose shutter at the side of the house. She went around to look at it and saw that a side door was slightly ajar. Did this mean someone was at home but perhaps hadn't heard her knocking? Maybe he or she was in the rear of the house.

"Hello?" she cried, and she waited, listening. She heard only the murmur of the stream and the clap of the shutter. "Hello? Anyone home? Mr. Levy? Mrs. Levy?"

She looked at the door and then approached it to open it a little farther and peer inside.

"Hello?" she called into the house. There was only silence.

Cynthia wasn't the kind of person who would snoop, but the side door opened to the kitchen, and she was admiring the old stove. She opened the door a bit further and took a step, and then another step.

"Hello," she cried to justify her invasion. "Anyone here?" She paused at the kitchen table and ran her hand over the maple wood. This was an antique, too, she thought, looking at the hand-carved legs. She turned to leave when she remembered something else the amateur sleuth in her detective story had done when he had entered a house.

She went to the refrigerator and opened it. Instantly she was greeted with stale odors. Did that mean no one was presently living in the house? She went to the bread box and saw that the bread within was as hard as stone and moldy. In the sink the dishes were crusted with old food, and the cups were stained from coffee that had evaporated. No one had been there for some time, she thought. The realization made her more aggressive, as if it gave her license to continue her exploration.

191

Cynthia moved from the kitchen to the dining room, again admiring the colonial furniture, the hutch, the table and chairs, and the small serving table in the corner. These were expensive pieces, she thought. She knew how costly antique furniture in this sort of prime condition could be. She went from the dining room to the hallway and gazed at the living room she had seen from the front window. Then she started to turn, intending to go out of the house the way she had come in, when she spotted the small marble-top oak table under the hat and coat rack. She froze in position.

There, on top of the table, was a now-familiar rich Italian leather case with the gold-embossed letters "LEON ENTERPRISES." The case was open, but there were no valuable jars of cream within. However, she saw what looked like a small pillbox.

Discovering the briefcase sent a chill up her spine but also confirmed that this was indeed the home of the Harris Levy who worked for Mr. Leon. But where was he or his wife, she wondered, and why was the food stale and spoiled in the kitchen? They must have been gone a while.

Her attention went to the stairway and the mahogany banister. Cynthia climbed the stairs, listening for sounds of anyone else after every step. When she reached the landing she turned toward an open door and gazed in at what she thought must be the master bedroom. The bed still had bedding on it. Oddly, on the bed were a pair of shoes with socks hanging out of them, pants, and a sports jacket.

She entered and noticed an empty pill bottle on the night table beside the bed. She looked at it and saw it was a prescription for tranquilizers from a Dr. Sacks. When she looked at an open closet she saw it was filled with clothing.

Maybe they had just left for a short time, she thought. It was best she get herself out of there before someone discovered she had broken into the home. She started for the stairway and stopped when she saw a shorter stairway leading up to what had to be an attic. The door of the attic was open, but the room within looked very dark.

Nevertheless, Cynthia was drawn to it by the same instinctive urges that had brought her there in the first place. Whatever the reason, she found herself climbing the short flight of steps, chastising herself all the way for being so nosy, for invading someone else's privacy, but recalling that she had always been a curious person, driving her parents crazy with questions, even more than Debbie or Stuart drove her and Drake crazy.

When she was only a little more than halfway up she was greeted by a foul odor. It reminded her of the stench that had come out of Debbie's toy chest when she had lifted the lid to get the doll to show to Richie. She paused. Rats and such creatures died in attics in country houses, she thought.

As horrible as the odor was, she continued up. When she reached the top step she leaned in. It was too dark to see anything. She expected to find an attic filled with interesting antiques, but it looked and felt empty to her. The smell, much stronger and more putrid, was enough to drive her away. When she started to turn her eyes adjusted to the darkness, and she saw the outline of what looked like a person standing in the dark.

She gasped, but whoever it was didn't move. She spotted the light cord dangling in the shadows before her and reached up to pull it.

She couldn't scream, not right away. For a moment she just stood there, locked in a mad gaze with a corpse dangling before her in the hangman's noose. The woman's skin had turned black and gray and had begun to flake off the skull within. The eyes had drained and dried in their sockets, their fluid leaking down the parched cheeks and creating bluish-red streaks. Her lips had pealed away from her mouth to reveal yellowed teeth in black gums. Yet her hair looked the same as it must have looked the day she died: brushed down over her shoulders, her bangs curled over her forehead, now mostly a sickly pale bone.

Cynthia turned and grasped her stomach as if she had just been punched. She brought her fist to her mouth and screamed.

She screamed all the way down the stairway, nearly tripping on the last small step before turning on the landing to continue her descent to the first floor.

Still screaming, she charged through the house to the side door and burst out into the warm, welcoming sunlight. She tried to catch her breath. Her pounding heart made her dizzy, but she didn't want to stay there a moment longer than she had to.

She ran to the car, started the engine, and backed up to turn out of the driveway, stopping only when she had finally reached a busy intersection. There she pulled off the road to gather her wits.

The world around her was so ordinary, so peaceful, so unaware. The contrast between where she was and what she had just been through was too much. She couldn't stop crying. Finally she pulled back onto the highway and headed toward the fire department so she could get directions to the police station.

— 13 —

What the hell were you doing there?" Drake shouted. His face was crimson, and he had hoisted his shoulders with such anger, he looked as though he might explode. Cynthia flinched and stepped back, actually cowering in a corner of the kitchen as he hovered before her. He came at her, looking so angry she thought he might even strike her.

"I wanted to speak to Mr. Levy," she cried.

"Why?" Suddenly, realizing how wild he looked and how frightened of him she was, he lowered his shoulders and took a deep breath. "For God's sake, Cynthia, why?" he asked in a calm voice, his arms out.

"I just wanted to see who he was and why he had recommended you," she said weakly.

"What? I told you who he was. Why would you drive a total of four hours to find out about that?" He grimaced in confusion and shook his head.

"He's not who you said he was," she replied. "The police in Weston gave me his description. He's missing . . . missing, Drake, just like Paul Stoddard's wife."

"You're absolutely bonkers," Drake said with amazement.

"I'm not bonkers. Harris Levy was a man no more

than fifty, so he couldn't have been the man who worked with your father.''

"So what?" Drake exclaimed.

"Well, aren't you just a bit curious as to who he really was, then?"

"No. He was someone I met somewhere. I've met a great many people selling insurance. Anyway, why would you drive all the way to Connecticut? I still don't understand."

She didn't want to tell him about her instinctive feelings, about her intuitive fears, because he wouldn't understand, so she skipped over why she had gone and decided instead to concentrate on what she had found.

"His wife might have killed herself, Drake, or her husband might have killed her. I saw that she was on tranquilizers, but the police can't say for sure yet."

"So?"

"Just listen. I thought about this all the way home. Paul Stoddard's wife was in a deep depression and disappeared, ran off. He says," she added pointedly.

"What's that supposed to mean? You think Paul did something to his wife because Harris Levy, whoever he is, might have done something to his? Cynthia, there are hundreds of murders of passion occurring in this country every day, every hour!"

"All I know is that he is the most cheerful heartbroken man I have ever met."

"Jesus, Cynthia, I—"

"Just listen," she repeated, gaining momentum. "Adrian Blake's husband died in the bathtub, accidentally electrocuted. Brad Peters's wife fell off a stairway because nobody noticed a railing was bad. Now we find out that Harris Levy's wife has been hanging in an attic. And all these people work for Leon Enterprises."

"So?"

"Why didn't any of those other people at the party have their husbands or wives with them, Drake?" She stepped toward him, her eyes wide. "Could it be that they're all dead, too, or missing?"

"My God, Cynthia, you really have gone wild. Just look at yourself. Listen to this paranoia."

"You weren't there. You didn't see that woman's corpse dangling from the ceiling."

"How could you break into someone's house anyway?" he responded, choosing to pick up on another theme. "What has gotten into you?" He blinked quickly.

"If I hadn't gone in, the police would never have known about Selina Levy. And another thing, Drake," she said, smiling madly, her eyes popping, "how come no one at Leon Enterprises knew that Harris Levy's been missing? Huh? Do you know how long that woman must have been hanging in that attic?"

"Maybe they do know. I'm not privy to all the things management knows," he whined.

"No one brought it up at the party, and I asked Paul about Harris Levy. Why didn't he say something then? Can you tell me, Drake?" she pursued.

Drake stared, his eyes blinking as if they were being irritated by smog.

"Maybe he didn't think it was any of your business. Or maybe he didn't know. Maybe only Mr. Leon knows."

"Well, now we know," she said.

He shook his head. "Jesus, what if the company finds out about this? How am I going to explain it?"

"I don't care about the company. The company, the company, that's all you talk about anymore. The kids have noticed it, too. You're obsessed with it and care about it more than you do about us."

"That's not true, Cynthia," he moaned. "I've deliberately made sure I was home earlier these past few days to spend time with them. I told you once I got settled into my routine I would be able to spend far more time at home than I ever did, and I'm beginning to. Just ask the kids."

She stared at him, trembling. What he said was true—he had been home earlier the past few nights and had been helping Stuart with his homework, just as he used to do. The children wouldn't side with her now.

"I don't know—you're different, Drake. You're just different," she said.

"I know I'm different. I'm happy in my work. I would have thought you would be happier, too. I just can't understand you, why you did what you did." He shook his head sadly. He was making her feel stupid, and she couldn't stand it.

"You don't know why I did what I did?" she began, her anger building toward a new crescendo. "You don't?" He shook his head in bewilderment as she came toward him. "Well, let me help you understand. First you go and quit a job you've had for more than twelve years, quit in a day without giving your former bosses any notice, and take a job with this cosmetics firm without so much as giving me a chance to discuss it. You come home and it's a fait accompli. Then you become immediately wrapped up and religiously devoted to the job to the extent that you neglect your family. Yes, you did, Drake," she added quickly when she saw he was about to protest. "Debbie was sick. All right, thank God it was just the flu, but you ignored her and went off to your workshop in Florida without leaving a number or an address, and you never called us the entire time to see how we were. Not to mention how weird you acted, wanting to make love every single night and treating me as if I were some . . . some prostitute."

"Now, that's not true, Cynthia," he responded.

"It's true, it's true," she said, shaking her head. "You think I've forgotten how you bound my wrists and started to torment me?" He shifted his eyes away. He was blinking madly again. "All right, you've calmed down, but for what reason I'm not sure. Perhaps you're getting your kinky sexual satisfaction someplace else these days."

"Huh?" He started to laugh, but it was a weak laugh and a weak smile.

"Don't think I didn't notice it when you came home reeking of Steffi Klein's perfume one day."

"What? Now that's—"

"The women love you, I know. You're giving them your miracle cream and changing their lives, so they all think you've become some wonderful person. Even Richie's noticed how you've changed. You weren't even apologetic that night you hurt him playing basketball in the driveway."

"I didn't hurt him."

"You did," she insisted. "You were like an animal out there. And that's not all, Drake. You don't want to have anything to do with any of our old friends. You've become a snob. And for you to refuse to go to Larry Thompson's funeral . . . Drake, it was the decent thing to do. You didn't have to love the man to attend his funeral."

Exhausted from her outburst, Cynthia paused and flopped in a chair. For a few moments Drake said nothing. He stared down at her. She lowered her head to her folded arms and began to sob. He put his hand on her shoulder.

"All right, Cyn, I'm sorry. I can see now you had reason to go a little bonkers. I was just so wrapped up in what I was doing and trying to do for us, I didn't see the effect it was having on you. I didn't realize how much pressure I have been placing on you. Really," he added, his tone apologetic.

She lifted her head slowly.

"I'm sorry, honey," he said again. "Just about everything you said is true. I was wrong. And I will apologize to Richie. I was just so full of energy that night, I lost control. I thought you wanted us to have nice things, a better house, more opportunities for the kids," he added, looking down at the floor.

"Of course I do, Drake. I want us to have things. I want you to be happy in your work and successful, but I don't want it to change who we are."

He nodded. "You're right. I let it all go to my head."

He smiled. "But I still can't believe you drove all the way to Weston, Connecticut, to talk to Harris Levy. What were you looking for? What were you going to ask the man?"

"I was desperate, looking for answers as to why you were changing. I wanted to understand what was happening. I know I seemed ungrateful after Paul Stoddard's party, Drake, but those people . . . frighten me."

He started to smile.

"No, Drake, it was weird there."

"Why?"

"People can like what they do, love their work and respect and admire their bosses, but it was different. It was as if they were a cult."

Drake shrugged. "I don't know. I guess everyone's so hyped up about this thing, they let it get to them and lose perspective. But Mr. Leon is a charismatic man. You're going to like him."

"I don't want to go, Drake."

"Now, Cyn—"

"No, I don't." She shook her head.

"Why not?"

"I don't know. I'm still . . . frightened. I'll see that woman's corpse dangling before me forever. I'm afraid to close my eyes."

"Well, what's that got to do with Mr. Leon and going to the compound?"

"I don't know. I just know I don't want to go."

"Well, that's not fair, Cyn. Now you're the one who's acting weird. I admit I've made mistakes, and I promise I'm going to change, but why should you do this to me now, just when I'm making great progress with this new firm? How do you think it's going to look—your not coming, throwing Mr. Leon's invitation back in his face? A special invitation, I might add. No one else from our sector has been invited, except for Paul Stoddard, of course."

"None of the others?"

"No. Just think, Cyn," he said, sitting quickly beside

her and taking her hand, "you and I will have plenty of time to be alone. When you see what's available to us . . . why, it will be like another honeymoon—swimming pools, whirlpools, racquetball courts and tennis courts, servants everywhere at your beck and call . . . and the grounds. It's breathtaking. I'd want you to go just to see the fountains and gardens."

She stared at him. His eyes were warm and loving. He was pleading.

"I'm so confused, Drake. I still can't stop shaking," she said, hugging herself.

"Don't worry," he said, standing up and drawing her up to embrace her. "Let's go down there and relax and get all the confusion cleared. When you meet Mr. Leon you can ask him anything you want about the company. He'll give you the grand tour, I'm sure. And if for some reason—any reason—you're unhappy, we'll simply claim you're not feeling well and leave. Does that sound fair?" He kissed her on the forehead. "Huh?"

"Well . . ."

"Then you'll go?"

"I suppose I should," she said, softening. "Maybe you're right. Maybe it will clear things up and make me feel better about all the things I have found strange."

"Sure it will. Now," he said, standing back and clapping his hands together, "after the day you've had, I think we ought to just pack the kids into the car and go someplace nice for dinner. What do you say? Can Drake Edwards take his family out to eat around here without looking too ostentatious about it?"

"Oh, Drake. You haven't been ostentatious. All right," she said. "I'm certainly in no mood to prepare anything."

"Great." He came forward to kiss her. "I'm really sorry, Cyn, but I'll work at making it up to you."

"Just be yourself, Drake. That's all I ask."

"Consider it done," he said firmly. "Now let's round up the kids. Stuart, Debbie," he called.

Cynthia watched him go. Then she rose slowly and

took a deep breath. Maybe all of it would be straightened out now, she thought. Maybe all she had really needed to do was to have this talk.

Drake announced his intention to take them to a fairly expensive restaurant. He took charge of the kids, getting them to put on some nice clothing, but when Cynthia looked at herself in the mirror she thought it would take a major overhaul to get her looking decent enough to go out. Her eyes were still bloodshot from all the crying, and her face looked bloated. She took a long hot shower and did her hair. While she was at her vanity table Drake came in to get dressed and put a new tin of Youth Hold on her table without making a comment.

She considered it and then dipped her finger in and rubbed some gently under her eyes and over her forehead. She even smeared some over her cheeks. After she chose her dress and put it on she went back to the mirror for a final check of herself and saw that the swelling under her eyes and in her cheeks had subsided. She looked more like her old, radiant self.

Say what you will about the people who sell this stuff, she thought, you can't take away its results. She knew that she would look even better the next day.

They had a wonderful dinner. Drake refused to let her see the bill, but some fast figuring in her head produced a number that would have floored them just a few weeks before. She saw how much Drake enjoyed spending his money, laying sizable tips on the maître d', the waiter, and the coat check girl.

That night Drake couldn't have been more loving. After they made love in the passionate but gentle way she had been accustomed to, she fell asleep in his arms quickly. The day's events had truly exhausted her.

But her eyes snapped open some time after three in the morning, and she realized she was alone in bed. Drake wasn't in the bathroom either. Puzzled, she sat up, listening. Had he gone to the children? Was Debbie sick again? Or had Stuart come down with something? She heard nothing, so she got up slowly and went out in the hall. The children were both fast asleep, but the light at the bottom of the stairway was on.

Poor Drake, she thought. He couldn't sleep and had probably gone down to get some hot milk. She returned to bed to wait for him, but she thought she heard voices coming from the front of the house, so she rose again and went to the window that looked out over the driveway and opened the blinds.

Another black Eldorado was there, and Drake was standing beside it in his bathrobe speaking to the driver, who was blocked from her view.

She leaned closer to the window and separated the blinds so she could see more. The driveway lights were off, but the bright headlights of the car reflected off the garage door and threw some illumination back. It was difficult to be sure, but it looked as though the front grille of the car was damaged. Finally Drake stepped back, and she saw he had been speaking with Paul Stoddard.

But why was the man there at three in the morning?

Drake waved to him as he began to back the car out of the driveway. Drake started back toward the house, so she returned to bed, crawling under the blanket to wait for him. She heard him turn off the light at the bottom of the stairway and come up. He moved slowly, quietly, obviously hoping not to wake her.

"Drake?"

"Oh, I'm sorry. I tried not to wake you."

"What's happening?"

He took off his robe.

"I guess some of that rich food got to me," he said. "I've been lying awake most of the night, so I went down and made myself some hot milk. Sorry," he added, and he slipped in beside her.

It was as if he had thrown a bucket of ice water over her. His lie drove the chill right to her heart. She didn't move, didn't say a word.

"You all right?" he asked suddenly, suspiciously. She hesitated.

If she told him she had seen him outside, he was sure to come up with some logical explanation for not telling her the truth. She almost could hear him saying something like, "I didn't want to worry you after all you've been through." But she was tired of logical, sensible replies and apologies and promises.

"Yes," she said. "I'm okay." She turned over so her back was to him, and closed her eyes, but she didn't fall asleep. She was wide awake when the first rays of sunshine came streaming in through the blinds she had opened to gaze down at Drake in the driveway. It hadn't been a bad dream.

The platinum blonde with the silicone-enhanced breasts stood waiting with a large, soft bath towel at the edge of the pool as Mr. Leon emerged from the warm, crystal-clear water. She was just a little heavy in the thighs, he thought, and he made a mental note to tell Rambo, his fitness trainer. As he stepped up and out of the pool he turned so she could wrap the towel around him, pressing her heavy bare bosom against him at the same time. He inhaled deeply. She pressed her hands against his chest firmly and then ran her right palm down his stomach, moving her fingers gracefully inside the separation of the towel to fondle him. He permitted it to go on for a few moments, and then, as if to torment himself, he stepped away from her.

"I want to watch you swim," he said. "Go on." He sprawled out on a lounge, adjusting it so he could sit up. Thor raised his head and looked out at the pool, too, the dog's eyes distrusting even in this sedate setting.

The blonde moved obediently into the water and began to do the backstroke, her breasts lifting and falling against her chest as she brought her arms back rhythmically. She had such a bright, healthy smile. He had forgotten her real name, so he had been calling her Bubbles, and she giggled. Beautiful but mindless, he thought.

But then, intelligent women intimidated him, and he

could see they resented being treated as nothing more than playthings. He had always found them dissatisfying and terribly competitive in bed. They were far too aware. Usually he ended up doing something sadistic to them, like binding them and tormenting them, fulfilling his need to dominate.

"Can I stop now?" Bubbles pleaded. "I'm getting tired."

"Do two more laps. You're a little heavy in the hips," he replied. She struggled to complete the command and afterward stood gasping for breath, her heavy bosom now looking more like a detriment.

"Come here," he said, and she stepped out of the water and stood by his side. He unfastened the ties that held her flimsy suit bottom, and the material fell away. Then he ran his hand over her soft rear and closed his eyes. She stood quietly, offering herself without complaint.

But his deep moment of pleasure was interrupted by the sound of footsteps on the patio tile. He opened his eyes as Gerald approached, carrying the portable phone.

"What is it?" he snapped.

"Sorry, sir," Gerald said. "It's Mr. Stoddard. He sounds rather agitated. Also," Gerald continued dryly, barely lifting his eyes to look at the naked woman still standing at attention beside Mr. Leon, "you told me to remind you about the ingredient. They're standing by at the factory and can do nothing until I bring it to them."

"Yes, yes, all right," he said, and he snapped up the phone. "What is it, Stoddard?" he asked, waving the girl away. She went to her own lounge chair. Gerald remained, waiting for the phone and instructions.

"But I don't understand," Mr. Leon said, sitting up quickly and flashing a look of concern at Gerald. "Why was she there?"

He listened, his face growing more serious.

"Hmm," he said. "A rather inquisitive woman. Maybe we chose the wrong member of that family to become immortal. No, I don't want you to do anything else. They are scheduled to be here soon. We'll take care of things then, just as we always do, just as we have," he said confidently. "But keep me informed if anything else occurs."

He handed the phone to Gerald without saying goodbye. Gerald waited, expressionless. Mr. Leon smirked and nodded.

"All right, Gerald. I'll fetch the ingredient now. Meet me at the usual place," he said, and he rose reluctantly from his lounge chair. Bubbles had a sun reflector under her chin, and her eyes were closed.

"Stop that!" he shouted. She opened her eyes and dropped the reflector to her bosom. "I told you what sun that intense can do to your skin. Are you a complete idiot?"

"But I thought . . . Youth Hold."

"You're just wearing out its benefit that much faster. Get rid of that thing. Besides, you're dark enough. I like some light skin around me, too," he declared. She folded the sun visor quickly and shoved it under her lounge. "Do another two laps," he commanded.

"Oh, I just did—"

He glared at her, and she sat up quickly. Then, with great reluctance, she stepped back into the pool. He waited until she began her first lap, and then he headed for the patio door that led to his bedroom, Thor following close at his heels.

He found his silk robe and put on his slippers. Then he went to a wall safe in his walk-in closet and, after checking to be sure no one was watching—especially Gerald—he worked the combination and opened it. All that was inside was a key. He clutched it tightly in his right fist and stood back smiling, as though holding that key brought him some deep, ecstatic feeling, an overwhelmingly pleasant sensation that traveled up his arm and quickly washed throughout his body. He always had that reaction when he went to fetch the key to the iron door that opened on the basement vault containing his fountain. Just knowing he had the precious liquid in his control enhanced his sense of security and made him feel immortal.

He closed the safe and started out of his bedroom, Thor still at his heels. His slippers clicked over the mauve Spanish tiles. They ran the length of the hallway to the rear of the hacienda. When he reached the stairway that led down to the basement he hesitated.

Gerald had come out of his quarters and started after him, maintaining the twenty-yard distance Mr. Leon had insisted upon whenever he descended the stairway to the vault. Hundreds of years ago Mr. Leon had built the hacienda over the fountain. What better way to protect and to hide it than to put a Spanish-style mansion over it, he had thought.

A little over fifty years ago he had installed refrigeration so his precious cache of bottles would remain cool and there would be little or no evaporation. The stock of water was the most valuable possession he had. In actuality, it was the most valuable resource on the face of the earth. And he had it! And all to himself, except for what he distributed to his disciples, and the amount he needed to keep Youth Hold effective. It was the Youth Hold that had built his financial empire, so he had to keep that going.

Thor, as though he could read his master's mind, began a low growl when Gerald drew too close. The dog took a step forward and remained poised. Gerald saw him take the position and stopped in his tracks.

"Yes," Mr. Leon said. "That's far enough, Gerald. I shall be up shortly." He looked down at his dog. "Stay, Thor," he commanded, and the animal sat back on its haunches but kept its attention fixed on Gerald Dorian.

Mr. Leon descended the stone steps, sinking into the cool darkness below the floor of his mansion. The walls gave way to stone, the original foundation. Finally he was on hard-packed dirt. He inserted his key in the door, looking back up the stairway and listening first, and then he turned the lock and heard the tooth snap back, permitting him to open the vault.

He flicked on the light switch and entered, turning quickly to his right to feast his eyes on the clear liquid that flowed out of an opening in the enormous rock.

His heart nearly stopped. He felt a surge of fear travel through his body with the speed of an electric current seizing his very soul and turning him into a mass of jelly.

There was nothing coming out of the rock, not even a tiny trickle. Nothing.

He closed his eyes and opened them as though that would wipe away the nightmare. Surely his eyes were playing some sort of trick on him. The abrupt movement from light to darkness . . . the poor light in there . . . anything but the reality of this. Please, he pleaded . . . this can't be.

He rushed forward to the basin that collected the precious liquid and saw that it was barely wet. He ran his fingers over the bottom and brought the dampness to his lips. Then he touched the opening in the rock. It was damp, but nothing flowed from it.

It was over; the nightmare he had dreamt a thousand times had taken form. He fell to his knees before the rock and pressed his forehead against his hands, the backs of which were against the granite surface. He did not pray; he had long since given up God or any hope of redemption and salvation. He simply knelt there, his mind reeling.

Deep in his heart he had always known this would happen. Whatever mysterious force had produced the fountain and kept it running all these years had run out of energy. But he had come to believe himself truly immortal, able to last as long as the earth itself. No man really faced his own mortality, lived with the realization that his life was terminal from the very day it had begun. It was simply natural, self-protecting to disbelieve in one's own death, even though there were continuous reminders on the obituary pages, reminders that his own death was impending.

We live; we get sick; we get older; we die, but not him, not Ponce de León.

He turned slowly and with great care disarmed the alarm that would result in a tremendous explosion should anyone ever get this far without him. He was determined that if he couldn't enjoy the waters of immortality, no one would. The disarming done, he opened the refrigerated cabinet. Hundreds of bottles of the precious liquid glittered like diamonds in the refrigerator's light. There was enough there to keep him young and healthy and alive for centuries.

But sharing it—even putting some into Youth Hold— that would have to end. He would use only enough to keep himself idolized and protected, to keep his little empire. But now there would have to be some changes. He would begin by cutting back on the disciples.

Reluctantly he reached in and took one of his precious bottles out of the refrigerated cabinet. He looked back at the dry opening of what had been the fountain of youth and then closed the cabinet door, taking extra care to be sure the door was locked and the explosive device was reset. He left the vault, slipped the key back into his robe pocket, and started up the stairway.

Thor was sitting just where he had left him, staring suspiciously at Gerald Dorian, who became alert as soon as Mr. Leon appeared. When he saw that Mr. Leon had only one bottle in his possession Gerald squinted, his forehead creasing with a frown.

"Weren't we to provide two bottles, Mr. Leon? The additional orders—"

"I don't care about additional orders. We're cutting back. Youth Hold is becoming too available. We'll lose our value and won't command the price."

Gerald almost laughed. He stopped at a wide smile.

"But no one else has the formula, sir."

"I don't care. Just do as I say. Tell them to make only what they can with this." He handed him the bottle with a reluctance and hesitation that drew Gerald Dorian's curiosity. "Careful," Mr. Leon snapped. "Don't drop it, or I'll have your head."

"I won't."

After he took it in his hands Gerald frowned again. "Now what is it?"

"This bottle, sir. It's unusually cold. Is this one from the stash?"

"Yes." Mr. Leon tried to hide his emotion. "I didn't have the patience to fill a fresh one. Just take it over and tell them to use it as sparingly as always."

Gerald nodded and started away. Mr. Leon watched him until he disappeared out of the hacienda. Then he patted Thor on the head while he continued to gaze after Gerald Dorian. The dog had no reaction to the gesture; he was not accustomed to any show of affection.

"He knows, Thor," Mr. Leon said. "He's been with me too long not to know. But I don't like that. I don't like it at all," he muttered, and he turned to go back to the dumb, big-breasted platinum blonde. More than ever, he needed the diversion.

Thor trotted after him, his tongue extended, his sharp teeth gleaming.

— 14 —

Richie eased his foot off the accelerator and came to a full stop when he reached Paul Stoddard's address. His fingers trembled a bit on the steering wheel, so he gripped it tighter. He couldn't believe he was doing this, but he had promised Cynthia that he would give it a shot if he had any spare time. He had made the time. Her voice had left him cold. He had phoned her from his bucket while he was up testing a line, but the light, humorous conversation he had intended had instantly turned heavy.

"Hi," he had begun, "I'm checking this line out and thought I would use you as the guinea pig. Am I coming through okay?"

She didn't respond.

"Cynthia?"

"Richie," she had whispered.

"What are you doing? Why didn't you answer me?" He leaned back in his bucket. There was a pleasant but strong morning breeze in Westchester. Some of the cloud formations were moving so quickly across the light blue sky, they looked motorized. The effect was to slide the long shadows over the street rapidly, washing him alternately in darkness and sunshine. Right now a chilling, deeper and darker shadow hovered. He raised his shirt collar and turned his back to the breeze, pressing the receiver tighter to his ear.

"I was just listening," she replied, still in a whisper, "to see if Drake had picked up. I thought I heard a click. He's upstairs dressing."

"So? What if he picked up? What's wrong?"

"Richie . . ." Her voice drifted off; he thought he had lost his connection and quickly checked his wires. "Drake might be involved in something bad," she finally said, speaking at a normal volume. She sounded strange, though, void of feeling, like someone who was drugged. The dead, matter-of-fact tone had a far more traumatic effect on him than any hysterical one would have had. His sister was in trouble, he thought, bad trouble.

"Why do you say that, Cynthia?"

"I've been thinking about his new company, Leon Enterprises, all night. In fact, I hardly slept," she said, which he thought explained the fatigue in her voice. "I feel certain it's a front for something, maybe drugs."

"What? Why? I mean, why do you think this?"

She described her trip to Weston, Connecticut, summarizing it in short, staccato, factual statements as if she were giving a police report. She left the grisly details out of her description of Selina Levy's dangling corpse.

"What made you drive to Connecticut to begin with?" Richie asked, amazed that she would have done such a thing.

Richie listened to her dry yet icy relating of events, enlarging the tingle of fear in his chest until it had become a tight, pounding sensation. Below him on the street traffic moved slower than usual because of his road signs. Most of the drivers looked up at him; all of the passengers did. He felt self-conscious about his long personal conversation, but he couldn't cut her off.

"Maybe they do something to the people who work for them, too, give them some sort of drug that changes them, that makes them obedient," she concluded. "You saw how strange Drake has become."

"Yeah, but drugs turning them into zombies? You're letting your mind run wild, Cynthia. Take it easy."

"I can't," she said. She told him about Drake's strange late-night assignation in the driveway and his lying about it later when she questioned him. "And I was almost sure that black Eldorado was damaged in front, just the way it might be if it had hit someone."

"Jesus, Cynthia. You think they killed Larry Thompson? Why would they do that?"

"They found out he was checking up on them. Maybe he found out something, or maybe they were afraid eventually he would. I don't believe this Paul Stoddard is who he claims to be, Richie. Richie," she said quickly, her voice finally gaining some energy, "you're down there. You could"—she lowered her voice to a loud whisper—"could you tap his line and listen to one or two of his phone conversations . . . just to see? Could you?"

"Are you crazy? I mean—"

"How would anyone know, Richie? You're working on the lines down there anyway. Please, Richie," she begged. "Maybe you will hear something that will help us, help me . . . please. If what I think is true, I must get Drake out of that company before it's too late for him, too late for us. It might be too late already," she added mournfully.

Richie took a deep breath and shook his head.

"Do you know this guy's address?"

She told him.

"I'll see if I get any free time," he said, "and if it's possible—but I can't promise anything, Cynthia."

"Oh, thank you, Richie. Thank you. Call me the moment you hear anything that might mean something."

"Even if I get to do it, it's just going to be a hit-and-miss thing, Cynthia. Chances are I won't hear anything."

"You might. Please try."

"I said I would try, but you'd better take it easy, Cynthia. You're going to get yourself sick."

"I'll take it easy. I promise. I will. Call me," she

added, and she hung up. He held the receiver a moment. Was there a second click? He was getting as paranoid as she was, he thought. Damn, what a mess. But he couldn't ignore her and her stories.

And so he had driven to Paul Stoddard's street and pulled his truck off to the side just before the street turned and descended a small hill to a busier thoroughfare. He was impressed with Stoddard's house and grounds. The kind of money these people were making with some cosmetic cream was like the money drug pushers were commanding, he thought. Maybe Cynthia wasn't just letting her imagination run wild.

He stepped out of his truck, trying to look as casual and businesslike as usual, but he was like anyone about to do something illegal. He thought he somehow appeared suspicious and overdid his routine behavior to compensate. He set out the MEN WORKING signs and then stood there studying a clipboard. He took his time gathering his tools and looked around every few moments to see if he had drawn any inordinate attention.

There was almost no traffic on the residential street, and the one or two cars that did go by went by as slowly as usual, the drivers not showing any interest in him or his work.

He gazed at Stoddard's house. It was quiet. It looked safe, he thought. No one would know the difference. There was probably no one home, and his tapping into the line would prove fruitless. Still, he had to give it a shot, at least spend an hour or so there for Cynthia's sake, he thought, and he began to prepare his bucket.

He stepped in and closed it securely, still keeping one eye on the house to see if he had attracted any attention. Satisfied that he hadn't, he manipulated the controls and had himself raised. It was obvious which line ran to the Stoddard home. In a matter of minutes he was listening in.

As luck would have it, he tapped into the middle of an ongoing conversation.

"Yeah," he heard a man say, "everything's set. It's

all occurring just as we anticipated. I'll tell you what," the man said, "if you will just give me a minute, I'll get what I need."

"No problem," the other speaker said. It wasn't Drake's voice, Richie thought. He waited and listened. Stoddard, if that was who was speaking inside the house, had put the receiver down to get something.

Richie took out a screwdriver and pretended to be checking a transformer. He didn't see the car slow down beside his telephone bucket truck, but he did hear Stoddard's garage door go up, and he saw the black Eldorado. Suddenly it came shooting out of the garage, its wheels squealing as the driver whipped it sharply to come out on the street behind his truck.

Just then he heard his truck door opened and turned to see the driver of the other car reach in.

"Hey!" he screamed down.

Whoever it was had released the emergency brake and taken the truck out of gear. Because it was already near the crest of the hill, it began to inch forward.

Meanwhile the black Eldorado pulled up behind the truck and tapped the bumper. The impact shook the bucket, and Richie grabbed onto the sides.

"Hey! What the hell are you doin'?" he screamed. The man who had been in the truck stepped back after he had made sure the steering wheel was turned so the front wheels were straight, and the black Eldorado increased its speed and pressure on the rear of the truck. In moments it was sailing forward.

Richie held onto the sides of the bucket for dear life as the truck picked up momentum down the hill. It hit nearly forty miles an hour before it reached the major thoroughfare. An oncoming sedan had no chance to avoid it and hit it broadside.

The impact spun the truck abruptly, and Richie lost his grip on the sides of the bucket and went sailing out. He landed on the roof of a second car, a coupe that had managed to come to a squealing stop just before hitting the rear of the telephone truck. Richie bounced off the roof and rolled over, slapping the macadam, falling on his right side and continuing his roll along the highway. A third vehicle squealed and spun to avoid him, but the left front tire caught his right leg just above the ankle. It had the effect of ending his slide across the road.

He lay there motionless on his back, his arms out in crucifix fashion as the vehicular bedlam whirled around him. At the top of the hill the black Eldorado backed up and turned into the driveway. It entered the garage, and the door came rolling down. Almost instantly the street in front of Stoddard's house returned to its imperturbable and serene air, the beeping horns and shouting voices at the bottom of the hill caught up in the hefty afternoon breeze, which carried them away as if it knew it shouldn't disturb the residents above. Even the screaming police sirens were drowned out by the chorus of mowers grazing over the lawns.

Cynthia felt as if she were playing musical chairs with the telephones in the house. Wherever she went and whatever she did, she made sure she was only moments away from seizing a receiver. She avoided using the vacuum cleaner because she was afraid the noise would drown out the ringing of the phone. She didn't turn on the television set or the radio, and whenever someone called her she made the conversation short, answering questions with monosyllabic replies. Everyone she spoke to heard the desperation in her voice, however. Even her mother was finally driven to ask if anything was wrong. Of course, she said no, she was just tired.

Mindy, Drake's brother Michael's wife, was the only one who became annoyed with her.

"It's obvious you're not interested in talking to me today," she said curtly. "Why don't you call me when you're in the mood?"

"Oh, I'm sorry, Mindy. It's not you. I'm very distracted today. I will call you."

"Do that. Oh, and tell Drake that Michael developed a little rash from that stuff he's selling. And it wasn't just a bad batch, because the second tin had the same effect.''

"Really? I'm sorry."

"Michael says he could open himself up to a lawsuit if he's not careful."

"I'll tell him," Cynthia said. It was the only thing that brought a smile to her face. Family jealousy had always been strong. Her guess was that neither Michael nor Mindy had really used the cream.

The children returned from school, and still she hadn't heard anything from Richie. He's not going to do it, she thought. It was silly for her to think that he would.

Drake called her late in the afternoon.

"I'm just telling you," he said, "that I could come home a little later and finish up this part of my territory today and not leave the house until noon tomorrow, or come right home and return here in the morning. I'll do whatever you want, Cyn."

"Finish up," she said. What did he expect her to say?

"We'll be able to spend the morning in bed after the kids go off to school. I'll make you breakfast, too. How's that?"

"Okay, Drake. I might feed the kids first tonight, though.''

"Sure. I'll make it as fast as I can."

"Just drive carefully."

"Right," he said. "I love you," he added. She hesitated. How her heart ached. She prayed there wasn't any deception, but she couldn't quiet the suspicions. "I love you, too," she said. If he had heard any hesitation in her voice, he didn't let on.

She had just begun to make the children their dinner when the phone rang again. She nearly leapt across the kitchen. This had to be Richie, she thought, it just had to be.

At first she didn't know how it was, the crying masked the voice so. Then she realized it was her mother.

"What? Mom?"

Her mother was crying so hard Cynthia couldn't

understand what she was saying. Finally her father came on the phone, even his normally strong, controlled voice cracking.

"What is she saying, Dad? I don't understand."

"Richie's been in a very bad accident. Very bad. He's in intensive care in a hospital in Westchester. They just called, and we're on our way."

"What accident? How?"

"He must have neglected to secure his truck before going up in the bucket. It rolled down a hill onto a busy road with him still in the bucket."

"Oh my God! Richie! It's my fault! It's my fault!" she screamed.

"What?"

"Pick me up! Pick me up! I'll go with you."

"All right, all right. Calm down. We're on our way," her father said.

She dropped the receiver and lowered her head. The phone bounced on the floor. Stuart rushed forward to pick it up and put it back. Debbie slid out of her chair and embraced Cynthia around the legs instinctively.

"What is it, Ma?" Stuart asked. "What was your fault? What happened to Uncle Richie?"

"He was in a bad accident," she said incredulously. She shook her head. "He's in the hospital. Grandpa and Grandma are on their way to get me." She brought Stuart to her and put her arms around both her children. "You'll have to be in charge until Daddy comes home, honey."

'We want to go, too, Mom."

Debbie started to cry harder.

"What?" She looked around, dazed.

"We want to go, too."

"No, I—"

"We want to go," Stuart insisted. "We're not going to eat," he said defiantly. "We want to go."

She nodded.

"All right," she said. "You can come along, but you'll have to wait in the lobby."

"Is he going to be all right?" Stuart asked, and both he and Debbie looked to her for the familiar reassurances she had given them throughout their lives whenever anything bad had occurred.

"I hope so" was all she could offer.

Her parents didn't want her to take the children, but she insisted.

"They love Richie, Mom, and I don't want to leave them alone."

"Where's Drake?"

"Out selling."

"Out selling? This late? Well, when is he coming home?"

"We're wasting time," her father said.

"I don't know when Drake's coming home. Get in, children," Cynthia said, urging them into the rear seat. She sat with them, no one saying much the entire trip to Westchester. Once they arrived she left the children in the lobby and followed her parents to the elevator that took them to the intensive care unit. The doctor on duty was waiting for them.

"He's a pretty strong young man," he began after they arrived and met him just outside the door of the I.C.U. "Miraculously, the only bone he broke was in his right leg. Of course, he's pretty banged up."

"But why is he in a coma?" Cynthia asked.

"Blow to his head. There's some pressure there. Most likely we're going to have to operate to relieve it. The surgeon is looking at him now."

"Will he be all right?" Cynthia pursued.

With a typical doctor's noncommittal face, he replied, "As I said, he's a strong young man. We'll see."

Cynthia got the children something to eat and then thought of calling Sheila. She figured it was something Richie would want her to do.

"I was wondering why he hadn't called me yet," Sheila said, her voice breaking. "I'll be there as soon as I can."

"You don't have to rush, Sheila. We're going to be

here a long time. We just heard that they have to operate to relieve the pressure."

After she made the call she told her mother.

"She's a very nice girl," she said. "Richie brought her to dinner twice."

"Oh?"

"Have you tried to reach Drake? He might be home by now and wondering what happened to all of you," her father reminded her.

When she called the house Drake answered.

"I've been going crazy here. I called everyone I know."

She told him what had transpired.

"God, that's horrible," he said. "I'm on my way."

Compounding the numbness she felt when she thought about Richie was the numbness she felt when she thought about Drake. How horrible it was to suspect that he might have had something to do with this, she thought. It couldn't be; it just couldn't be, and yet she couldn't help harboring some suspicion.

Sheila and Drake arrived while Richie was still in the operating room. Afterward they met the surgeon outside the recovery room.

"The operation went well," he told them, "but it will be some time before we know the extent of the injury. All of his vitals are good. You people might as well go home and get some rest."

The children had fallen asleep, and Debbie had to be carried to the car. Stuart woke but remained groggy all the way home. Cynthia invited Sheila for coffee.

"You're all pretty tired," Sheila said. "I'll call you in the morning, and maybe we can go to the hospital together."

"Sure. Call."

"He's going to be all right," Sheila, said hugging her. "I just know he will." She pulled back and shook her head. "I just can't believe he was that careless."

"Neither can I," Cynthia said, eyeing Drake, who was already in the car.

"Call you in the morning," Sheila repeated, and she left. Cynthia got into the car with Drake.

"What a damn freak thing to happen," Drake said after they had started for home.

"Was it?"

"What do you mean?"

"Richie's not that careless, especially when it comes to trucks and cars."

"So? Jesus, Cynthia, you're not talking this mad paranoia again and applying it to Richie, are you? I know you're upset, but—"

"You know where the accident happened?" she asked him. He looked at her and then turned back to the road.

"I wasn't listening to the details when your father told me. All I could think about was Richie. So?" he said when she didn't elaborate. "What's the mystery? Where did it happen?"

"Banning Way."

"Banning Way," he repeated. She watched him. His eyes blinked rapidly. "So where's Banning Way? Why is that significant?"

"Don't you remember, Drake? We took it to the party. It's just down from Paul Stoddard's house."

"So? He was working in Westchester. That had to be just a coincidence."

"Was it?"

"Oh, Christ," he said. "This is really ridiculous. You know what? I think you need some professional help." He shook his head. "I mean it. Professional help."

"So do I," she said. "So do I."

But she was thinking of the police.

Richie was still in a coma when Cynthia, her parents, and Sheila arrived at the hospital in the morning. Drake had promised to meet her there as soon as he had taken care of some things.

"But I thought if you worked late last night you

wouldn't have to go out until late in the morning," she reminded him when he told her at breakfast.

After they had come home from the hospital the night before she had taken a sleeping pill and gone to bed. They had had very little conversation. Drake saw to the children. She didn't even hear him come in and get into bed, so she didn't know what time he had gone to sleep.

"Right, but now I intend to stay with you at the hospital all day, so I'll just make the few deliveries I have to make and join you. I won't be but an hour or so behind you," he claimed.

Sheila arrived, so she didn't have a chance to question him or complain. She wasn't in the mood for any of that anyway. All she cared to think about that morning was Richie. Drake left before her parents arrived, and they all drove down to the hospital.

"It's not unusual for him not to have regained consciousness immediately," the doctor told them, but that didn't relieve their anxiety. They sat at his bedside and stared, she and Sheila taking turns talking to him, hoping that the sound of their voices would break through whatever wall had been thrown up around his awareness.

Drake arrived just before noon. They went to lunch and returned, but Richie's condition hadn't changed.

"It could go like this for some time," the doctor advised them when he made his afternoon rounds. "This will take its toll on all of you. His vital signs remain excellent. My advice is for you all to go back to your regular routines as soon as possible. We have your phone numbers. As soon as there is some significant change we'll let you know."

"Very sensible," Drake said. Cynthia glared at him, but he didn't notice.

"Maybe the doctor's right," her father admitted.

"You want to get home for the children, anyway," her mother said.

"Drake can go home; I can stay," Cynthia declared.

"But why?" Drake asked. "You heard what the doctor just told us."

"Why? Why?" She looked toward her brother.

"Cynthia, get hold of yourself. You will just compound our problems," her mother said, gazing around to be sure their conference hadn't attracted the attention of other hospital visitors. "Go home, rest, and we'll plan out our visits intelligently."

"Always logical, always intelligent, never emotional," Cynthia muttered, but no one heard her, or if anyone had, no one commented. Reluctantly she agreed, and they all left the hospital.

"I'll go back with your parents, Cynthia," Sheila told her. "They drive right by my apartment."

"Okay. Call me later." They hugged, and she got into Drake's company car. When he approached the entrance to the hospital parking lot she leaned forward to tell him to turn right.

"Right? For what?"

"I want to see someone."

"Who?"

"Make a right and go to the first traffic light," she commanded dryly. "Then make the first left."

"What is this, Cynthia?"

"Just do it," she snapped. He shook his head.

"You're really frightening me, you know that? You really are."

Drake followed her directions. After they made the left she told him to go to the next traffic light and make a right. Two turns later they pulled up in front of the police department.

"What is this?" Drake asked.

"I want to see what they've found out about Richie's accident," she replied, and she got out. He followed and was surprised when she asked for someone by name.

The desk sergeant directed them to an officer sitting casually behind a desk on the right. He had a seasoned look with graying dark brown hair and sleepy brown eyes. He was on the phone, but from the expression on his face it was obvious that it was a personal call. He signed off when Cynthia stepped up.

"Officer Douglas?"

"Yes?"

"I'm Cynthia Edwards, Richie Parker's sister. I called you this morning."

"Oh, yes. Please sit down."

"This is my husband Drake," she said quickly, and she took the worn, scratched chair on her left. Drake hesitated a moment and then sat down beside her, a look of irritation on his face.

"Well, Mrs. Edwards," Officer Douglas began, sifting through some papers on his desk as he leaned forward, "we've gone over the preliminary investigation, eyewitness reports, and so on, and everything we've found so far points to just an unfortunate accident."

"Did you check the truck?" she asked. The policeman nodded and shrugged. "Nothing sinister about it. He could have just left it in gear and it popped out . . . pressure, whatever. He simply didn't back it up with the emergency brake."

"That's not like my brother, Officer Douglas."

"People make mistakes, Mrs. Edwards. That's why we have so many automobile accidents," he replied calmly. He looked at Drake, who nodded in agreement.

"Not Richie," she insisted. The policeman, a bit embarrassed by her intensity, looked down and shook his head. "Did you do what I asked? Did you question people in the homes on the street above Banning?"

"No one saw anything unusual, Mrs. Edwards." He turned to Drake. "Why are you so intent on there being something else here?" He turned back to Cynthia. "Was someone threatening your brother?"

"Not exactly."

"Cynthia, for God's sake," Drake said softly. The policeman's eyebrows lifted. When he looked at Drake, Drake shook his head and closed his eyes. The silent gesture was understood.

"I realize why you are upset, Mrs. Edwards. It was a terrible accident, and it's not easy to have someone you love in critical condition, but—"

"I'm not overwrought. I know what I'm doing," she replied quickly. He nodded.

"Well, ma'am, that's all we have."

"And you're not going to investigate any further?"

"No reason to, as far as we can tell, Mrs. Edwards. If something should come up—"

"It won't," she said, standing abruptly. "But my brother is not this careless, not when it comes to such things," she insisted, turning away. Drake rose.

"I'm sorry," he said, "but she's—"

"That's quite all right. I understand. It's not the first time we had someone swear that white was black or black was white when it came to someone they love. How's he doing?"

"Still in a coma, but the doctors are hopeful."

"Good. Best of luck, Mr. Edwards."

"Thank you," Drake said. Cynthia was already out of the police station by the time he turned to follow.

"My God, Cynthia," he said, sliding in behind the steering wheel, "what did you expect them to find? Someone's fingerprints on the back of Richie's truck? It was an accident."

She didn't reply. She was tempted to, tempted to tell him she had asked Richie to tap Paul Stoddard's phone, but something held her back from revealing that information. Something instinctive told her to wait and not to reveal how deep her suspicions concerning Paul Stoddard and Leon Enterprises were.

"You've really messed yourself up, honey," Drake continued. "That foolish trip to Connecticut, your paranoia—all of it, including the things I did—has left you so high-strung, you're like a bomb waiting to go off. You need rest, relaxation, a prescription for recuperation, but not from me."

She turned to him inquisitively. He smiled.

"I mean, you don't have to worry about us affording it."

"Affording what, Drake?"

"What I mentioned yesterday when we left the hospital. It can't hurt, it can only help."

"What?"

"Seeing someone, a professional."

"A therapist?"

"Exactly. And it's not like we'd be groping in the dark here. Fortunately, I have someone Paul Stoddard recommends, the doctor his wife was using."

"Not very successfully, if she wandered off never to be heard from again," she said dryly.

"Her problems were far more serious than yours are, honey. This man's quite respected in his field. Two or more sessions with him might do you a world of good, and if it doesn't have any significant effect, nothing ventured, nothing lost."

"Why? We won't have to pay? It's another one of the benefits of working for Leon Enterprises? That's why we don't have to worry about affording it?" Her sarcasm made him laugh.

"Ridicule it all you want, but it's there, and most people would love the opportunities and, yes, the benefits."

"Um," she grunted.

"Will you at least consider it?"

"I don't know," she said. She was tired, and who knew? Maybe he was right, maybe she was going off the deep end of things and needed to regain a sense of perspective. Could Richie have forgotten to put on his emergency brake? Was it just an accident? She wouldn't know for sure until he came out of his coma. What if he didn't? She shook her head and embraced herself to ward off the chill.

"Here," Drake said, reaching into his inside pocket. "Paul gave me his card. Hold on to it, so if you decide, you can make an appointment. You know how these guys are—booked up for years. Just mention Paul Stoddard, though, and they'll fit you in whenever you like."

She took the card without looking at it, but just before she slipped it into her purse she gazed at it, and some-

thing familiar about it caught her eye. She read it quickly
and thought. Then it came to her.

Dr. Sacks.

That empty bottle of tranquilizers that had been prescribed for Selina Levy, Harris Levy's deceased wife—
it had been prescribed by a Dr. Sacks.

Paul Stoddard's wife and Harris Levy's wife had had
the same psychiatrist, and they were both gone. And
now Drake, with Paul Stoddard's advice, was recom-
mending she see the same man.

Nothing—not a shot of brandy, not a hot bath, nothing—took the chill out of her the rest of the day. Cynthia
remained in bed under a quilt. Concerned, the children
came to see her.

"Maybe you got the flu I had, Mommy," Debbie told
her.

"Maybe," she said, smiling.

"Dad and I are going to make dinner, Mom," Stuart
announced proudly. "I'll do most of it."

"That's nice, honey. You guys eat. I'm not too
hungry."

"You've got to eat something. How about some toast
and tea?" he asked. She nearly laughed at the way the
roles had been reversed. He sounded more like a parent.

"Maybe later."

"You guys should let Mommy sleep," Drake said,
coming in on them. "She's tired."

"It's from worrying about Uncle Richie," Stuart
declared, nodding.

"Sure it is," Drake said. "Stuart, you might just
become a doctor."

"Maybe," Stuart said, seriously considering it.

"Come on, kids," Drake urged. They were reluctant
to leave her side, but she promised she would be all
right after a good rest.

She did fall asleep for an hour or so. After she woke
up she called the hospital and spoke to the nurse in
intensive care, who told her Richie's condition was the

same. Stuart returned with a tray of tea and toast and jelly, Debbie at his side. She took the tray and listened to their description of the dinner, laughing at Debbie's critique about how "gooey" the mashed potatoes were. Relieved she was looking and sounding better, the children decided to go down to watch television.

"Where's Daddy?" Cynthia asked them as they started to leave.

"He's in his office on his phone," Stuart said, his face grimacing. "He's been in there a long time again."

She nodded and waited for them to go. Then she leaned over and carefully, slowly eased the receiver out of its cradle. She pressed it to her ear quickly and listened. Drake was in the middle of a conversation with Paul Stoddard.

"But I don't have enough to last me until next weekend," Drake complained. She heard the underlying note of hysteria in his voice. "What if we don't go?"

"You have to go, Drake. I've told you—I can't give you the next dosage; the second dosage comes only from Mr. Leon. It's always been that way. And he insists on giving it to you personally, at the compound in Florida."

"But she's not up to a trip, and with her brother still in a coma—"

"It's your problem, Drake. Solve it. Mr. Leon does not take kindly to anyone refusing his personal invitations. It would be . . . disastrous. Do you understand?"

Drake was silent.

"Yes," he finally replied.

"That's good, Drake. We're all proud of you, very proud. Mr. Leon wanted me to tell you that."

"Thank you," Drake said.

"I'll call you soon with more definite arrangements. Happy sales."

She heard the click and waited because she didn't hear Drake hang up. She thought she heard him breathing heavily into the phone. He sounded like someone on the verge of a heart attack. She was tempted to call to

228

him, but she didn't want him to know she had overheard his conversation.

Finally Drake hung up, and the line went dead.

Cynthia sat there with the receiver in her hands, her heart beating madly, her mind in a turmoil. She was pulled by feelings of pity and fear.

What had they done to him? What did Stoddard mean by the second dosage? Dosage of what? Was he on some kind of drug after all? Who were these people?

Somehow she had to find out and put an end to it all.

— 15 —

The tension of the days that followed wore away at everyone. Even Drake, whose energy had seemed endless, began to show signs of wear. One day Cynthia saw him limping a bit, as if his old basketball injury had returned.

Sheila accompanied her to the hospital often. When she was there she was good company and always optimistic, but Richie's condition did not change significantly. The doctor's stock response to any question was "We'll see."

Ellen and Steffi came to sit with her a few times. Both her friends continued to blossom and look radiant under the continual therapy of Youth Hold. When they made mention of Drake she listened keenly. Neither seemed to want to dwell on him, but the way they glanced at each other whenever his name came up made her suspicious. Cynthia felt certain that when he called on them to sell Youth Hold his visit involved more than merely his marketing the wonder product. He was marketing himself as well, and if he was doing it with them, who knew with whom else?

"Drake's so worried about Richie," Steffi told her.

"You can see it in his face these days. He looks so tired." She turned quickly to Ellen for confirmation.

"I agree," Ellen said. "You poor dears."

Cynthia knew the mental and physical exhaustion was taking its natural toll on her looks. Her face became drawn, sallow; her eyelids drooped; she felt drained; and she plodded along in an almost mindless fashion, completing her chores and looking after the children as best she could. Most of her depression resulted from her sense of guilt. She was convinced that someone had tried to murder Richie, and only because she had cajoled him into spying on Paul Stoddard.

Nearly every day Drake made mention of Dr. Sacks, now claiming it was foolish not to make use of something at their disposal.

"I'm sure you're having trouble dealing with what happened to Richie as well as all the rest," he told her. "You need a professional to guide you."

She continued to say she would think about it. Finally he used her reluctance to see the therapist as more reason for their need to go to Mr. Leon's compound.

"Richie's stable, but it looks like we're in this for the long haul," he said. "You've been going down there every day, living under constant tension and mental fatigue. You won't go to the therapist. All right, but let's at least steal away for two days of R and R, Cynthia. You'll lounge by the pool, eat great food, be entertained, and for forty-eight hours put all the problems behind you. It will make you stronger and more able to cope when you return," he reasoned.

Ever since overhearing his phone call with Paul Stoddard she had been trying to think of something she could do to expose Leon Enterprises. Perhaps this trip would provide her with the best opportunity, she thought. She would go there, observe, listen and learn, and as soon as she arrived at some hard evidence she would pounce. Of course, she was also afraid, but her desire to find something significant and to solve some of the mystery was greater.

"Okay," she said. "I'll go, but only for the two days. I'll make arrangements for the kids to stay with my parents."

Drake's face lit up. "We're going to have a great time. I can't wait until you see the place."

He made a fist and shook it near his temple. "We're going to make a comeback here. You'll see. Everything is going to turn out all right."

"I hope so, Drake," she said. "For everyone's sake," she added, but he didn't hear her innuendo. He was off to make phone calls and see to arrangements.

I'm going into the lion's den, she thought, but there doesn't seem to be any other way to defeat the lion.

As their weekend trip drew closer Drake became more and more excited, his high energy level returning. During the past week he had slowed down considerably, actually falling asleep one night on the couch watching television. He hadn't done that since his days at Burke-Thompson. She thought he had been forgetting to use his own wonder product, too, because his face lost some of its shine, and some of those premature wrinkles began to reappear.

If she asked him how he was feeling, he became very self-conscious, but all he did as a result was bring up their impending weekend at the Leon hacienda in Florida, repeating with urgent desperation that they both needed the getaway.

Once she had agreed to go he returned to what had become his new self. He made more time for the children, arriving home closer to the time they would return from school. If he wasn't tossing a ball with Stuart or playing basketball with him, he was taking the children for rides, filling in the slack, as he said: shopping with them for shoes and clothes and other things they needed so she didn't have to do it. He wanted them to go out to dinner every night, insisting she shouldn't have to cook with all she was doing. At night he couldn't have been more solicitous, waiting on her hand and foot, seeing to any needs or wishes she might have. She began to feel like royalty, but when she protested, he insisted.

"I haven't done enough for you, Cyn. Let me make up for my bad behavior."

Not a day went by that he didn't describe and redescribe the Leon hacienda. He made it sound so beautiful that for a while she lost track of what her real intentions were. It was as if the compound and its beautiful grounds could begin to mesmerize her even before she had arrived. It drove a cold, thin pin of fear into her heart. Perhaps she was underestimating the power of these people. Perhaps the danger was far greater than she could imagine.

It was not without the greatest trepidation, therefore, that she went up to her bedroom and began to pack the night before. Her hands trembled, and every once in a while she stopped herself to reconsider. But Drake was bouncing around her, asking her to take this and to take that.

"Don't forget your necklace, of course. You want to be wearing that when we arrive. He'll expect it and be disappointed if you're not wearing it. Bring the dress you wore to Stoddard's house. There'll be a party. There's a party there almost every night. Oh, and that new bathing suit I bought you."

"But Drake, that's so revealing."

"You look great in it. Why not be proud of your figure? You have to realize," he said, "Mr. Leon has guests from other parts of the world there—women from France, for example, who are used to bathing topless."

"Topless? You don't expect me—"

"Nobody pressures anyone there, honey. You will do what you feel like doing. Okay?" He slapped his hands together and looked around the room, his eyes so full of excitement that he looked as if he were on uppers. "Well, I'll see how the children are doing."

They were driving the children over to her parents' house that night because the limousine was going to pick her and Drake up very early in the morning.

Although Drake made no attempt to make love to her the night before they left, she noted how restless he was. Sometime in the middle of the night he had to get up to take some aspirin, which was something he hadn't done in a long time.

"Are you all right?" she asked.

"Just a little hyped up is all. I'm okay."

She closed her eyes and fell asleep again. When she woke up in the morning she discovered that Drake had been up for some time. In fact, he had showered and dressed and brought their suitcases down to the front door. She couldn't imagine anyone, even a child, being more excited about going on a trip. She might even have laughed at him if she didn't sense the desperation in his face. He was so hyper he couldn't sit still. Every few moments he went to the windows to look out in anticipation of the Leon limousine. Finally, she heard him cry out, *"It's here!"*

She paused to look at herself one more time in the mirror, but he had come running up the stairs and was at the bedroom door.

"The limo's here, honey."

"All right, Drake. I'm coming," she said. She gathered her things together and followed him down the stairs. He was already out in the driveway with their suitcases.

"Come on," he called.

She stopped and looked around her house, getting the ominous feeling that she might just be seeing it for the last time. And then, smothering all hesitation and caution, she turned and walked out to get into the waiting limousine. The driver, whom she recognized from previous occasions, smiled at her before closing the door behind her. Drake was sitting with his hands in his lap, grinning like an obedient schoolboy. As soon as they were out of the driveway Drake took her hand.

"You're never going to forget this, Cyn. Never."

Her heart pounded so, she thought she would lose her

breath, but she forced a smile and looked back only once.

They were on their way.

Paul Stoddard met them at the airport and led them out on the tarmac to board the Leon Enterprises jet. Cynthia couldn't help but be impressed. She looked at the empty plane and then at Drake, who was beaming. They sat about midway, Drake taking the window seat. Paul sat across the aisle from them.

"The weather's going to be perfect all weekend," Paul said. "Sometimes I think Mr. Leon has control of that, too. It's always perfect when I visit."

"Did you ever visit with your wife?" Cynthia asked quickly.

"My wife?" He smiled, but she thought it was a very weak, insecure smile. "Yes, once. But that was before things turned bad for her," he added.

"Haven't you heard anything from the police?" she pursued. Drake squeezed her arm gently, but she ignored his warning. "Surely after so long a time there has to be some trace of her somewhere."

Paul's smile wilted.

"Nothing," he said. "It's as if she disappeared off the face of the earth."

"Considering the state of mind she was in at the time, couldn't she have done something harmful to herself?" Cynthia continued.

"Cynthia, please," Drake said. "Paul's suffering enough as it is without us reminding him."

"No," Paul said, forcing a smile, "it's all right. Yes, I've thought about that, Cynthia. It's very possible."

"That she committed suicide?" Cynthia was relentless. Stoddard stared at her a moment, his eyes narrowing. Then he softened.

"We have to consider that possibility very seriously, I'm afraid."

Content with his admission, Cynthia turned to Drake. She fixed her gaze on him, but he turned to look out the window. The remainder of the trip was filled with small talk. Every once in a while Cynthia tried to bring the conversation around to Paul's wife, asking questions about her personality, what he thought had depressed her. Paul's answers were curt, and Drake always inserted some digression to get them off the topic.

Another Leon limousine awaited them at the airport in Florida.

"Nice to be treated so specially, isn't it?" Drake said. "Especially when it's all free."

"Are you sure it is, Drake?" she asked sharply. He simply laughed, behaving as if he had missed her point.

"Of course it is. Everything belongs to the company."

"I hope that doesn't mean us, too," she muttered, but neither Drake nor Paul heard her.

When the compound came into view Paul explained the reasons for the high electric fence and the security patrols and dogs, but she was overwhelmed with the beauty of the grounds—the fountains and pretty cottages, the elaborate gardens, fruit trees, and tall palm trees that bordered the property on every side. It was all so plush and colorful, with sprawling bougainvilleas threaded in and over the fencing. There seemed to be a small army of gardeners working on the flowers and bushes.

"How many people are employed here?" she asked.

"Counting the people who work in the Youth Hold factory, which is that building there," Paul said, pointing, "about a hundred. There are nearly a dozen household employees alone. Mr. Leon has two chefs, one French, one Spanish, both world class."

The limousine stopped at the gate, and the windows were lowered for the security guard to gaze into the car.

"Hello, Mr. Stoddard," the young man said. "Welcome back."

"Thank you."

"Mr. and Mrs. Drake Edwards?"

"That's right."

"Okay, sir," he said, stepping back. He nodded to the

driver, who proceeded up the driveway. Cynthia leaned forward and gazed in awe at the sprawling hacienda with its atriums, its marble steps, its stained-glass windows and colorful tiles.

"Isn't it beautiful?" Drake said.

"Breathtaking."

The moment the car came to a stop two attendants rushed forward to get the luggage. Another security guard greeted them with the metal detector as they emerged. All of the security precautions frightened Cynthia.

"What are they looking for? I don't think they protect the President of the United States any better."

"Probably not," Paul said, laughing, "but he who throws caution to the wind is blown away with time." He turned to Cynthia. "Mr. Leon told me that himself last time I was here." He pointed to the front steps, and they approached the doorway.

Gerald Dorian was there to greet them.

"Ah, Gerald. How are you?" Paul asked.

"Fine, Mr. Stoddard."

"You've met Mr. Edwards before."

"Yes. How are you, sir?"

"Fine, thanks."

"And this is his wife Cynthia."

For a moment Gerald said nothing. He riveted his eyes firmly on Cynthia's, making her feel as though this man knew of her suspicions and fears.

"Welcome, Mrs. Edwards," he said, and he lowered his eyes and bowed his head.

"Thank you."

"Busy weekend?" Paul inquired as they stepped into the great arched entryway with its Spanish tiled floor. A giant oval mirror in a gold-plated frame caught everyone's reflection. The hacienda was so deep and wide, their voices and footsteps reverberated. The melodic sounds of flamenco guitars was heard through stereophonic speakers planted high in the walls.

"Actually, no, sir," Gerald said pausing. "Mr. Leon

wanted this to be a special weekend, so he has invited no other guests."

"Really?" Paul sounded disappointed but quickly flashed a smile. "Well, that's an honor, Cynthia."

"I'll show Mr. and Mrs. Edwards to their suite first," Gerald said.

"Of course."

"As soon as everyone's settled Mr. Leon will greet you in the library. He asked that you go there directly, Mr. Stoddard."

"Wait until you see that library," Drake whispered. "It's as big as any public school's, even some college libraries."

"Please follow me," Gerald said, and Drake took Cynthia's arm. Gerald led them down a corridor to the left. Cynthia turned every which way to look at the paintings and wall hangings, the vases and crystal on the marble tables. The furniture looked old but authentic and in immaculate condition.

However, the suite they were shown was totally modern, with its king-size bed with black lacquer head- and footboards, its lacquer dressers and nightstands, and its wall decorations: abstracts and cubist paintings. There was a white satin drape over an enormous picture window that looked out on some of the gardens, and a patio door that opened to the tile decking of the sun deck and great free-form pool. The floor of the room was covered with a white rug so plush and thick, Cynthia felt as if she were wobbling as she walked.

The bathroom was as big as their bedroom at home. All the walls were mirrored. There was a long white marble vanity table with cushioned vanity chairs, a glass-enclosed stall shower, and an oval hot tub.

"I think we might just be comfortable here," Drake said, smiling. The attendants brought in their luggage and set it by the closets.

"Unless you want to freshen up a bit," Gerald said, "you can follow me to the library. They," he added, nodding toward the attendants, "will see to your things."

"I don't know. Want to brush your hair or something, honey?"

"No, I'm all right," Cynthia said. Now that it had come right down to it, she couldn't help being nervous about meeting Mr. Leon.

When she turned she found Gerald staring at her again, his eyes delving, inquisitive. She felt a surge of heat come into her neck. Under such intense scrutiny she couldn't help but become self-conscious and worry that her thoughts were obvious. Gerald Dorian seemed capable of mind reading.

"Then if you will follow me," he said, "I will take you to Mr. Leon."

Gerald took them back to the front of the house and then off to the left, through a lobby, past a magnificent living room with a wall made of granite splattered with rainbows of color, out of which a stream of water flowed into a small whirlpool. All of the furniture was over-sized. Cynthia felt as though she had entered the home of a cyclops or some similar mythological giant. Some portions of the house, because of the skylights and windows, were airy and bright, but others were cool and dark.

Gerald paused at the library doors and looked back at them as if every entrance had to be timed dramatically. He caught Cynthia's eyes with his, nodded knowingly, and then opened the doors.

"Mr. and Mrs. Edwards," he announced, and he stepped back to let them enter.

Paul was standing at Mr. Leon's side. He was at the end of a long, dark hardwood table, a large volume opened before him. The library was indeed impressive, with shelves of books that ran the entire length and height of the room on both sides. Skylights in the ceilings provided a splash of illumination that trickled down over the tomes and illuminated the tables at the center.

Mr. Leon was wearing a pair of riding pants and riding boots. He was also dressed in a black silk shirt opened at the collar. Around his neck a thick gold chain glittered. His eyes caught the sunlight and sparkled with a supernatural brightness that for the moment overpowered any other feature in his otherwise unremarkable face.

He sat back, smiling, and lifted his hands from the table, turning the palms upward.

"Drake, welcome," he said.

"Thank you. Mr. Leon, my wife Cynthia," Drake said, moving forward. Almost immediately there was the sound of growling, and Thor came into view at Mr. Leon's feet.

"Quiet," he commanded, and the great muscular dog was silent, but its eyes burned with suspicion, and the muscles in its jaw twitched. "Don't mind him," Mr. Leon added. Then he smiled again.

"Cynthia," he said, nodding. "At last we meet. Welcome to my humble casa."

"Humble?" Cynthia almost laughed. "It's magnificent. I've never seen anything like it, even on 'Lives of the Rich and Famous.' "

Mr. Leon leaned back and laughed.

"You hear that, Paul? Come, my dear. Sit for a moment, and let me get to know you before I get involved in more mundane matters with these businessmen."

Slowly, unable to take her eyes from the dog that glared angrily at her, Cynthia approached the table and took the seat he had indicated just off to his right. When she did so the dog rose to its haunches at Mr. Leon's side. The way it leaned forward, it seemed primed to pounce. She had never seen such a vigorous and intent guard dog. He was like a loaded gun, pointing, hammer back. But no one else seemed to notice it or care, so she turned back to Mr. Leon.

"I hope your accommodations are suitable."

"Again, magnificent is the only word," she said. He beamed.

In person Mr. Leon looked even younger to her, but there was something in his eyes and in the way he smiled that suggested age. Perhaps it was the calmness, the confidence, she mused. He was certainly not an exceptionally good-looking man, but he had the demeanor of one who thought he could have anything he wanted any time he wanted it. That self-assurance was impressive and gave him the authority and magnetism she knew the others, including Drake, felt.

"I'm happy you find it so. I want you to treat this house as if it is your own home. Go anywhere you like; use anything you want. The servants are here for you as much as they are for me. I know you need a good, restful weekend, and I want to be sure you have one," he added, his expression turning serious and concerned. When it did he looked more like a fatherly figure, despite his youthful skin, his shiny black hair, and his young physique.

"Thank you."

"In fact, I've chased everyone away so you could enjoy a peaceful time. You have the pool area to yourself. If you and Drake like tennis, it's there for you. Do you play golf?"

She shook her head.

"Well, if you did, there is a nine-hole course on the grounds and a driving range. We have a racquetball court here, too. So choose your favorite distraction and enjoy.

"I promise you a dinner tonight the likes of which you have never seen. I've instructed both my chefs to come up with prize-winning entrées."

He leaned forward and put his long hand over hers. He had a diamond pinky ring in a platinum setting. It looked enormous, maybe five carats, she thought.

"No two guests who have come here are more important to me than you and Drake, Cynthia. I have high hopes for Drake, and I want you to be happy."

He sounded warm, friendly, even loving, but when she looked into his eyes she saw something cold, chilling. There was an almost unnatural hunger visible, the same sort of licentious appetite she had seen in Drake's eyes during the times he'd made love to her violently. Something instinctive triggered a surge of fear. She wanted to take her hand out from under his, but he was holding on firmly.

"Is there anything I can do for you? Anything you want, or"—he paused—"want to know?" He took his hand off hers and leaned back. She looked down at Thor. The dog seemed to be studying her with a human intelligence, waiting to hear her reply as if he understood every word spoken and would leap up at her if she even suggested something negative.

"I . . ."

"Yes?"

"Was wondering how long you've been here," she said. Mr. Leon's eyes widened, and his face broke out into a grin.

"How long?" He laughed. "Seems like ages and ages to me, Cynthia. I've been here so long, I forget how long. Why do you ask?" He glanced at Drake, but Drake only smiled stupidly.

"The furniture, the artwork . . . it looks priceless with age."

"Some of it is. Years and years of collecting," he explained.

"And Youth Hold? Has that been around a long time, too?"

"Oh, no. That's a relatively recent thing. My father made money in other ways. You might say he was something of an explorer, in the classic sense of the word. So," he said, leaning forward, "why don't you go make yourself comfortable, put on your bathing suit, and lounge about at the pool? Someone will be there to bring you snacks and drinks, and I promise I will keep Drake from you only a short while."

She nodded and looked at Drake and Paul, who stared down at her. She realized she was being excused. They wouldn't talk in front of her. She rose slowly. Thor shifted his weight from one side to the other.

"See you soon," Drake said as she started away.

"Gerald," Mr. Leon snapped, "please escort Mrs. Edwards back."

"Oh, I can find it all right," Cynthia said.

"Gerald," Mr. Leon repeated.

Gerald looked at Paul Stoddard and then at Mr. Leon. "Of course, sir," he said, and he followed her out.

"It's all right, Gerald," Cynthia said as they started down the corridor. "In fact, I might just dwell on some of the artwork and furnishings. I'm sure I can find my way."

"Very good, Mrs. Edwards. If you need anything, just pull the cord in your suite." Once again his scrutinizing eyes unnerved her. She turned and walked away quickly. When she looked back he was gone.

He had not returned to the library, however. Instead he hurried down the corridor to Mr. Leon's office, shutting the doors softly behind him. Then he went to the great desk and stared up at the bank of monitors, concentrating on the one that covered the library.

Gerald looked down at the controls, found the dial for sound, and turned it to pick up the dialogue in the library. He had to listen only for a few minutes to realize that he had been right to be suspicious.

"Come sit beside me, Drake," Mr. Leon said. "You look tired," he added with a wry smile. Drake moved into what had been Cynthia's seat.

"I sure feel the difference," Drake said. He turned to Paul, who nodded with a silent laugh. "When do I get my second dosage?"

"Then you appreciate the benefits of my little wonder pill, eh?"

"Yes," Drake said quickly. "Very much so." He looked at Paul again, but Stoddard was watching Mr. Leon, his eyes riveted.

"I'm glad," Mr. Leon said. He was silent a moment, and then he reached into his jacket pocket and produced a capsule, placing it before him on the table, his two long hands resting comfortably on either side. Drake eyed it covetously and then looked up at Mr. Leon in anticipation.

"I like your wife, Drake. She's a rather interesting-looking woman. I know you haven't been sharing your capsules with her, but she looks so young. Did you ever notice," he continued, turning to Paul as well, "that some people are born with a hold on youth? They have an innate resistance to age." He laughed. "It's as if they worked for me."

Paul laughed, too, but Drake could only stare at the tablet.

"Your wife's an intelligent woman, too, isn't she, Drake?"

"Yes, sir, she is."

"She asks pointed questions, and she's been somewhat more observant than most women. I can't decide whether that comes from an exaggerated paranoia or an intellectual curiosity. What do you think, Paul?"

Paul smiled weakly, as if the question were beyond him. Mr. Leon turned to Drake.

"Drake?"

"I . . . guess she's just a bright person. She did very well in school."

Mr. Leon laughed.

"Yes, I imagine she did. Right from the start she was curious about why you left your old position and took one with us, even though the benefits are far superior. She was anxious to have Mr. Thompson investigate us, and then she drove to Connecticut to speak to Harris Levy," he recited, turning his mouth up at the corners when he paused.

"I . . ." Drake looked at Paul, but Paul looked down.

"And then asking her brother to tap Paul's phone!" Mr. Leon slapped the table. Both Paul and Drake jumped back. Mr. Leon's anger was instantly wiped off and replaced by a cold sneer.

Drake sat with his back against the chair. He felt as though he were growing more and more tired every moment, almost at an accelerated rate.

"I didn't tell her anything that would make her so paranoid." He glanced sharply at Paul. "Things upset her. What happened to the doll . . ."

"The doll." Mr. Leon shook his head and looked at Paul. "No one appreciates my sense of humor anymore, Paul. What am I to do?" He sighed. "It has become something of a mess, hasn't it, Drake? And just when I was thinking of moving you up the ladder in my firm. You see, I've grown somewhat disappointed in my assistant, Gerald," Mr. Leon said. "Some of what has happened is his fault. Anyway, I wanted the two of you here this weekend because I have a new proposal. I want more than one right-hand man, so to speak. I'm looking to create something of a partnership. All the members won't be equal in power, of course," he added, smiling, "but I want to share some of my responsibility and all of what was Gerald's."

"What's happening to Gerald?" Paul asked in a voice barely above a whisper. He was obviously overwhelmed by his good fortune.

"Gerald is . . . going. His time has come. Unfortunately, he won't be the only one."

"What do you mean?" Paul asked.

"I've decided to trim down my staff . . . get rid of dead wood." He turned to Drake. "Only those who prove they are most loyal will remain with me." He put his right hand over the capsule so it was out of sight. Drake caught the action and swallowed hard.

"I will need new demonstrations of that loyalty," Mr. Leon added. "You understand, don't you, Paul?" he said, turning to him sharply.

"Yes, sir. Just ask."

Mr. Leon smiled with cold satisfaction.

"You've already made a significant show of your loyalty, Paul. That's why I want you to be one of my trusted advisers."

"Thank you, sir." Paul beamed. Mr. Leon turned to Drake.

"But you have yet to demonstrate your loyalty, Drake."

"Why?" Drake protested. He looked to Paul. "I told you about Larry Thompson. I told you about my brother-in-law and what he was going to do. I thought you were only going to warn them off, but—"

Mr. Leon waved Drake's complaint off.

"We appreciate that, but I need something more, a sacrifice as significant as the one God asked of Abraham."

Drake's face reddened. He looked at Paul, who was staring at him hard, imitating Mr. Leon's expression.

"I don't understand."

Mr. Leon lifted his hand from the capsule and smiled.

"I like your wife, Drake. She interests me, and it's so hard for me to find pleasurable diversions these days. Oh, I surround myself with beautiful women, but they're like clones. Rarely does one come along that really interests me. Sexually," he added.

Drake swallowed. His knee was aching, and he felt so tired, so terribly tired. He gazed longingly at the pill.

"Tonight, after dinner, I'd like you to bring her around to my suite. We'll have an after-dinner drink, and then you will leave. Without her," Mr. Leon added.

"I can't do that . . . I mean . . ." He turned to Paul, but Paul was going to offer him no assistance. "She won't want to stay."

"We'll have something in the drink . . . something of an aphrodisiac, which will confuse her."

"But later, when she realizes what happened . . . she'll hate me," Drake said, shaking his head.

"What of it? You will find a way to rationalize, and even if you don't, look at what you gain," Mr. Leon said, taking the capsule between his forefinger and thumb and holding it up before him as he twirled it. The clear liquid visible within caught the light from above like a precious diamond. Drake felt his mouth water.

"What will you do to her?"

Mr. Leon smiled widely.

"Come now, Drake. What do you do to her?"

Drake looked to Paul again, but he offered no sympathy.

Mr. Leon put the capsule down but kept his forefinger on it.

"You've gone pretty far with us, Drake," he said. "And you're in deep. Admittedly, the way Mr. Thompson and your brother-in-law were handled made things a bit awkward," he added, glaring at Paul, "but what's done is done. Now think of yourself, Drake. Immortality is within your grasp. Health and happiness forever and ever."

Drake bit down on his lower lip. His heart was pounding. Slowly he brought his hand up to the table and moved it toward the tablet. He hesitated and then continued his forward motion until he reached Mr. Leon's hand. When their fingers touched Mr. Leon lifted his hand, and Drake plucked the capsule off the table. He brought it to his mouth and held it there. Mr. Leon was smiling and nodding.

Drake closed his eyes and quickly swallowed the pill.

"Thank you, Drake. There will be another one for you tomorrow. And another for the day after and the day after that . . . forever and ever," Mr. Leon said.

— 16 —

Cynthia did not go directly to the suite to change into her bathing suit and lounge at the pool. With the men involved in their business discussion back at the library, she thought she would look around. She did not know exactly what she hoped to find, but she was there alone, able to explore. She thought it would be foolish not to take advantage of the opportunity.

There were so many rooms in the sprawling hacienda. Many were simply guest suites, the decor different in every one; some colonial, some southwestern, some modern. But some rooms had their own special themes—one looking like a bedroom in a Roman palace, one looking like a bedroom in an old English inn, one (she had to laugh) designed to appear like the inside of a large tent. Did Mr. Leon dress in Arab garb and pretend to be the sheik of Araby to seduce his women? She had the sense she was looking in on different movie sets.

There were a number of sitting rooms, some looking unused and more like rooms in a museum exhibiting Old World furniture. She came upon a large game room with pool tables and backgammon tables, chess tables and Ping-Pong tables. One door opened to the indoor racquetball court Mr. Leon had described. She even discovered a small bowling alley. She found the steam rooms and hot baths and met some of the fitness staff. All of the servants she encountered smiled and were friendly. No one challenged her foray into the various corridors and rooms. She was beginning to lose hope of discovering anything. There didn't seem to be any secret chambers, no skeletons in closets, no guards outside of doors preventing her entrance. There were only guards on the outside of the hacienda policing the grounds to prevent anyone from compromising the fences and gates.

Somewhat discouraged, Cynthia made her way back. However, when she returned to the lobby she pulled herself into the shadows to watch Gerald Dorian emerge from what she could see was a rather large office. He closed the door softly behind him, looked both ways as if he wanted to be sure he hadn't been spotted, and then turned and disappeared down the corridor.

Cynthia crossed the lobby and went to the office door, listening for a moment, and then knocked gently. There was no response. Did she dare? Mr. Leon had invited her to go anywhere she wanted. *Mi casa es su casa,* right? Why not, then? She turned the knob slowly and opened the door. For a moment she simply stood in the doorway, panning the large office. Then she started toward the desk.

The television screens on her left caught her attention immediately. The security monitors covered every corridor and a number of rooms, one of which, she saw, was the library. She couldn't hear what was being said, but Drake, Paul, and Mr. Leon were having some wine, toasting something. She watched them for a few moments and then went to the desk.

She had never seen one this large, she thought. It had to have been custom built. Everything on the desk was neatly organized. She riffled through some of the documents. All of it had to do with Youth Hold: sales reports, etc. There were some documents dealing with real estate holdings and, from what she could peruse quickly, documents and letters from other businesses and enterprises with which Mr. Leon was involved.

She looked up at the monitor again. They were all still in the library, talking.

She began to look in the drawers. In one she found a pistol, but it looked more like an antique than a working gun. She didn't touch it. She went to another drawer, which was filled with office supplies, and then another. The third drawer contained something of interest—a very old-looking leather-bound book.

She took it out slowly and opened it after gazing again at the monitors to be sure she was still safe. The first written words caught her attention. She settled into the large desk chair and continued to read a list of names. The numbers next to them didn't make any sense. They couldn't be dates, she thought: 1616, 1703, 1788 . . . but across from each was something listed as their sacrifices and their eventual dispositions. According to what was written, some were killed in accidents and some were murdered. It was Mr. Leon's Book of the Dead.

She flipped the pages quickly to reach the last few entries and found Paul Stoddard's name and Harris Levy's. She read what was entered under Sacrifices. Stoddard's wife had been buried alive, and Harris Levy had hanged his own wife. Oh, God, she thought. She read what was under Drake's name. The words left her cold. She closed the book quickly and returned it to the drawer.

After she closed the drawer she looked up at the monitor and saw the three men had already left the library. She looked about frantically for a moment and then decided to exit through the patio doors. She went out as quickly and as quietly as she could and crossed the patio to the swimming pool sun deck. She was able to recognize her suite from the curtains in the patio window. Fortunately, the doors were unlocked, so she slipped in quickly and caught her breath.

Before Drake arrived, Cynthia changed into her new string bikini and went out to the pool. She had to play along and pretend to be enjoying herself. Now she knew even more than Drake, she thought, although she still didn't understand why Mr. Leon had such a firm grip on everyone who came into his fold. That was all that was left to understand.

As soon as she lay back on the lounge chair a Haitian man approached her to offer her a tropical drink. He brought a tray of barbecued shrimp and some hors d'oeuvres made from potatoes that were absolutely delicious. She sat back and rubbed suntan oil over her face, shoulders, and arms. With so much of her breasts exposed, she thought she had better cover them as well.

The waiter returned with her drink. She sipped it, lay back, closed her eyes, and wondered just what she would do next.

Finally Drake joined her, looking more chipper than he had before they had arrived. He ordered a piña colada for himself and ate nearly the whole tray of shrimp. Obviously something had brought back his voracious appetite, she thought.

"Isn't this wonderful? A paradise. What did I tell you, huh?" He ordered a second drink and asked for more hors d'oeuvres. "What about some tennis before dinner? Mr. Leon and Paul want to play doubles."

"I think I'll just rest," she said. "How did your meeting go?"

"Oh, great. There are so many possibilities opening for us. There's even a chance we might be able to move down here."

"Down here? Why?"

"Mr. Leon is replacing some people . . . dead wood," Drake said. "Don't worry. We don't have to make any decisions overnight, but it's something to consider. Naturally, the company would find a home for us—a big one with a pool and tennis court. What do you think? Think you could get used to all this on a regular basis?" he asked, holding his arms out.

"Right now I just want to enjoy the weekend," she said.

"Sure, sure. I'll vegetate a while with you and then join the others at the court," he said. She caught him staring at her.

"Is everything all right, Drake?" she asked.

"What? Sure, why not? Perfect."

"Is it perfect, Drake? Is it what you really want?" She hoped he would suddenly shake his head and propose they simply run out of there, but the pensive look died away, and that wide, almost clownish smile returned.

"Of course. Who could ask for anything more than this? It's more than anyone deserves."

"Maybe that's true, Drake."

"Just an expression, Cynthia." He lay back and closed his eyes. "Just an expression."

She watched him for a moment and then lay back herself, waiting, wondering, hoping.

Shortly after Drake left, Cynthia gathered her things together to return to the suite and rest before dinner. She thought she would shower after she had a nap. Actually, she was quite impressed with herself and how well she had done keeping herself calm and cool so far.

Before she stood up she felt someone's eyes on her and swung around to see Gerald Dorian standing inside of her suite, looking out the open patio door. She pressed her towel to her bosom and started toward him.

"Is something wrong?" she asked, hovering back a few steps. Perhaps he had discovered she had been in Mr. Leon's office.

"I think you know something is wrong, Mrs. Edwards," he said, and he stepped back so she would enter. She hesitated. "Please," he said. "Don't be afraid."

She walked in, and Gerald closed the patio door and drew the curtains quickly.

"I wanted to talk to you," he said, "while they were all at the tennis court." She stood staring at him, her arms still pressing the towel to her body protectively. "Please relax, Mrs. Edwards. I want to help you."

"Help me? What do you mean?"

252

Gerald smiled, his eyes full of that strange, knowing look he had had when she first met him.

"Mrs. Edwards, the company—Mr. Leon—knows that you have been suspicious right from the start. We know you discovered Selina Levy's corpse. We know," he added slowly, "that you sent your brother to tap Mr. Stoddard's phone."

"Oh, God," she said, stepping back.

"It's all right, Mrs. Edwards. I'm not here to hurt you. I'm here to help you and your husband. Isn't that why you came here?"

She nodded and sat on the bed.

"Why do you want to help us?"

"Why?" he said, as if it were the deepest philosophical question of all time. "Why?" he repeated, shaking his head softly. "Mrs. Edwards, I have been Mr. Leon's personal assistant for a long time, a very long time, and I have, I am sorry to say, been part of some terrible, terrible things. The man is sick. He is perverted, sadistic. Very, very evil. I'm not proud of the things I have done, despite how well he has treated me. As corny as it might sound to you, Mrs. Edwards, my conscience is bothering me. I am remorseful, and I want redemption. In short, I want out of all this."

"Why don't you just leave?"

"For the same reason you and your husband can't just leave, Mrs. Edwards. Mr. Leon and his people wouldn't permit it. Not with what we know."

"How did he do it? How did he get my husband so hypnotized? What kind of a drug is he taking? It's not like cocaine or heroin."

"No, Mrs. Edwards. It's something entirely different. It gives your husband and people like him a sense of invincibility, elation, fills them with the illusion of . . . of immortality. They think they will never get sick, never suffer the aches and pains that accompany age. I call it the illusion drug, Mrs. Edwards. The thing is, it's very addictive. Your husband is no longer in control of himself, and he will be unable to do anything to help you when the time comes. In fact, he will deliver you to evil.''

"I know," Cynthia said. "I sneaked into Mr. Leon's office and read his leather-bound book."

Gerald smiled.

"I thought you were an exceptional woman the moment I set eyes on you—actually, as soon as I began to hear about the things you were doing. I'm glad you've come, Mrs. Edwards. I think you are just the person to help me end this."

"I don't know," Cynthia said. "It's taking all my strength to keep from running out of here."

"It would do you no good, Mrs. Edwards. You wouldn't get very far, even if you somehow managed to get past the dogs and the guards and got off the grounds. They would hunt you down. Your husband, the poor fool, would lead the pack."

"My God."

"Yes, Mrs. Edwards, my God. Are you willing to help me help you?"

"What do I have to do?"

"Tonight, after dinner, Mr. Leon is going to invite you and your husband to his suite for an after-dinner drink. Your drink will contain a drug that will leave you virtually at Mr. Leon's mercy. I've seen its effect before, on other women. You grow dizzy and then drunk and confused, but very willing to be passionate, indiscriminately passionate. Do you understand?"

"Yes. I read what he wrote in the book."

"You can't depend on that, Mrs. Edwards. He has often gone beyond what he has written and planned. He might spontaneously add something sadistic. I know he despises women with any sort of intelligence. He likes to reduce them to blubbering fools and torment them. He'll have you doing rather—what's the word?—oh, yes, kinky things."

Cynthia nodded, her heart pounding.

"What do I do?"

"Obviously, you don't drink what he gives you. Pretend to, though, and dump it when he's not watching. You mustn't let on what we are doing, what we know. Okay?''

"Yes, but then what?"

"Your husband will leave you. That's the plan. Mr. Leon will then approach you. By this time you would be dizzy, confused, willing. Only I want you to do one thing. I want you to show an exaggerated fear of Thor."

"Thor?"

"His dog. I can't effect your rescue smoothly with Thor still in his presence."

"But why do we have to wait until I am in his suite? Can't we work out an escape before?"

"We could, but I need the evidence. What you found in his office means nothing to anyone. We need what's in his wall safe in his suite. I must get him to give it to me. I can if the dog is not a problem."

"You make the animal sound so intimidating."

"He's truly an unusual animal, frighteningly wise. Sometimes I think he can read human minds. He's trained to attack anyone who so much as points a gun at Mr. Leon. And he is blindly devoted to his master. I can't get near him with that dog loose, Mrs. Edwards."

"What do I do?"

"Be unwilling until the dog is out of sight. Suggest he put it in his bathroom. He'll do it because he'll feel safe and he'll want you."

"But what will you do once the dog is locked away?"

"I'll come in and force Mr. Leon to let us all go. I know the security system and what he must do to make our escape possible, and I will bring enough evidence to have the authorities finish him and this mad business for good."

Cynthia studied him. Could she trust him? He had a strange look in his eyes. At times he looked like someone under the influence of some drug himself. Perhaps Mr. Leon had sent him; perhaps this was the beginning of the sadistic and perverted plan.

"How will you know when to come in?"

"I'll be waiting just outside the patio door. You come to the door and open it for me."

"How do I know I can trust you?" she asked. "How do I know this isn't part of Mr. Leon's original plan?"

"You don't know, Mrs. Edwards. But what is your alternative?"

She stared at him a moment. He looked devoid of feeling, inscrutable, the walking dead. It gave her the chills to scrutinize such lifeless eyes.

"Okay," she said. "I'll do my best, but what happens if he refuses to put Thor out?"

"He'll have his way with you one way or another, Mrs. Edwards. Once he realizes you didn't drink the aphrodisiac he will most certainly turn violent, and neither I nor your husband will be able to come to your aid. Not with that dog there."

"Oh, God. What if I just appeal to Drake to leave right now?"

"The moment you do so, you will be letting him know all you know, and Mrs. Edwards, I think your husband will turn you in," Gerald said coldly. "I know he will."

Gerald advised her to keep as busy as she could before dinner.

He then showed her to the spa, where he instructed the staff to give her a mud bath. Her spa treatment took up most of the afternoon, and ironically, despite what was happening around her and what would happen, it left her feeling rather wonderful. Gerald's suggestion had been a very good one. He had seemed so calm, so assured; it was as if he had rehearsed the plan or something like it for years.

When she returned to her suite she found Drake had returned and was taking his shower so he could dress for dinner. He asked her what she had been doing, and she told him—without any mention of Gerald, of course. After that she avoided him by busying herself with her own preparations.

"I'm glad you're enjoying the facilities here so much,

Cynthia," Drake said, standing behind her at the vanity table and looking at her in the mirror. "I knew you would. This weekend will do wonders for us. Once it's over—well, once it's over we'll be like two new people with a whole new and wonderful future ahead of us."

He leaned down to kiss her on the neck.

"You sound like we're going to sell our souls to the devil, Drake," she said pointedly, speaking to him in the mirror as well.

"What?" He looked at his watch. "We'd better get a move on. We're having cocktails and hors d'oeuvres in the small ballroom. There's going to be music, too."

She stared at him a moment, seeing how he had to shift his eyes away quickly and distract himself, and then she finished dressing. She put on the dress she had worn to Paul Stoddard's, with the diamond necklace. When she studied herself in the mirror she thought the spa treatment had done wonders for her skin, and despite her trepidation, the constant pitter-patter of her heart and the trembling in her limbs, she looked radiant. She hoped that no one would see through her buoyant facade.

The small ballroom, as Drake referred to it, was a large chamber illuminated by grand chandeliers. The floors were black marble with thick mauve and aqua throw rugs in front of the round black leather sofas and oversized leather chairs. The furniture faced a small landing on which there was a flamenco guitarist and a flamenco dancer. Behind them three men dressed like Spanish gypsies played castanets and tambourines.

The dancer, adorned in a flowing floral-pattern dress, had a classic dark-skinned face with ebony eyes and long, flowing coal-black hair that gleamed under the bright chandeliers. The music, the singing, and the dancing had already begun before they arrived. Paul and Mr. Leon were seated at the center of the largest sofa facing the musicians and dancer. Thor was sprawled at Mr. Leon's feet, his great head up, his eyes following them as they entered the room. Servants were bringing around trays of hors d'oeuvres and the glasses of champagne.

Paul and Mr. Leon rose to their feet when she and Drake entered. Mr. Leon stepped forward to take her hand and kiss it.

"You're absolutely beautiful, Cynthia," he said. "The diamonds have found an appropriate home."

"Thank you."

"Please sit beside me," he said, leading her to the sofa. Thor moved farther to his right and sprawled out again, this time turning toward her.

"I've never seen such a devoted dog," she said.

"Yes, he is devoted. Man's best friend," Mr. Leon added, smiling. He nodded, and a servant brought her a glass of champagne. Drake and Paul watched the dancer for a moment and ate some of the hors d'oeuvres.

"He looks so cold, though, and not like any household pet I've ever seen."

"Please don't let him bother you. He's perfectly harmless until he has to be otherwise."

"I'm sorry," she said. "I have this thing about dogs." She said it quickly so Drake wouldn't hear.

"How do you like them?" Mr. Leon asked, nodding toward the entertainers.

"It seems a pity to have so many talented people for such a small audience," she said. Gerald Dorian was off to the side speaking softly to a servant. He gazed at her for only a moment to see if she was all right. She tried to indicate that she was.

"Oh, but it's the quality of the audience, not the quantity that matters," Mr. Leon said. "And tonight they feel they are playing for royalty."

What a charmer, Cynthia thought, wondering how strong she would have been had she not known his intentions.

After their cocktail hour they walked down the long corridor to the dining room. Mr. Leon had taken her arm in his and, with Drake's permission, led them to the enormous long room. Cynthia understood now why Gerald was so intent about Thor. The dog walked at Mr.

Leon's heels as if there were an invisible leash between his wrist and the dog's collar.

They paused briefly in the dining room doorway to take in the room. Like the small ballroom, the dining room was illuminated by chandeliers hung from the ceiling directly over the table. The windows were draped in bone-white silk curtains, and the floor was a highly polished hardwood. The dinner staff stood waiting behind the high-backed dark pine chairs that were adorned with hand-carved leaves and branches.

"That shield"—Mr. Leon pointed to the one directly ahead of them—"bears my family's coat of arms."

"Really? I always wondered how anyone could be absolutely sure about something like that," Cynthia said.

"Oh, I can be sure, my dear. Believe me, that is indeed my family symbol."

The table had been set at the far end with Mr. Leon at the head, she to his right, Drake to the right of her, and Paul across from them. Thor sat on his haunches just to the right of Mr. Leon to observe everyone. He did have almost human eyes, she thought.

Cynthia noted that Gerald was not sitting with them. He moved about, however, overseeing the servants, tuned in to Mr. Leon's every gesture, every look. He read some unspoken instructions from them. The way Gerald anticipated Mr. Leon's thoughts sent a chill down her spine. Could someone who was so in sync with someone else really betray that person?

The dinner was as elaborate as promised.

"My chefs are terribly competitive," Mr. Leon remarked, "so you will have to taste each entrée."

Cynthia confessed she had never eaten anything as wonderful. One dish was duck, and one was veal, but she had no idea what ingredients were used to arrive at such flavors. The pièce de résistance was the Viennese table filled with desserts.

No one seemed to care about calories, fat, or cholesterol. All three men ate voraciously. The wine flowed; the waiters buzzed around them filling glasses as soon as they were emptied, every one working with a frenzied hysteria, as if the slightest mistake might result in his beheading.

"Have you had enough of everything, Cynthia?" Mr. Leon finally asked.

"I couldn't eat another thing," she said, watching Drake sample his fourth dessert.

"I know what you mean. But I have just the remedy," he said. "The perfect after-dinner drink. It has the effect of enhancing digestion and ridding you of that stuffed feeling. It's a very rare and expensive liquor. Consequently, I keep it in my own suite. Shall we adjourn to it? Is that all right with you, Drake?" Mr. Leon asked.

Drake looked up sharply. Cynthia noticed the way he looked from Paul to Mr. Leon and then at her.

"Fine," he said.

Mr. Leon nodded toward Gerald, who was in the doorway.

"Gerald will escort you," he said. "I just want to pass our compliments to my chefs and see to some matters here quickly. I'll be right along," he added.

They all rose and started out. She exchanged a knowing look with Gerald but looked away when she thought she caught Paul studying her.

"That's what I call a meal," Drake said. "Huh, Cynthia?"

"Yes, Drake."

She couldn't stop the trembling in her legs and wondered if she would simply sink to her knees. She held on to his arm as they walked and wondered if he could feel the shivering that traveled through her body.

Gerald led them down the corridor, moving, it seemed to her, from brightness into darkness before arriving at the great double door that opened to Mr. Leon's suite. They entered a large sitting room with a great bedroom visible through another set of double doors left wide open. Cynthia could see the patio doors on the other side.

"Make yourselves comfortable," Gerald said. He cast

a quick glance at her and went directly into the bedroom to open the curtains on the patio door. Then he returned and set out the glasses.

"Only Mr. Leon pours this after-dinner drink," he explained. "We'll have to wait for him."

Cynthia looked at Drake. He wore a worried expression. She hoped that what Gerald had described wouldn't come to pass. She muttered a silent prayer. Drake smiled at her, his lips trembling.

"How are you doing?" he asked.

"Okay," she said softly.

"Beautiful suite, huh?" he said, looking around.

"Everything is beautiful here, Drake. It's all that you said it was."

"Yeah."

Mr. Leon entered, Thor trotting beside him.

"It's rather a wonderful night tonight," he said. "Perhaps we should all go out on the patio."

Cynthia turned quickly toward Gerald. He shook his head slightly to indicate she shouldn't be concerned. Mr. Leon went to his bar and began to pour the drinks. Just as Gerald had predicted, he kept his back to them, effectively hiding whatever he was doing.

"First Cynthia," he said, turning and approaching her with a tumbler half filled with a clear liquid. She took it and he smiled. "Just taste that," he said. She looked at Gerald. His face was glum, his eyes riveted to her.

"I'll wait for everyone," she said diplomatically.

"Of course," Mr. Leon said, smiling, and he returned to the bar.

"May I look at your bedroom?" she asked.

"Pardon? Oh, of course, my dear. Go right in." He swung his eyes at Drake and smiled. Drake shifted his weight from one foot to the other and watched Cynthia. Then he looked at Paul, whose eyes were fixed on him.

"What a magnificent bathroom!" Cynthia called from the bedroom.

She walked into it and quickly dumped the contents of her glass into the sink. Then she rinsed it and filled it with cold water. She had managed step one. When she returned to the sitting room she telegraphed her success to Gerald, who revealed his satisfaction with a slight smile on his lips. Mr. Leon had handed Drake and Paul their glasses.

"To everyone's health, happiness, and long life," Mr. Leon toasted.

Drake hesitated. Mr. Leon seemed to anticipate that hesitation and turned to him abruptly. Then Drake drank. Cynthia drank her water, closing her eyes as she did so.

"This is very good," she said, and she downed the remainder of the liquid. Mr. Leon beamed.

"I knew you would enjoy it," he said.

Cynthia looked at the four men who were all fixed on her. Gerald was watching to see how credible a performance she would create; Paul looked curious, interested; Drake looked terrified, regretful; but Mr. Leon looked satisfied, full of anticipation. Was it too soon for a reaction? she wondered, glancing at Gerald. He closed his eyes and opened them.

"Oh, dear," she said. "I suddenly feel so dizzy."

"Really?" Mr. Leon said. "I'm sure it's nothing. Maybe you should just lie down a moment. Drake, would you escort Cynthia into my bedroom? Let her lie down on my bed a few moments."

Drake stood his ground. He's going to refuse, Cynthia thought. She was happy, but she suddenly thought about the things Gerald had told her, especially how Mr. Leon wouldn't let them escape. If Drake showed courage now, ironically, it could ruin things. And yet she wanted some sign from him that he wasn't going to sacrifice her. Their love was too strong even in the face of all this temptation, wasn't it?

"Sure," Drake said, and he crossed to her. "Are you okay?" he asked.

She laughed, acting giddy.

"I don't know. I feel like I'm floating." She laughed again. Out of the corner of her eye she saw a pleased look on Gerald Dorian's face. "Maybe I'd better lie down, Drake."

He escorted her into the bedroom, and she lay back on the enormous bed. She laughed again, louder this time.

"Cynthia?"

"Oh, I feel so strange, so . . . warm. Isn't it warm in here, Drake?" she said. She saw Paul and Mr. Leon standing in the doorway. Drake turned and saw them, too. "It is warm," she said, and she laughed. "Even for this skimpy dress." She reached back and unzipped it so the bodice would fall away from her breasts.

"Perhaps you should let her rest, Drake," Mr. Leon said tersely. Drake looked down at her. Cynthia laughed again. "Drake?" Mr. Leon said.

Drake turned with some reluctance and walked back to the doorway.

"Paul," Mr. Leon said, "perhaps Drake would like a game of pool about now."

"Yeah, what about that, Drake? You play pool?"

"Not really," Drake said softly.

"Sure. He's probably a hustler, Mr. Leon."

"Of course he's a hustler. That's why he's here," Mr. Leon said.

They were inches apart, eye to eye. Drake looked back at Cynthia, who had turned on her side, her dress slipping down a little more. Suddenly she got up and laughed.

"I wonder if I could be a flamenco dancer," she said. She spun around, holding her dress out, and laughed again.

"Ready?" Paul said. Drake lowered his head and followed Paul out.

Mr. Leon turned to Gerald, who stood waiting in the sitting room.

"That will be all for now, Gerald," he said, and he walked into the bedroom, closing the doors behind him as soon as Thor entered, too.

— 17 —

Drake paused in the corridor and turned to look back at Mr. Leon's suite as Gerald emerged and walked quickly in the opposite direction.

"Don't worry. You're making the right decision," Paul said, stepping up beside him.

"Am I?" Drake replied dryly. He continued to look back.

"Of course. And to show you just how much confidence Mr. Leon has in you, he asked me to give you this in advance," Paul said, holding out his fist. Drake turned and looked down as he opened his hand to reveal the next day's capsule. "You can take it as soon as you get up in the morning. Is he a man of his word or what?" Paul said, smiling.

Drake stared at the clear pill in Paul's palm.

"Come on, take it," he urged. "Before you leave he'll give you enough to last a long, long time."

Drake looked back once more and then snatched the pill quickly and slipped it into his pocket.

"Good man. Listen," Paul said, taking his arm and moving down the hall again, "don't worry. You're not making that much of a sacrifice. Who knows how many times she has cheated on you without your getting anything for it?''

''Cynthia's not that type.''

''They're all that type eventually,'' Paul said. ''Look, this way Mr. Leon gets to believe you would do anything for him, and he rewards you. Just think about the things he told us earlier,'' he added in a whisper. ''He's going to get rid of Gerald and promote us in the company. Just imagine the power, the wealth. Wine, women, and song forever and ever,'' Paul sang.

''Cynthia's not going to understand. She would never understand, even if I told her the truth,'' Drake said, shaking his head.

''That's because she can't participate. But maybe, once you're one of the higher-ups, you can get permission for her to be one of us, one of the immortals,'' he said. ''If you want her to be, that is,'' he added after a beat.

''Of course I would want her to be. I love her.''

''Come on, Drake. Love is for—for mortals, for people who don't have our vision. Our futures are unlimited. Why do anything to restrict yourself?'' He smiled lasciviously. ''You had a taste of what could be the last time you were here, didn't you?''

''Yes, but—''

''So? Don't tell me you didn't enjoy it,'' Paul said, squeezing his shoulder. ''I've been here for one of Mr. Leon's weekends, buddy. I know.''

''I didn't even know what was happening. Before I knew it I was practically raped,'' he protested.

''Sure, sure. Look Drake, save the false morality for inferior people. As I said, you're talking to someone who has been where you are now and knows the score.''

They walked on. Suddenly Drake stopped and seized Paul's arm.

''What exactly happened to your wife, Paul? What did Mr. Leon demand of you?''

''What's the difference?'' he said. ''It's over and done

with," he added, and he started ahead again. Drake seized his arm once more to stop him.

"I'd like to know. How did you prove your loyalty? It's not the same for everyone, is it?"

Paul stared at him a moment. Then he smiled.

"No. But Mr. Leon was making me a regional leader. Do you know what that meant right off—the money, the authority? Brenda, my wife, was a lot like yours in the beginning—always complaining, suspicious. Oh, she didn't go as far as Cynthia, but she was becoming a problem very quickly, and I was afraid Mr. Leon would find out and get very upset."

"So?"

"Mr. Leon wanted a sacrifice, proof of my complete loyalty," he said nonchalantly, as if it were all self-explanatory.

"What happened, Paul? Where is your wife? She didn't wander off in any depression, did she?"

"No. She's here," he said, smiling.

"Here? I don't understand. She's locked up somewhere in the hacienda?"

"No, not exactly. She's out back, buried."

"Christ! You killed her? For him?" Drake asked incredulously.

"It wouldn't have worked out with her anyway," Paul said in that same casual tone. "My youth and vitality overwhelmed her. In time I would have had to do something to rid myself of her. I mean, even with Youth Hold, she'd still get old. And how would that look? We'll outlast dozens of women, Drake." He laughed. "Dozens."

Drake stared, events of the recent past now crystallized with meaning. These were the things Cynthia suspected, even with her limited knowledge of what was really happening, he thought.

"The others—all the others who were married—Brad, Adrian—Cynthia was right," Drake said, but more to himself. "Because that's what happens if they're not part of it, right?" he asked, looking up at Paul. "You have to get rid of them. Even if Mr. Leon demanded something else."

Paul shrugged. "You made your choice. Put it behind you," he said. "Be like me. Think of the future." He started away, but Drake did not move. Paul stopped and turned back to him.

"Coming?"

"No," Drake said determinedly. "I'm not." He started back toward Mr. Leon's suite. "I'm not going to let this happen," he muttered.

"Drake!"

"I can't do it," he cried without turning, and he continued toward Mr. Leon's suite, but Paul hurried after him and seized him at the shoulder, spinning him around abruptly.

"Look, Paul, I—"

Paul stood there with a revolver in his hand.

"Mr. Leon suspected you might back out at the last minute. He said, 'Paul, there's something weak about Drake. I want you to watch him,' and sure enough, he was right. What a guy," Paul said, shaking his head. "Very perceptive when it comes to people."

"Paul, listen—"

"Get moving. Don't worry, we'll make you into one of us yet."

"Where are we going?"

"You'll see," Paul said, smiling. "Move." He gestured with the gun. Drake looked at it and at Paul, whose eyes were cold steel. There was no doubt in his mind that the man would pull the trigger. He walked ahead. "Turn left at the end of the corridor," Paul directed.

They walked until they reached the doors of Mr. Leon's office.

"Go inside."

"What for?"

"Mr. Leon has a video security system here. There are cameras everywhere. Even in his suite. We can watch."

"Watch!"

"Yes. He thought you might learn something. Now go on, walk in," he said, waving the pistol toward the door.

"Cynthia," Drake moaned, but he opened the door and walked in ahead of Paul. What have I done? he thought. What have I done?

Cynthia spun out of Mr. Leon's embrace and laughed. He had brought his lips to her neck and kissed his way down over her exposed bosom.

"Want to tease me, huh?" he said, smiling. "Just like most modern women, you enjoy tormenting a man."

She laughed again but this time stopped abruptly and looked down at Thor, who lay panting on the floor, his eyes on her as if he could appreciate human sexuality, too.

"You're a very bright young woman, Cynthia," Mr. Leon said, gazing at her appreciatively. "Do you put your brains to work when you make love, too? Do you think of more creative ways to make your lover happy? I bet you and I could find new heights of ecstasy."

She brought the bodice of her dress up over her bosom and pouted.

"Your dog is staring at me. I don't like it."

"Forget my dog," he said, approaching.

"No," she replied, sidestepping him. "I can't. I can't stand the way he looks at me. I don't like dogs. He makes me nervous." She embraced herself more tightly.

Mr. Leon studied her.

Does he realize I didn't drink what he gave me to drink? Cynthia wondered.

"Now, now, my dear," Mr. Leon said, starting toward her again. "You must put everything out of your mind, everything—"

"He looks like he wants to bite me," she cried, stepping back.

Mr. Leon sighed.

"You intelligent women do have trouble putting your thoughts to rest, don't you?"

He looked down at Thor and then up at her.

"All right," he said. "We'll give Thor a rest. I don't see you as much of a threat anyway."

He went to the bathroom doorway.

"Thor," he called. The dog rose instantly and walked to him. "Go on in, Thor. Go on. Our prima donna can't let herself go with you gawking at her."

The dog hesitated as if he knew he shouldn't go in. Cynthia held her breath. Finally he trotted forward, and Mr. Leon closed the door.

"Now," he said, turning, "are you happier?"

"Yes," she said, moving toward the patio. She unlocked it and looked out. What if Gerald wasn't there? What if this really had been all part of some ruse? They could be toying with her for everyone's amusement. She saw no one outside. Mr. Leon came up behind her, put his hands on her shoulders, and brought his lips to her neck. He kissed her and slid his hands down under her loose bodice, cupping her breasts.

She was about to panic just as the patio door was jerked open and Gerald Dorian stepped in.

Mr. Leon backed up, surprised.

Gerald had a pistol in his hand.

"What the hell are you doing, you fool?" Mr. Leon demanded. Cynthia pulled away instantly and began to tighten her dress. Mr. Leon looked at her and saw the awareness and clarity in her eyes. Surprised, he turned back to Gerald.

"Yes, sir, she's part of this. She knows," he said coolly.

"What? But how—"

"I didn't want to—how did you put it?—go. What did you tell them? My time has come?"

"Now, Gerald," Mr. Leon said, smiling, "you know I said those things just to get those two committed to me. You know I could never think of getting rid of you. Why, we have been together for so long, I wouldn't know what to do without you."

"Really? I didn't think you needed anyone but yourself, Mr. Leon. Go over to the wall safe," he commanded.

"You're making a big mistake, Gerald. An eternal mistake," Mr. Leon warned.

"Go over to the safe," Gerald repeated as he pulled back the hammer on the pistol. "If I have to shoot you first and then break it open, I will."

"It won't do you any good."

"Just open the safe."

"Very well." He started toward the safe and then veered off toward the bathroom door.

"Get away from that door. You'll never open it before I shoot you, Mr. Leon."

Behind the door Thor began to growl and bark. Cynthia started toward the entrance to the suite.

"What did he tell you, my dear, to get you to become part of this ridiculous thing?" Mr. Leon said, moving to the wall safe. "What did he promise you? Because whatever it was, it was a lie."

"Shut up," Gerald said, "and just open the safe."

"You're a sick, vicious man," she said. "I don't know what you've done to my husband, but this is all going to end."

"You little fool. I thought you were a bright woman. You think he's going to let you and your husband out of here?"

"I said shut up and open that safe," Gerald repeated.

"And I told you," Mr. Leon said as he began to work the combination, "this won't do you any good." He opened it.

"Step back," Gerald snapped. Mr. Leon obeyed. "The others don't know," Gerald began, "but I realized it—you're drawing on the stash now. Something's happened to the fountain, hasn't it?" Mr. Leon didn't reply. "You don't have to answer. I'll see for myself shortly, but I know I'm right. You wouldn't have rationed what we give the factory for Youth Hold if that were not so. In time you would rid yourself of everyone else. You would spare no one, because the supply has become limited." He reached in and took out the key.

"You hear what he's saying, Cynthia? If I would do that, what do you think he will do? Open the bathroom door," Mr. Leon pleaded. "He'll kill you and Drake. I never meant to kill you."

"Don't listen to him," Gerald said. "These are the words of a desperate man."

"I thought you were going to get evidence from that safe," Cynthia said. "Why do you want a key?"

Gerald turned to her.

"He's lying," Mr. Leon repeated. "Open the bathroom door. Quickly."

"Get back," he told her. "Stand away from the bathroom." He pointed the gun at her, so she moved away quickly. Then he turned back to Mr. Leon.

"That key won't help you," Mr. Leon said. "You have to know how to disarm the cabinet. Otherwise it will begin an explosion that will bring down the entire hacienda."

"Don't even try," Gerald said. "You wouldn't do anything to endanger the supply and the fountain. Do you know," he said, smiling coldly, "I once thought you were God? I thought nothing could stop you, and I was happy to be virtually your slave, watching you enjoy."

"You enjoyed, too, Gerald. I never forbade you anything," Mr. Leon said, his hands out with the palms turned up. Gerald laughed.

"Yes, but it was always your leftovers or second choices, wasn't it? You never really shared with me. You never really respected me. My only regret," Gerald said, "is that I waited so long to do this."

"Gerald, listen, I'm not lying about the cabinet. If you open that door—"

Gerald pulled the trigger. The gun's report set Thor pounding against the inside of the bathroom door. Cynthia pressed her hands to her ears and screamed. Mr. Leon looked up from his fatal wound with shock and then crumpled to the floor.

For a while Paul Stoddard, watching the scene on the monitor with Drake, didn't understand what was happening. His thought was that this was all part of one of Mr. Leon's plans, a scene he had created to heighten his pleasure with Cynthia; but when Gerald mentioned what Mr. Leon had told them in the library, Paul realized they weren't acting.

"Don't move," he told Drake, and he shot out of the library, running as fast as he could to the suite. He charged through the door just after the gunshot.

Mr. Leon looked up from the floor helplessly; he was still breathing, his eyes wide. Thor scratched madly at the door. Gerald and Paul confronted each other, but Paul had his gun pointed, and Gerald had his at his side.

"What have you done?" Paul said. "Drop your gun. Drop it!" he commanded.

"Wait. Don't do anything rash," Gerald said. "I have the key," he added, and he held it up. "The key to the supply. Do you know what this means?"

"But . . . Mr. Leon," he said, looking down.

"He's dying: He's gone. Now you and I will be as great as he was," Gerald said, backing up toward the bathroom door. "We don't need him anymore."

Paul's face hardened. "Drop the gun and throw me that key. Do it!" he shouted, snapping back the hammer of his pistol.

"All right, all right. Calm down." Gerald dropped his pistol, but when he lifted his hand to throw the key he reached behind him and opened the bathroom door.

Instantly Thor shot out. Trained to go for the man holding the pistol, he lunged at Paul Stoddard, who managed to get off a shot, but because the animal was so fast and so close he missed. Thor went directly for his throat, tearing it open with one bite. Stoddard spun around to the floor.

Gerald scooped up his pistol and lunged for the entrance to the suite.

On the floor Mr. Leon's body had begun to degenerate. Cynthia saw his skin flake off and his eyes dry up

272

and crumble in the sockets. His mouth fell open, the lips peeling off. The sight mesmerized her, and all she could do was scream.

Drake, who had been coming down the corridor carefully, pulled himself into a doorway when Gerald came running out. But when he heard Cynthia's screams he shot forward and rushed into the suite. He didn't stop to look down at Thor tearing Stoddard apart. He went directly to Cynthia and embraced her. Then he led her to the patio door, looking back to see Mr. Leon's skeletal frame disintegrating.

Thor, finished with Stoddard, turned and ran toward the patio door.

"Drake!" Cynthia screamed. He closed it just as the animal lunged. It struck the glass and fell back, growling furiously at them, its teeth dripping with Stoddard's blood. Finally it turned and ran out the door.

"Oh, God, Drake," Cynthia said. "It's still coming after us. How could you bring me here?"

"Shh. It's all right; it's all right. Cynthia, I'm sorry. I can't explain . . . the pills . . . all of it . . ." He started to embrace her.

"How will we get out of here, Drake?" she asked, looking around. The bright lights illuminated the grounds immediately around the building. The protection of darkness seemed far away. Fortunately, it was a partly cloudy sky, and there was no moon.

They could hear the other guard dogs yapping. Security men were shouting to one another. Somewhere an alarm sounded. Afraid of Thor, they couldn't reenter the house.

"We'll have to take our chances going around the house," he said.

They ran across the patio and down behind the cabana. The barking of the dogs grew louder, so Drake pulled her into one of the changing rooms, and they waited. The dogs charged toward Mr. Leon's patio door, two security men following. The shouting within the house grew louder. More men and animals were converging on the ghastly scene inside Mr. Leon's suite.

"We won't get away, Drake," Cynthia cried. "We'll be electrocuted if we touch the fence."

"Come on," he insisted, and he led her out. They moved through the darkness to the corner of the hacienda and ran toward the front, keeping as far away from the building as they could so they could remain in some shadows, but just as they got to the driveway they heard a guard shout after them. He fired a warning shot over their heads. The bullet whizzed by and smacked into a tree.

"Oh, Drake."

The two of them crouched, frozen.

In the basement below, Gerald Dorian fumbled for the switch to put on the light. It had to be near the bottom of the stairway, he reasoned. He had never been this far before. Mr. Leon had never permitted it, and that damned dog had made sure of it. He felt along the wall and found the switch. The light illuminated the entryway to the vault, but just as he started for it he heard Thor coming and looked up to see the dog charging down the stairs.

Gerald crouched and began firing. His first two bullets went too high, but the third and fourth found their target. One bullet crashed into Thor's skull and another into his neck. His front legs collapsed, and he rolled head over hind down the remaining steps to fall at Gerald's feet.

Gerald straightened up and smiled. Nothing could stop him now; nothing would prevent him from being Mr. Leon.

He inserted the key in the door, but before he turned it he hesitated. What if Mr. Leon hadn't been lying? What if there really was an explosive device? No, he thought, he wouldn't have put anything that volatile next to the fountain and the stash. Besides, what alternative did he have now? He needed the fluid to survive, didn't he?

He turned the key and opened the vault. Seconds went by, and nothing happened. He smiled to himself and continued inside. Before him was the rock from which the fountain had once flowed. He knelt at the basin and felt inside. It had dried up. His suspicions had been correct. He smiled to himself. He had faith that there was plenty of the fluid inside the refrigerated cabinet. He opened the cabinet and looked in at the cache of bottles glittering in the light.

To Drake and Cynthia, crouched above and waiting for the approaching guard, it sounded as if the whole world were exploding. The impact threw them back, sending chunks of the hacienda in all directions, shooting through the air like guided missiles. Some struck the dogs that were charging toward them and sent them fleeing in all directions. The guard was hit in the head, his skull cracking open like an eggshell.

The first explosion set off another and then another, traveling down the length of the hacienda. Everywhere people were in commotion, fleeing for their lives. Some emerged with their clothing on fire; some managed to get clear unscathed.

Drake did not wait a moment longer.

"Are you all right?" he asked Cynthia. She nodded, and he helped her to her feet. "This way," he said, and he led her down the driveway toward a parked limousine. Behind them flames shot upward like a fountain of fire from the center of the hacienda. People were screaming, but no one noticed them or cared. Drake pulled the limousine door open and looked inside.

"There's a key in the ignition. Quick," he cried, and Cynthia got in beside him. He started it up and drove down the driveway. Behind them the small explosions continued. The fire raged voraciously, lighting up the night sky. But neither of them turned back.

When they reached the front gate the guard at the

security building was waiting. He drew his pistol and began firing, but Drake did not stop. The guard jumped out of their path, and they crashed into the gate. It snapped open, and they sped through it as if they were entering a tunnel carrying them from one world to another. Minutes later, when Drake finally slowed down and stopped, they looked back.

The sky was red. It was as if the fire had grown so great it had reached the stars.

Cynthia and Drake looked at each other.

"Cynthia, I don't know where to begin. I—"

She put a finger on his lips.

"Don't say anything," she said. "Just take me home, please." He nodded.

"I will," he said, "gladly."

—— Epilogue ——

Richie's eyelids fluttered but remained shut. Everyone had come at the same time today: her parents, Cynthia, Drake and the children, and Sheila. In two days it would be Richie's birthday, although no one mentioned it. Cynthia's mother almost did, but she stopped herself, knowing that it would bring tears to her eyes. When they were at Richie's bedside they spent most of the time talking to one another or to the nurses. It was as if Richie were an afterthought. Every once in a while they would stop speaking and look at him.

Cynthia kept expecting the sound of their voices to work miracles. The continuous flow of words to his brain would eventually break through. He would sit up surprised and ask where he was and how he had gotten there. It got so she had the same daydream in the car every day they traveled to the hospital.

Drake couldn't have been more remorseful. Since they had returned from the Leon compound, and since he had stopped taking whatever they had given him, his old personality had returned. He heaped apologies on her, sat staring for hours if she let him, and collapsed in her arms every night. She felt the tears on his cheeks but never mentioned them. At the hospital he would sit by Richie's bed and stare at him. Sometimes he would just stare down at his hands in his lap and not say a word the entire time.

For a while he was receiving phone calls from Youth Hold customers. He told them he was no longer with the firm, but some called back anyway, refusing to believe him, accusing him of being selective as to who could buy the cream. Ellen and Steffi were especially disappointed and immediately called Cynthia to find out what had happened.

"It turned out to be a scam after all," she explained. "Drake found out before he got too involved."

"But it works!" Ellen insisted. "Without the cream my face is returning to the way it was."

"That's just it, Ellen," she said. "It doesn't have lasting value. You're literally chained to the stuff and at their mercy. They can raise the prices any time they want, and people will pay. It's a kind of drug."

"I don't care," Ellen said petulantly. "My looks are most important. If Drake isn't working for them anymore, does he know someone who is?"

"No," she said sharply. "There's no one else in this area."

"I can't believe that," Ellen said, "and neither can Steffi. He shouldn't have just cut us off like this. I told him I was very upset with him, but he didn't seem to care. What's happened to him?"

"He's regained his senses," Cynthia said. Ellen didn't appreciate it, and neither did Steffi. For the next few days neither friend called. Eventually all the calls from old customers stopped.

As far as Cynthia knew, Drake heard nothing from the other salespeople. It was as if they had gone up in the explosion with Mr. Leon and Paul Stoddard. Cynthia envisioned them popping like soap bubbles at the moment it all went up in flames. She asked Drake about it, but he said he had no idea what had happened to the others and didn't care to find out. Nevertheless, whenever the telephone rang they both stopped and looked at each other in anticipation. It was never anyone who had anything to do with Leon Enterprises.

One morning Drake received a call from Mr. Burke, who said he had heard that Drake was no longer with his new company. He wanted to know if Drake would consider returning to the firm—as a vice-president and partner, of course.

"I told him I would come in and talk to him on Monday," Drake told Cynthia.

"I'm glad, Drake."

"With the improved income we can consider moving closer to the city and shortening my commute," he mused. It was the beginning of a real recuperation as far as Cynthia was concerned. Their conversations were filled with plans and hope again, and the shadows that hung over them began to dissipate.

On Richie's birthday they all went to the hospital as usual, everyone feeling the pain and sorrow far more intensely. They tried not to talk about it, tried to distract themselves. Drake, who took his seat at Richie's bedside as usual, waited until Cynthia, her parents, and Sheila walked off to get some coffee. Alone with Richie, he stood up and leaned over his brother-in-law. He watched the nurses to be sure none of them was looking his way, and then he reached into his pocket and produced the capsule Paul Stoddard had given him that fateful night in the hacienda.

He had been tempted to ingest it a number of times. Every morning when he woke up with an ache, or when his old knee injury reintroduced itself, he would think of the capsule. It took all his self-control to refrain from swallowing it. What would he do after it wore off? he asked himself.

Still, he wondered about its miraculous power. He had no idea what its potential was, but he saw no harm in giving it to Richie. Satisfied that no one was looking his way, he brought the capsule to Richie's mouth, opened his lips, and broke the capsule over his tongue, permitting the clear liquid to drip out. Then he sat down again quickly.

Richie didn't make a miraculous recovery that afternoon. Cynthia and Drake returned home as usual, driving for long periods in regretful silence. But shortly after dinner, while Drake was just sitting down to review some math homework with Stuart, the phone rang. He watched Cynthia go to it.

"Hello?" she said.

"Mrs. Edwards?"

"Yes?"

"This is Sue Cohen, nurse in I.C."

"Oh, yes."

"I have someone who wants to speak with you," she said.

"Pardon?"

Drake rose from his chair.

"Who is it?" he demanded. Cynthia widened her eyes and shrugged. "It's a nurse from the hospital. She said she has someone who wants—"

"Cynthia. What the hell am I doing here?" Richie asked.

"It's Richie!" she screamed. Debbie and Stuart ran to her.

Drake took the receiver from her because she was crying so hard she couldn't speak.

"Hey, Richie, how are you doing?"

"Drake?"

"Yeah, it's me. And don't think that just because you've been in the hospital a while you're going to get any breaks when we play one-on-one in the driveway," Drake said.

Richie's laughter brought forth Drake's own long-imprisoned tears. They flowed freely, lifting the final weight from his shoulders. The family hugged one another and gathered around the phone as if it were a small campfire that would forever keep the darkness outside.

* * *

The bulldozers bore down on the rubble in the hot Florida sun. When the small army of construction workers assigned to the job first arrived they thought they had been brought to a war zone. They shook their heads in amazement and began their work. Steam shovels lifted the debris and dropped it into ten-ton trucks to be carted off. A continuous cloud of dust rose up as though the great fire were still smoldering.

Once in a while a worker would stumble upon something that had survived the fire—a piece of crystal, some metal artwork—but for the most part there was nothing of any value left. The bulldozers moved forward, gobbling up the debris, pushing it into piles for the steam shovels. After a while the work became monotonous, mindless, seemingly interminable.

The bulldozer operator who dipped into the gaping hole to scoop up some of the debris did not notice the large rock. He grazed it with his machine, nudging it gently with one pass.

'What the hell you doin' in there?'' The foreman called to him. "It'll be easier just to bury that."

The bulldozer operator scratched his head and nodded. "Right."

"Shove some of this crap in there," the foreman ordered. The operator turned his bulldozer around and began to do so. The chunks of stone and debris rushed into the hole eagerly. Some of it struck the great rock.

At the opening from which the fountain had once emerged a tiny trickle of water reappeared. For a few moments it sparkled in the bright sunlight, but the bulldozer operator was oblivious to it. He bore down on the debris and drove it in and over the rock. The dirt plugged up the hole, and the momentary resurrection of the wonderful fountain was ended.